RUNNING AWAY

VAMPIRES OF FATE BOOK TWO

JULIE HUTCHINGS

inked **entertainment**

E-Book - ISBN 978-1-912382-28-6

Paperback - ISBN 978-1-912382-29-3

Hardback - ISBN 978-1-912382-30-9

ALSO BY JULIE HUTCHINGS

Vampires of Fate

Running Home (Book 1)

Running Away (Book 2)

Crawling Back (Book 3, coming 2020)

The Harpy Series

The Harpy (Book 1, coming 2020)

The Harpy: Evolution (Book 2, coming 2020)

Five Poisons

The Wind Between Worlds (Book 1, coming 2020)

They're all for my family. Everything is.

CHAPTER 1

Kat's death turned me into a haunted house. The lights were on, but nothing good was home. Inside, was an infestation of hornets.

I sat at the handmade kitchen table in Nicholas's log cabin, watching the first clear day of the new year out the window. It was dead calm, quiet. Lifeless. Even the birds didn't know what to do without the constantly falling snow we'd had that winter in New Hampshire. Nicholas put his hand on my shoulder from behind me. Instinctively, I leaned my head into it.

"I'm ready to go to Japan."

Nicholas sighed. "Eliza, you're not."

"You showed me my fate, but it doesn't mean you get to call the shots. I say I'm ready, and I am."

"You only think you're ready to become *Shinigami* because you feel so horrible right now."

"I barely feel anything now!"

"Eliza—"

Rage coursed through me, propelling me out of the chair. "No! The reason everything's horrible is *because* it's time for me to become a vampire! I've been stripped of any reason to go on alive, in true *Shinigami* fashion! Right? That's how the world you know works, right? Some hand of fate does everything it can to make sure I have nothing to live for, that I'm all alone? Nothing ties me here anymore. I have no job, thanks to your well-thought gift of getting me fired, my apartment is gone, everybody that ever cared I existed is conveniently dead, and now my best friend, my only true friend—gone. We were together every day!" Acid tears ate at my lids, my voice was broken glass. "Kat is dead. *Your* best friend killed her. And if Roman hadn't, you would have. Despite that, I still love you more than I thought possible. Do you know what that does to me?" Like gasoline mouthwash. Like a bed of nails in my brain. Like termites in my gut, cockroaches in my heart. A flesh-eating disease.

Pain crossed Nicholas's beautiful face, but he couldn't deny my words.

My voice evened out, fueled by crude determination. "My whole life has been a tool to make sure I would have nothing left. It's my fate to be alone, except for you."

I approached him slowly, like he was some scared rabbit, and took his hand. It was as limp as I felt.

Softly, I said, "I cannot survive another day like this, knowing everyone around me will be destroyed, will be ripped apart, away... I'm a cancer here. I don't belong. It's time for me to go to Japan. We've got the tickets, our bags are packed. It's time for me to become a vampire."

CHAPTER 2

I was as lifeless as the cold, gray morning that Nicholas and I left for Japan. It was miserable boarding that plane, early so that the sun wouldn't burn Nicholas in his frailness. He missed the sunlight; I could see it in the longing, Jesus-like stare upwards through the plane window. I pictured his skin bubbling and turning to ash in the morning light. Since Kat was killed, the continual cloud of death that followed me had nested inside me instead, giving me morbid visions. I was too empty to be worried about it.

Nicholas held my hand in both of his on the plane. I looked over to find him staring at me, a panicked look of worry about him. He'd been doting on me like some worried grandmother. It was getting on my nerves.

"Eliza?" Nicholas whispered, like he was talking to a child he just found in the woods.

"Yes?" I whispered back.

I studied his face with detachment. He still looked

rugged, even though he was gaunt. His lips were paler. His chocolate eyes weren't the inhuman, ever-swirling storm of caramel and cocoa; they were still, as if they didn't have the energy anymore. His cheeks were hollow, his skin dry. His dark hair, a mix of well-groomed and tousled curls, fell across his forehead, limp. Denying himself the blood of the human he'd been fated to kill had diminished him. It happened to all *Shinigami* that dared defy the call of fate. It didn't seem right that Nicholas had to play by those rules, but I saw him decaying before my eyes. Roman was certain that Nicholas wouldn't survive the plane trip to Japan, but that was before he took away Nicholas's remedy. Before he killed my best friend himself.

I wasn't so sure he'd make the trip to Japan either. Only that realization shocked my feelings into play.

Nicholas was all I had left. And he was destined to make me immortal; I was his *unmei fumetsu*. I didn't feel much like *his Eliza* just now, only Ellie Morgan. I was the teenager again, abandoned in a world without anyone to love me but a ghost of decay that clung to me like a leech.

He leaned closer, murmuring, "You should try to sleep. You haven't slept since Kat—"

I cleared my dry throat. "Oh. Really?" Sheer pity emanated from him. Glaring, I turned away. The last thing I wanted was pity. I was the reason Kat was dead.

Nicholas kissed my hand, and held it to his clammy cheek. "Eliza, I don't know how to make this right." His voice broke. The thought of him suffering should crash like a falling boulder into my heart, but not this time.

"Well, Nicholas, you've lost your best friend, too." I couldn't control the spite in my voice. I didn't want to.

"Roman isn't gone for good; Kat is. It doesn't matter who drew the blood, the guilt is all mine," he muttered.

Volatile as I was, I couldn't let Nicholas take all the blame. My spine stiffened as I told him with cold calculation what I knew was the truth. "Kat was *unmei nashi.* No fate." The words stung like poison through my gritted teeth. "She was doomed from the day she met me. It's my fate to become a vampire, and the only way that can happen is if nobody misses me. It's why everyone around me dies. Why I'll be forever alone if I stay human." I squeezed his hand. *"Not your fault.* It's not even Roman's fault that he killed her. He only did it so you wouldn't have to." I swallowed. "He was trying to do us a favor."

Nicholas's sharp bite of breath substituted for his disagreement. He knew better than to disagree with me, and on this point, what argument could he really make?

A flight attendant with bouncy hair like Kat's stopped by our seats.

"Can I get you—"

Her question ended abruptly when she saw my face. To look so truly frightening that you can stop the essence of perkiness mid-sentence with the slightest of eye contact must be the worst superpower a person can have.

"Miss, I'm sorry to bother you," she said quickly and quietly, and moved on to the next passenger, ignoring Nicholas completely.

I put my head back and went to sleep.

I let Nicholas tote me through the crowded airport to

switch planes, jostling obnoxious people coming down from vacation highs, all brightly colored and loud and pushy. There were so many people bustling about, they became a blur. It wasn't hard to tune them out.

Nicholas bought me a coffee for way too much money, and we found our way to a quiet spot that had been overlooked by the masses. I watched the boards change times and destinations. I sipped the coffee. I tasted nothing.

"Eliza?" Again he stared at me with unmasked worry. He shifted in the seat next to me so he could hold my gaze, and make me pay attention. Kat used to get my attention by giving me food. "I want to talk about what you'll come across in the temple."

Nicholas's eyes burned with the discomfort of thirst and guilt. Rage bubbled inside me again, that any of this was happening, and that I couldn't be more kind to Nicholas now that he needed me. I needed too much and had forgotten how to process the void of losing everything.

"What do you need to tell me?"

"The temple is completely off the map. It technically doesn't exist, but is actually at the top of Mount Daisen." He paused to rub his forehead with his palm. "A lot of vampires call the temple home. *Some* of them are well adjusted," he said with a crooked smile, "but most are dangerous. They leave only to feed, and have no interaction with humans besides. The humans that are chosen to become *Shinigami* are reluctant exceptions."

I was surprised to find myself interested. I hadn't bothered to think of anybody else in the temple, vampire or human; I had no intention of making friends. It was interesting to think there were other people who repelled companionship the way I did, though.

"Tell me more."

He smiled tightly, the only way he really could now that his lips were so constantly dry and cracked. "The vampires there are the most primal of us. Don't expect a fruit basket. But you need to be there."

When I realized that was all he had to say, I got up the energy to respond. "I don't want a warm reception. I just want to leave my life behind."

The Kyoto airport held staggering amounts of tourists buzzing with energy. I longed for Boston, where you could get lost in the crowd on purpose, and nobody made eye contact. Despite the bustle, nobody here bumped and pushed and grumbled. Some of them nodded politely, acknowledging that I was real. It felt like everyone was watching me. I had no right to be there.

The train looked like it should be robot operated. It was a city that someone made up but hadn't gotten quite right. Landing in Japan was like falling into a video game, where there were vending machines for everything, and glaring lights, pulsing music, but the buildings looked like they were too old, and too clean. It wasn't the opposite of Ossipee, New Hampshire, it was a different planet. In Ossipee, everything felt familiar and warm; but that town didn't want me anymore, if it ever did. So, now I help-lessly allowed Nicholas to navigate me through the train

7

and bus routes that would bring us to the base of Mount Daisen.

When we began traveling through the countryside, when the strangeness began to fall away, I allowed myself to slowly attempt to repair. I didn't deserve peace, but the world of snow that greeted me was too like the New Hampshire winter for me not to fall in love with it. A fire was put out inside me as I took in the streams, hot springs, and mountains that belonged in a fairy tale. Snow-covered pagodas perched on hillsides, overlooking skeletal forests. Tiny villages spotted the landscape, and I could imagine families inside around their tables, together. Forest animals fearlessly showed themselves in this place.

For the first time, I felt like it hadn't been only desperation that made me ready to come here. I was *unmei fumetsu*, chosen to be immortal, a vampire, *Shinigami*.

"Amazing, isn't it?" Nicholas asked me in a low grumble. I'd almost forgotten he was with me.

I looked at him, really looked at him like I wanted him to see me, too. I wasn't afraid for him to see the wretch I was, because being here, I knew that the feeling would end. "It's the most beautiful place ever."

He smiled, and a pang of missing him swallowed me. My eyes swam with tears that I'd held back too long.

"You'll be okay, Eliza." He pulled my hand into his rough, warm ones, and smiled more. "This is where you'll be okay."

The tears fell as the train skidded to a stop. Two more hours until arrival at the temple.

~

Yonago Station was surreal. At first, I thought I must have dozed off on the train, and this was one of the half-dreams I'd been suffering. But it was too pleasant.

Boston's stations were muted burgundies, grays and other dirt-encrusted dull shades, the worst of New England fall colors plastered to dirty city things. Here, my eyes couldn't stop moving from the vibrant hues that painted every surface. Drawings of Japanese families and royalty in traditional robes that belonged in a museum covered the buses, the walls, the tiny shops, every sign and window. There were even standups with holes cut out to put your face into for photos, like you'd see at a carnival. The colors came to life in the people here, all of them wearing tulip yellows, deep sea greens, sunset pinks, blending like flowers in a colossal garden. Simple, sweet, harmonic. I'd walked into a children's book.

The bleakness in my heart edged off, letting a little of this light in. For the first time in days, I noticed Nicholas's scent from beside me. Today, it was fresh fruit and cinnamon that complemented this incredible place.

I wished I wasn't a pock mark on its beauty.

"Eliza," Nicholas whispered in my ear. His breath sent the first rumblings of desire through my body that I'd gotten in a while, but the black hole in me consumed it.

"This place is so alive," I hissed, yearning and contempt kicking the seeping warmth from my body, beating each other in my heart.

Nicholas sighed and leaned his forehead on my shoulder. I leaned the side of my head against his, trying not to crumble. "I can feel the pain throbbing from your heart, and Jesus, Eliza, I want to heal it for you, would do anything to heal it for you. The death in you—it's killing me."

"Nicholas, I love you." My voice was hollow. I meant it, I knew it the way I know what the state capitals are, but I felt nothing.

"Your love for me chokes you, and I don't know how to fix it."

I stared straight ahead into the blinding colors of life.

CHAPTER 3

Daisenji Temple was perched on the mountainside like it had been there since the dawn of time, emanating serenity and power, but welcoming. Nicholas smiled wide when it came into view.

I was afraid of it.

The fear invaded all my other warring emotions, making itself real more real. Nicholas didn't notice, thank God; it was embarrassing, and he was babysitting me enough.

"Let's go," Nicholas said, and started up quickly, tugging me behind.

He took his boots off at the door, motioning for me to do the same. As soon as I did, I wanted to run away.

The peace inside the temple punched me in the face. A Japanese woman with the hint of a smile was silently adding incense to an urn, and it made me want to cry with inexplicable anger. Only the terror that stung my chest prevented it.

"You look like you've seen a ghost. What's up?" Nicholas said.

"I want to leave."

Nicholas shook his head in disbelief and ran his fingers through his hair. "Okay, let me pay my respects quickly, and we'll go." I tried to stay still and not fidget like the devil in church as I watched him place incense in the burner, nodding a quiet greeting to the woman before him. My stomach turned as the subtle scent assaulted me.

"You must go."

I gasped, spinning around to face the owner of the voice behind me. A tiny man in brown robes stared up at me, his face solemn. I could only think one thing.

This man can see inside me.

"Grief consumes you. It burns everything in its path. Your fire is impure. You must go. *Aitou.*"

Mourning. I knew the word in my heart. I was panting in fear, shaking as this man's soul peered deep into my own, and nothing should be in there, nothing.

"I—I'm sorr...sorry."

I ran barefoot from the temple out into the snow, desperate for that place to be behind me, away from me and the spirit of death that haunted me. A half dozen crows met me, black ash marks on the snow.

Nicholas appeared at my side like a stream of energy, making me yelp with shock, my nerves were so electrified. He grabbed my arms, and I struggled, whimpering, but couldn't match his strength.

"Sssshhh, Eliza. Eliza, it's okay." He smoothed my hair, and bent at the knees the way he always did when he wanted to look deeply into my eyes. He calmed me like that, like a wild horse back from the brink of a destructive panic. My breathing was so erratic that it hurt as it slowed down. Hot tears poured down my cheeks as I tried to erase the temple in my mind, screaming at me with its tranquility.

Nicholas pulled his gaze from mine with a long breath. I answered his raised eyebrows with a nod, that yes, I was settled. Only then did he kneel to put my boots on. Like a little kid, I let him. The crows watched his every move.

"Your feet are soaked, love," he whispered, drying my numb toes them with his coat.

Standing back up, the snow crunching under him, he pulled me close, smothering me with his arms and chest. His scent was like home, our home; cinnamon and chocolate, vampire-tailored to suit my needs and make me his, but it wasn't working.

"God, I'm sorry. I should have known," he murmured.

"Known what?"

"People in mourning don't belong in a temple. Here, grief is an impurity of the soul." He shook his head, his fists clenched. "Your heart hurts too much right now."

Cold stung like bile in my throat. "I have no heart now."

The incident at the temple left me emotionally scorched. I sat in the snow with Nicholas, the image of the old man's eyes burned into my mind. This stranger that was repulsed by my frozen soul.

Nicholas rubbed my back like my mother used to

when I couldn't sleep. His touch made me hurt more. I wanted nothing good near me, no one else to touch me that I could ruin. But Nicholas was no better than me. His mere appearance in my life brought the destruction of it, gave a name to the death that I created just by existing; *unmei fumetsu*.

"There's an inn not far from here. Let's head there so you can rest."

My head was an anchor that I had to pull up out of the sea just to meet his eyes. Nicholas was emaciated. "You need to feed, Nicholas."

He ran his hands through his hair. "I won't get any weaker before we get to the temple."

"If you fed, you'd be stronger, though."

"Not right now. Anything but *unmei nashi* right now won't be enough anyway. Waiting until I have another one won't hurt."

Silence sat in the air while I thought, *So Kat just gets replaced then, by someone else to kill.* "Where do you think Roman is, Nicholas?"

He sucked in a breath. "He doesn't want us to know. What difference would it make? Kat's still dead, and we are still this."

CHAPTER 4

C rows circled overhead at the inn. They must have known I was coming.

The burning in me subsided as Daisenji Temple vanished from sight, and my fear with it. It left me drained. Grayer than Nicholas looked.

He led me to a modest little inn hidden by trees, that looked like part of the mountain itself. The fresh smell of the place was so different from the heady scent of incense in Daisenji that I breathed a sigh of relief. There were vegetables being cooked nearby, and a fire was burning strong and bright to welcome us.

"I'll find the inn keeper," Nicholas said, and left me waiting. He headed to a back room like he knew exactly where he was going. I could hear him speaking Japanese with a man over the sound of pots clanging, followed by laughter from them both. It felt like home, home with Nicholas and Roman, where I could rest. Finally rest my soul.

I wasn't sure I wanted a soul anymore.

Nicholas came out of the room with an old smiling man clapping him on the shoulder. The man easily was two feet shorter than Nicholas, his back hunched. He walked with a cane that looked like it had been cut right out of a tree, probably by his own hand. Happiness filled me when the old man looked up with the most beautiful toothless smile.

"This is Ayumu," Nicholas said. Ayumu smiled up at me, now so close that I could smell the scent of the kitchen on him, and of the earth.

"*Konnichiwa,*" I said, bowing, but Ayumu grabbed me in an embrace with more strength than I thought his tiny body could muster. I blinked back tears from the simple humanity of it.

When he pulled back, I was surprised to see him still grinning. He took my chin in his gnarled hand and said, "*Unmei shinsei.*"

I looked at Nicholas over the old man's head.

"Chosen for new life," he said quietly.

I looked back down to the little inn keeper, and this time I embraced him first.

Our room was dim in the fading afternoon. A low table in the center dominated it, covered in a pale blue blanket, thin enough to reveal a glow from underneath. It promised warmth to my aching muscles and freezing limbs, and pulled me in fast.

"Put your legs under the blanket," Nicholas said as I

sank to my knees in front of it. Sure enough, it was heated underneath. I could have crawled inside. I groaned, closed my eyes, and put my head down on the tabletop.

I sat up what I thought was moments later, but the sky was dark. I'd been woken by a soft sound at the rice paper door. Nicholas emerged from behind an ornate room divider at the rear of the room, wearing black sweatpants and a gray thermal shirt. In an instant he was in the doorway, bowing to a young girl and taking a tray from her hands, though she wanted to bring it in herself; he knew I couldn't see anyone. Not yet. A delicious scent wafted towards me.

"I'm ravenous!" I belted out.

Nicholas grinned, a hint of his former self shining through. "There's my girl."

The prospect of food coupled with a nap changed my attitude quite a bit. It's the little things, sometimes.

"I like you better when you eat," Nicholas said.

"Mmmph," I mumbled as I shoveled fish and steamed veggies in my mouth like I hadn't eaten in a week. Actually, I wasn't sure when the last time I'd eaten was. "I'd still kill for a box of Funny Bones."

"I could give you horse shit and you'd eat it right now. For your first victim I'll try to arrange for a Hostess factory employee."

I laughed hard, choking. "Come on!" I said, wiping tears from my eyes. "That shouldn't be funny!"

"You eat like a starved bear, and it's really sexy."

"What every girl wants to hear."

"You're not every girl."

"If I was every girl, there'd be a lot more stomachs

being sucked in all around the world." It was hard not to sing the Oprah theme song, but I wasn't about to stop eating.

"My God, it's good to hear you laugh again." His voice thickened. "I miss you, Eliza."

I stiffened. "Well, Nicholas, I was always here." The cold fire crept out in my voice, refusing to be forgotten entirely.

"You haven't been and you know it."

"That's not my fault. It's one thing that's not my fault."

We ate in silence for a few minutes, but a couple of glances over the table confirmed neither of us was ready to let go of this peace. My belly wasn't churning and screaming, finally. Nicholas watched me, the cream and coffee spinning of his eyes as warm as the heat on my legs. He looked so tired, so pained, but beautiful, flickering in and out of existence in his worry. He reached across the table to tuck a black curl behind my ear. My momentary contentment and that single touch stamped down my rage and sadness; I leaned into his hand, surprising us both. Nicholas actually took a sharp breath.

"Eliza," was all he said, but it forced a sob out of me as my former self broke the surface of the despair I'd ingested. He was around the table, holding me from behind, and rocking me, but I was already still. I had no tears left.

His lips grazed my ear through my mess of curls. "I promise you, I'll make this better—"

"You can't."

Nicholas stopped moving. "You'll be *Shinigami* legend, Eliza. One day, you'll see there's nothing more important."

He stiffened, betraying his fear of saying what he'd say next. "This life that you're leaving behind was never really yours. And you never really wanted it."

I wasn't offended by what he said—he'd always said what he wanted to, and I knew it was the truth. It was the deadbolt on a door I'd already locked.

CHAPTER 5

Never had the sun sparkled that way, until I witnessed it kiss the snowy cherry blossom trees surrounding the temple. My own steady breaths were the sole sound to interrupt bird songs. The world breathed a sigh with a cold wind ruffling my hair.

This was the place I would die.

Nicholas inhaled deeply. My heart jumped to my throat to look at him. I hadn't seen his face in the sunlight in so long, it took my breath away. I tried to see him as he'd been, before all the death that crushed us. The close, bouncing dark curls had a tint of gold here. I loved how his eyes were the most dominant feature on his beautiful face; they were at their widest staring at the temple, and their warmth encompassed me over the distance. The ever-present five o'clock shadow was rugged, but managed to make his face even fresher against peach pearl skin. Subtle furrows framed the berry lips that I dreamed of, still plump like a child's, smooth and inviting.

Even wilting like he was, he was spectacular.

He caught me out of the corner of his eye, and flashed a smug smile.

"Home," was all he said in his lion's growl.

My world was coming together.

Climbing the stairs embedded in the mountainside, Nicholas told me about the creature who waited at the top inside the temple.

"Records of the Master date back over 1700 years, but still no one knows when he was made, or how."

"What? Hasn't he ever told anyone? Not even you?"

"He's too old to remember." Nicholas shrugged.

When the only the sound was snow crunching with our steps, I blurted out, "I'm scared." I hated that it was true, and shocked myself by saying it out loud.

Nicholas stopped and turned to me. The mountain wind carried the scent of peppermint and brownies to swirl around me while his cocoa cream eyes looked into mine; sedative made just for me. I pushed the emptiness, anger, and fear away as hard as I could, and let Nicholas comfort me.

"He's fierce, but kind, and he'll be pivotal in deciding the rest of your existence, so, yeah, be nervous. Nothing surprises him, nothing escapes him. But he'll show you the way."

Nicholas's admiration and love rang clear. It must have shown on my face how it touched me, because Nicholas bowed his head shyly.

"Oh my God, you're like, overcome with emotion," I said like a jerk.

"I'm not."

"Are too."

A smirk twitched his lips, but it faded in his sincerity. "The Master saved me from myself. He took me under his wing while all vampires were under his care, he took care of *me*. I owe him everything." He swallowed, and his eyes never left mine when he said, "Without him, I wouldn't have you."

I tried not to let the emotional door slam that I'd built recently. "Nicholas, you were fated to be my creator whether the Master existed or not. You don't owe anyone for what we have. Nobody made this happen, not even him."

"He made me believe there was more for me. And that's you. So stop arguing with me."

"You're still happy you found me?"

"Happy? Yes. Yes, I am. Tortured, disturbed, but happy." He looked at me harder. "You're not happy you found me?"

I was pinned, motionless by this all too simple question, even though I was the one who brought it up. How the hell could I be *happy* to have found him, after my life and Kat's and everyone's had been destroyed because of it? I suppose if the Master wasn't responsible for what Nicholas had become, Nicholas wasn't responsible for what my life had become.

Bells clanged at the top of the mountain, and it sent a flurry of birds flying. Not crows, for once. I was lying to myself if I said I wasn't happy to be here. I was happy to know what I was meant for. I'd spent my entire life wondering what it was. I wasn't fool enough to think I got a higher purpose in life for free. There had to be sacrifices.

Mine was my best friend, and I made that sacrifice to save my own destiny, and Nicholas; they were one in the same.

"Silence is answer enough for me," he said, more ice in his voice than under my feet, more cold coming from the frost he gave off than from the cold wind around us. His brownie scent was gone. He didn't want to comfort me anymore. There was nothing but hurt and anger from him to match my own.

Finally, we felt right together again.

Once inside the temple, I understood right away that the vampires I knew in Ossipee, even the psychotic Lynch, were refined and humanized. This place was as primal as it came, closer to the Earth and Heaven than anything I'd ever imagined, bare of anything except soul.

The temple itself exuded a life of its own, formidable and ancient. I was shocked to feel as though it was wrapping its arms around me, but I shouldn't have been; this was the only place that welcomed death.

Flames flickered in orange lanterns lining the walls in the womblike darkness. They lit a path along the red runner down the enormous length of the place to an altar sitting atop a short flight of stairs. Incense created wisps of smoke, shrouding the sole figure.

For as singular with the Earth as the temple was, the

creature before me couldn't have been more otherworldly. He was so still it gave the disconcerting illusion that the ground was moving. His presence defied his slight stature. A force of silent will, he emanated power that filled the hollow hall, seemed to shake the very walls. He wore a simple white robe with his hands tucked into the bell sleeves. Waist-length white hair with matching mustache gave the impression that he'd never been young. And his eyes—they bore into me across the length of the temple. They were a glowing, colorless shade of milky white, no pupils. At once, I realized I shouldn't be able to see such details so far from him, and gasped at a disarming sensation that he was standing right in front of me, like he was in both places at once. Goosebumps sprang up on my arms under my layers of shirts and coat.

"Holy hell!" I screamed. The Master was in front of us with not so much as a flicker or the flash I would see from Nicholas when he moved with vampire speed. The Master was up there, then he was down here. My head spun like I'd been put under a spell.

"Shhh," Nicholas hissed at me.

The Master's face was smooth as glass, but rippled inhumanly with joy as Nicholas bowed to him. I followed suit. Ignoring me, the Master pulled Nicholas upright to embrace him.

"Nikorasu," the Master said in a voice rich with age and love. "I've missed you. And now you only come on official business." The Master focused his eerie eyes on me, and I smiled. My discomfort was like another person in the room, it was so overwhelming. "Ah, but *she* is not all business," the Master said into Nicholas's ear, milky eyes never leaving mine.

Nicholas pulled gently away. "You see too much sometimes," he said to the Master.

The old vampire continued to stare at me, and my soul squirmed.

"It is simple to see the death in her," the Master said. After a cryptically long pause in which I realized that vampire pauses are longer than regular ones, he finally looked back to Nicholas. I was able to exhale.

"I'm ready. I'm ready to be done with my awful life, and to see how *you* can somehow make it all better by teaching me karate? I guess?" I spat.

"Eliza," Nicholas started, but I turned on him. Being sized up didn't suit me.

"Shut up, Nicholas. I won't be censored. I'm here on good faith, and I have every right to—"

I didn't get to finish. My teeth began chattering, and I shook like mad, attacked by cold. The kind of cold Nicholas gave off, that I was familiar with, but intensified to a dull ache. It came from the Master.

I squirmed, sending needles to my head that morphed into a throbbing eye pain. I forgot everything except how afraid of this ancient vampire I was. He glowered at me, and Nicholas had been right; all I saw was a god, beyond human or animal.

"Master," Nicholas pleaded quietly.

Warmth flooded me so quickly that I buckled in half like a dropped marionette. I sucked in the cold air, wincing as it stung my chest.

Point taken. Don't mouth off, and don't screw with Nicholas on the Master's watch.

CHAPTER 6

The Master left without explanation, just vanished, leaving a cold mist in his wake. I'd never seen anything move like him.

Nicholas and I were alone. I dreaded looking at him, but I did it.

He was deathly serious, the lines around his mouth making him look sadder now that he was so malnourished. But as I watched him, he burst into laughter that echoed up and down the long space, and had me looking around like we were going to get caught.

"What the hell, Nicholas! Shush!"

"You're not the boss of me," he said, lips trying to stay still.

I tried not to laugh with him. "What's so funny?"

"What's so funny? You! What were you *thinking?*"

"Yeah, yeah, I know I shouldn't have yelled. We just met. Yelling should wait for a second or third meeting."

Nicholas ran his fingers through his hair, and shook

his head. "Eliza, nobody talks to him like that." He laughed again, and it was beautiful. "Who the hell do you think you are?!" I hadn't seen him laugh so hard in a long time. His now-bony shoulders shook with it.

"I'm screwed, right?" I said, holding back laughter.

"Yeah, you so are," he wheezed.

I crouched down, suddenly very tired. It might have been from the emotional exhaustion but more likely because of climbing a million stairs. "What now?"

Nicholas recovered himself and crouched next to me. "You're going to learn."

"Karate?" I said skeptically.

"Martial arts are a way of life defining the most enlightened people in history. And the Master," he said, his lip twitching again to a smile, "has been *the* Master as far back as martial arts are recorded. Trust me when I tell you, he has plenty to teach." Nicholas glanced around. "He's waiting for me to talk to him. You stay here, I won't be long. Then we'll get you fed, get some rest." And he was off with that *crack*, leaving a streak behind him.

The silence enveloped me. I'd have burned the place down for a nap, but I stayed awake, cross-legged, alone, in this strange place—and it was right. No matter how scared I was, this was right.

Then, the feeling filled me, like it had never done before. It seeped through me like oil, into every limb and thought. It was different, more intense than ever, and I recognized it as soon as it entered me. That shadow of death, the thing all too real, like an old friend that nobody wants, but the only one I ever really had. It was always with me, after my parents' death, the rest of my family. It left me after Roman killed Kat, but by then, I'd already knew what it was; the *Shinigami* coming to claim me. The ever-present chill down my spine that was fate itself.

I breathed slow and deep through the presence of death overcoming me, catching myself *smiling,* smothering the oppression and guilty that had ruled for so long...

A shadow flickered impossibly on a wall already too dark for shadow, behind a column. Finally, after all these years, a body to go with the presence of death invading me, embracing me. I wanted it, and wanted to hit it, and was so happy to see it was a real thing. I didn't dare move.

The shadow moved again. A person, but death. I couldn't understand.

"Hello?" *Real smart.*

The shadow darted out of view, giving me a glimpse of a bare chest, loose white pants, and waist-length black hair. Human? I stayed still and waited for more, but nothing and no one came. Only Nicholas.

"Someone was here," I whispered.

"Okay."

"You left me alone."

"Not really."

"Was I safe?"

"Probably not. But you could handle yourself until I got back."

I just gaped at him. He'd left me to be vampire fodder. "Thanks, Nicholas. You just told me the *Shinigami* weren't going to love me, then you left me for dead. I was feeling awesome already."

He smirked. It pissed me off. "I'm not into your ill-placed mockery."

Nicholas looked unfazed. "The Master did it on purpose. He wanted me to leave you to your own devices."

I should have been mad that Nicholas was amused by it, but instead I was just irritated that I'd acted like such a girl in the face of the challenge. What did I do, call out *hello?* Me, horror movie buff—I pulled a Classic. Then bitched at Nicholas about it. I should have gone to check the shadow out. I should have confronted him—it—but I chickened out. Fail.

There could be no failing here. I had to get over myself if I wanted to be rid of this life that didn't want me. I had to see things the way the *Shinigami* saw them if I was to be ready.

"Nicholas—" I started, looking back to where the shadow had been. The presence of death had gone with it, leaving a vacancy in my chest.

Though Nicholas was beside me, I smelled nothing from him—which meant he wasn't trying to be close to me, to capture me. It hurt me more, and I had no right to be hurt, not the way I'd been treating him.

He waited, looking at me distantly.

"I saw someone over there," I said, pointing to the column, "and it felt like death. Like the feeling I always had, but more."

Nicholas was completely still, emotionally, in every way, and I grew more disconnected from him as I realized he would never know that specter that haunted me. No, that belonged to me alone.

"I imagine death will find you a lot more now, Eliza, so get used to it."

Hot-headed as he was, Nicholas's odd anger threw me

for a loop when he got up and walked away. I glared at the place death had been, and followed Nicholas; my own path was too dark to forge.

Nicholas walked ahead of me until I asked him to slow down.

"Where are we going?" My feet ached, and my eyes were crossing with exhaustion.

"Where you'll live."

My eyes snapped open with that one.

"Where *I'll* live? Not you?" I hadn't thought about where I'd be staying, but I wouldn't have thought alone.

"Not me. I have my own place here. You need to find yours."

"Shit, don't say I have to go on some scavenger hunt."

He stopped and hung his head in front of me, something I'd gotten used to seeing him do. Here he was immortal, and I was making him old.

"This is a place for you to be alone, as much as you can," he said quietly. "You don't need me as much as you tell yourself."

I swallowed. "Good, because I think I lie too much."

It was dark, and I burst into waking frantic, with no idea where I was. But there were sounds.

"Nicholas? Nicholas?!" I whisper-shouted.

Noises again, and worse, I got the sense of something. Not just anything—death again, lurking, as invasive and comforting as always.

My limbs shook when I flung off the blankets and

threw my legs over the side of the bed, only to discover the bed was on the floor. The noise of my feet hitting the bare floor made me gasp. My small room, alone, on a mountain top.

Japan, I'm in Japan, and in my own room. Nicholas isn't here.

Eyes adjusting, I saw nothing in the room but for the bed I'd been in and a few very pieces of simple furniture. Shadows flitted across the walls from outside, the trees swaying in the winter night. I steadied my breathing, knowing I was alone, and knowing anything could be waiting for me. The vampires had kept themselves hidden during the day, and now they were out, looking for blood.

No. These are Shinigami. They're not horror movies.

I wanted light but couldn't find anything and didn't want to draw attention to myself. Hide from the dark in the dark. Try to deny that you *are* the dark.

"Perfect time for some crap karate test, Nicholas, for the love of—"

A branch snapped. Two thin walls framed a sliding paper door to outside, and there was enough snow on the ground that a branch would have to be stepped on to snap.

The silhouette of a man appeared on the other side of the door, inches from my face, and I screamed, stumbled backwards, and fell onto the bed.

He didn't move. Didn't try to run or come after me. He waited. Like death itself. The death that always knew I couldn't resist. The only horrible thing that was familiar to me here. It owned me. When I stood and moved to the door, I never doubted I should open it. Sliding the screen door open, the figure made no movement, didn't even blink. The full moon illuminated him.

He was breathtaking in his darkness.

The night made him brighter somehow. A full head taller than me, bare-chested with only thin white karate pants, the same crispness as the snow. Perfectly chiseled, smooth, strength in every pore. Beautiful and fearsome. He looked down at me with onyx eyes, shining black hair falling around his cheeks and chest, the front held up in a traditional knot.

He smelled like red wine and roses. Rich, heady and slightly nauseating. The scent of looking into something beyond.

The smell slapped me with memory, one I hadn't touched since it occurred. I knelt at my mother's casket, eyes on my father's next to her. The room felt too heavy, stagnant. Wine heavy on her breath, the scent of withering roses succumbing to it from too many wreaths and bouquets, my grandmother leaned close to me.

"There's shadows all around you," she'd whispered in my ear.

My mouth was opening and closing, no sound coming out as I stared at the man in front of me.

He was *Shinigami.* And he was looking at me with as much wonder as I was him, all in his eyes. The rest of him was rigor mortis still. Until a *crack* resounded, one I knew all too well, and the Japanese man was gone. Scared away.

I slid the *shoji* screen shut as snow drifted in over my bare feet, and turned to run back to the bed, only to smack into Nicholas.

"You're late," I muttered when I'd stopped my scream

of shock. I breathed in his cinnamon plum scent. A mix of New Hampshire and my new home, Japan.

"Who was that?" he asked, like I'd answered the door to Girl Scouts, not a vampire, and like he'd been here the whole time.

"The same vampire from earlier."

Nicholas flashed to the doorway and looked out, but we both knew nobody was there.

I collapsed back onto the bed. I didn't know what day it was, or what time it was, but I knew that Nicholas was in the room with me, and that I wanted him to stay. "Please stay. I know I've been a pain in the ass to deal with, but, please."

His shoulders either relaxed some, or they sagged. I had both effects on him these days. I didn't see him turn around or come to me, but he was there, kneeling at the edge of my bed.

"I'm not a man who needs apologies for everything to be all right."

"Good. Apologizing is awful."

He sighed heavily, his eyes glinting in the moonlight. "But necessary. Look, I didn't want to come here tonight, I wanted to be alone. Because I've nearly killed myself for you, Eliza Morgan, and you resent me for it. Feelings don't die any faster than I do, and it's agonizing trying to kill them."

"What are you saying?"

"I'm dying, and you're spending the time we have hating me for something I had no control over."

I stopped breathing. This spite towards me—I didn't know what to do with it. And I didn't know what to do with the notion of Nicholas being gone from this world, from my world.

"What is it, Eliza? All the times you said to me 'it's not your fault, this is my fate,' you didn't mean it? You seemed so sincere."

"Your sarcasm isn't making this easier."

"Nothing is easy! *Nothing!*" Cold nipped at my legs and feet under the blanket, and I wanted to die. I was terrified that he was calling my bluff. I was terrified that I'd pushed him too far. But I was pissed that he was treating me this way, knowing what I'd seen, what I'd been through, and what I was leaving; my life.

"I lost my best friend," was all I said.

"And so did I. I spent my immortal life with Roman. Until you. Do I hold it against you? No. Because it's not your goddamn fault. And for the number of times you've said to me that it's not my fault, it's yours, maybe I started to believe you. You and I both know we need this to be somebody's fault."

The wind was knocked out of me. It felt like I was losing him, and of course, I was. He was melting into nothing because Roman took Kat's life and he hadn't. And I was pushing him away. All this death for nothing. No explanation except that there was no choice.

"I think we both need to remember what it's like to be alone," he said, and in a sickening flash, he was gone.

The only scent that lingered was red wine and roses.

CHAPTER 7

The silence was heavy, the room warm when I awoke, despite the rice paper walls and the snow that was basically a notebook's thickness away. There were woods behind those doors, close, just like New Hampshire. The trees were different. Dead of winter, no flowers on them. And this room—it should have been colder, with such simple texture and sparseness, but the lack of clutter made *me* uncluttered.

A plain, white wraparound jacket and baggy pair of white pants hung from a hook on the wall. I wished I knew who left them. I was sure people were watching my every move here but I'd only caught one.

Where was everyone? How many vampires were here, at the temple? Were they hiding from me? I got the distinct impression I was the rabbit on the racetrack.

A bucket of clear, cold water was next to a basin on the floor, and I washed up in it. "This hotel sucks," I muttered to myself.

Today I had to get my bearings, gain myself back. I wanted control again, as if I'd ever had any.

The karate clothes were not me. I sighed looking at my cargo pants and hoodie. Time to give up a little bit of me. A little bit more.

Still nobody was visible when I went outside into the snow, and looked around at the other little dwellings like my own. No shadows moved behind those walls. No noises came from within. I didn't know where I was going, and nobody was going to help me.

And I didn't need any help.

A flashback of the strange night before with Nicholas made me shudder, but I wasn't letting go of him that easy. I needed him. Not because I was a stranger in a strange land, but because I'd woken up believing something.

I believed Kat's death wasn't my fault. And I needed him with me, to feel the same way.

I should never have said I didn't blame him when I did. I shouldn't have told him it wasn't his fault, like some bitchy wife trying to get her way. I was ashamed, but had to put that away. I couldn't change it. I had to let myself *feel*.

Unable to give up my Converse All-Stars this morning, I walked on winding boardwalks with overhung trees and iced-over fish ponds. Breathing in the mountain air, I knew what this place was; magical. Heavenly. A gift to me.

If I wanted to share it with Nicholas, I had to find him. Wandering aimlessly wasn't working.

I stopped in the middle of the boardwalk, closed my eyes and listened to my own breathing. It had been a while since I let myself *see* Nicholas this way, to watch him in my mind. I tried to brush off that part of my brain and wake it up by just standing there, concentrating on nothing else, and I wasn't surprised when the picture of him snapped into view.

But I *was* surprised by what I saw.

He was in the snow, in the morning sun, wearing a pair of black sweatpants. His bare back was so bony, he didn't look like the same rugged man I knew that could build a house in a month, who looked so strong just moving.

He was on all fours, retching blood into the snow.

His agony was my agony, and it drew me to him, running down the boardwalks, slipping and falling all over the place. Finally, I fell into the snow at his side, my feet moving too fast for the rest of me, and was almost sick myself over the stench of regurgitated blood as it pooled and clotted in the snow.

"Nicholas, Jesus Christ!" His back was slick with sweat, but it was covered in a frost that came from within him. Hunching over to look in his face, I saw his lips were blue. Frost clung to his eyebrows, and the stubble on his sunken cheeks.

He tried to answer me, but all that came out was a grunt that sounded so painful, tears sprung to my eyes.

I pulled him to me, wishing I had never let go of him before, and rocked him like he'd done to me so many times, always taking care of me when I didn't deserve it, always loving me when I didn't deserve it.

He could tell me all he wanted that his thrall drew me to him, or that it was the unbreakable bond between *Shugotenshi* and their chosen, but we needed each other every way there was.

"Cold," he said through chattering teeth.

"Okay, okay, let's get inside."

I pulled him to standing with effort. He was the weight of a corpse and about as much help in getting up. He stumbled more than I did, and all but fell through the paper doors of his room, which was thankfully heated by a fireplace. We struggled to cross the small room, falling with a thud to the floor.

"What happened?" I asked, as I searched the room, knowing he had a thermal shirt thrown somewhere, he always did. When I found it at the foot of his bed, I threw it at him to put on as I pulled all the blankets off of the bed and dragged them across the room.

"Just f-f-ed."

He was still wiggling into the shirt when I sat with him. Every movement was molasses-slow when he should be able to do this simple thing before I even noticed. I wrapped myself and the blankets around him, hoping my body heat would help restore him. But this cold came from inside.

"This happened from just feeding?" I asked him quietly, rubbing warmth into his hands.

He nodded. "Not m-mine. Not my *unmei nashi*. I can't t-trick my body anymore." His teeth smashed together with every word, his body trembling while mine sweated. "E-e-eliza, I don't th-think I have l-l-long. My b-body is re-rejecting blood."

My throat hurt from sucking back tears. This was the most hopeless a person could be. The kind where you knew you could have done better.

"What can we do, Nicholas?" I sobbed, rocking him

39

like a baby, my heart turning black at how small he felt in my arms.

He only shook his head, though I could barely tell the difference from his spasms.

"I'm going to the Master. He'll know what to do for you."

"He won't," Nicholas croaked.

"He's not going to let you die, or become a vegetable or..."

"This is my fate. I f-f-found you, but—p"

"Enough. You called me a hero once, and goddammit, let me be one."

Sweat dripped from his frost-coated hair as he lifted his head to look at me.

"Let me taste what a hero is."

His cracked lips parted, and slowly his fangs protruded while his eyes stayed on mine.

"Nicholas?"

"Ssshhh," he said. The shaking was gone, the sweating stopped. His eyes glazed over, as if he'd seen an answer in me.

He put his hand, still clammy, on the back of my neck and pulled my lips to his. Once his lips met mine it was like a hot cup of tea after a long, cold day. The scent of him enthralled me, and I couldn't get away from it.

That's when he bit me.

Right under my jaw, just lightly, and then another further down, and then a deep, forceful one on my jugular. It had purpose, and it was selfish; draining, and fulfilling. I couldn't get away from the slow poison of his lips and tongue and teeth, pulling the very life from me, wrapped in sugarplum chocolate scents. If I were to die right then, it would all have been worth it.

He grunted, winding my mess of hair through his fingers and pulling my neck closer. The blood running out—I savored every drop. Ecstasy. I could let him drink until there was nothing left.

But he drew back, leaving me gasping for air, stars swimming in front of my eyes, heart pounding erratically. He smiled, the grin that sang of confidence, happiness and sarcasm, and licked blood off his teeth. I took a sharp breath.

"That was worth near death," he said, and wiped a drop of blood off my collarbone with a rough thumb.

I nodded dumbly. "You're not shaking anymore." My voice sounded too far away.

"Nope," he said, and shot up. He stood straight, something I hadn't seen for a while and not even realized it.

I stumbled to my feet, dazed, and dizzy. Nicholas became a blur of beauty in front of me, catching me as I fell.

"Sitting down is great. Let's sit down," he said, and put me on the bed gently.

"Oh, man. This is why I don't donate blood."

"You do now."

My head cleared up quickly with that statement. "Do you think drinking from me will fix you?"

He sat next to me, hard. It meant he wasn't himself, that existing still hurt. He needed the right blood, and I'd thought it could only have been Kat's. It's what we both thought.

What if we were wrong? What if another's blood could

restore him? There was more than one kind of right in this world.

"Your wheels are spinning. It's hot, but scary. What are you thinking?"

"I need to go to the Master."

"What for?"

"Because, Gatekeeper, I need answers and I want them from him."

He ran a hand, now steady, through my hair, and did the thing he always used to do, before I took myself away from him and anything that wasn't sadness. He put his finger under my chin to lift it up, to make my eyes meet his.

"Feeding from you was great, but I don't think it's permanent, and I don't think the Master will like it at all. Wouldn't have stopped me, but he wouldn't like it."

Seeing the beauty restored to his face, knowing it was my blood that did it, made me angry that we hadn't tried this to begin with. And I was angrier to think that the Master wouldn't want this for him.

"What's not to like? Look at how much healthier you are!"

"Your proposal is to be my blood donor? You're here to become a vampire, not exactly conducive to donating blood. We're more takers."

"I don't have to be *Shinigami*. I don't need anyone to tell me what my destiny is. It's you, and if I can save you—"

He absentmindedly ran his thumb over my lip, sending shivers down my arms. "Your fate isn't to save me or serve me. It's not what you're for. You're bigger than this."

All the emotion I'd held prisoner since we left New Hampshire escaped in my voice. "I. Am not. *Strong* without you."

He bit his lip, and smiled through it. "I'd tell you that you're stronger than me, but you'd tell me to shut up. I'm glad you need me again. I've needed *you* all along."

I kissed him hard, winding my fingers through his thick hair. He needed my blood. But he needed my heart more. I rested my forehead on his, tasting my own blood as I pulled from his lips, and I breathed our salt in deep. "Don't you ever forget that I love you. However lost I get, when I drift away, it's always you I need. Nothing else. No one else."

He tilted his head and took my lips again. The scent of oranges and cinnamon made me ache.

"I love you," was all he said.

"Then let me take care of you. While you need me."

He nodded, and I was out the door.

CHAPTER 8

Guided by an inner sense that had only awoken in Japan, in this temple, my mind ran as fast as my feet, over boardwalks and bridges, down stone steps and snowdrifts. I reached the top of stairs overlooking a clearing between elaborately carved pagodas and doorways straight from a Kung Fu movie.

"Holy hell."

Dozens upon dozens of vampires. They sat in an enormous circle, quietly watching two others sparring in the center.

What the hell had I been thinking, running around Vampire Village, knowing I was being spied on by at least one of them in the middle of the night? What, was I just going to go say hello? What a clown.

But Nicholas needed me and the Master was down there. I took a deep breath and started down the stairs. The Master stood straight and tall, no matter how small he really was, with a long stick-weapon-thing, watching the fight. I kept my eyes on him as the eyes of the mass of *Shinigami* stayed on me.

Breathe steady, suck your stomach in. Don't be a wuss.

The Master slammed the bottom of the stick on the ground when I reached the clearing, and the fighters stopped at once, turning to bow to him. He bowed back, before turning his cloudy eyes on me.

"Master," I said awkwardly, and bowed.

I heard vampires making noises at the sound of my voice, predators forced to sit like nice, quiet pets. I sucked in my stomach again.

"Eliza Morgan," the Master said. "She belongs to Nikorasu."

The murmuring stopped, and only then did I dare look around me.

The *Shinigami* all looked up at me. They exuded a cold mist that chilled me and made this already foreign world a little more foreign.

But I belonged here, and they knew it. I could see it in all of their eyes. Some gritted their teeth, fangs protruding, but I didn't move. I might as well have been naked behind a podium while they all waited for me to talk. I didn't let my voice betray how unsure I was.

"Master, please may I speak with you?" *Stupid and formal and ridiculous sounding.*

With one nod of his head, the *Shinigami* were silently on their feet with not a hint of movement. They bowed in unison, and were gone with flashes, cracks and bangs like colorless fireworks.

And I was alone with a vampire so ancient even he didn't remember where he came from.

He barked out a Japanese word, making it very clear I was to come closer. I did, reluctant though I was to let him know I was afraid and would probably have done anything he said.

"Nikorasu has fed from you," he said with a voice as cold as the snow underfoot.

"Yes," I sad breathlessly.

"It is not to happen again."

So, Nicholas was right. Shocker. Wasn't he always?

And yet...

"If I may, why not, Master?"

"Look at me, *onna*," he said, ice in his voice. With a magnetism that reached into my head and wiggled around, I was made to pull up and look into his blank eyes.

"You are here for you. Not for him. His path is his own. Yours is yet to be seen. Do not turn from it so quickly."

His words were gentler than I expected, and they pierced my heart. It was like a stroking of the soul.

"But I can heal him, I think. The others' blood is killing him, faster than before."

"It is his path."

"No."

He didn't move at my boldness, but the chill in the air became a little colder. I continued.

"It doesn't have to be his *path*. We can fix him, we can bring him back. He doesn't have to suffer."

"He has chosen to suffer."

"He didn't! Roman—" I took a deep breath, steadied myself before my emotions ran me over. "Roman fed on Nicholas's *unmei nashi*. Nicholas never chose that."

"Nikorasu chose to allow it by not attending to his destiny."

"I won't believe that. It's a cop-out." He stiffened, and my breath caught.

"*You* would teach *me* what fate is?" he said, bemused.

I gulped. "You can't know everything. And forgive me, but I don't see how learning karate is going to help prepare me for being a vampire, and I don't see why I should want to if Nicholas isn't with me."

He pounded his staff on the ground again, and a shockwave rumbled through my feet.

"*Baka!*" he bellowed, but I heard it in my head in English; *fool.* "You question the need to learn, no matter what the subject matter? Ignorant American! To think you cannot grow simply from the act of learning. Or did you not think of that at all? Your lessons begin today, and let this be your first. *Learning is change, and change is the only thing that can save us.* Shut your mouth if you don't understand. There is such a thing as a stupid question."

The wind had been knocked out of me with his vehemence. When I finally found my breath, shutting my mouth was not a problem. I'd solved nothing except pissing off an ancient vampire and Nicholas's father figure. He turned his back on me, and even I knew it was meant to be an insult.

A prickling across my scalp and down my spine, as if darkness itself had run its fingers over my skin, and it loved me. Death, back again, to defend me this time.

The Master spun back to me in a lapse of motion, and something rippled across his terrible eyes.

So, you sense it too, I thought.

47

The Master's mouth worked up and down, and I could have sworn he was *scared*. I let the dark sensation wrap around me and hold me. There was little else it could take from me. It was time for that lurking death spirit to pay me back.

"You feel it?" I said to the Master, in a voice from deep inside me, that was inhabited by something else.

"It can't be," the Master said dreamily. He spoke in Japanese, but I understood. He looked like a little old man then. Not a god among men; a man. Until, in his fear and hostility, his fangs found their way between his lips.

They were so long they touched his chin, and they were matched by two more on the bottom, like a viper. I had no doubt he could move as fast.

I took advantage of his slight senselessness. "There's more to me than just blood, and fate. I'll take care of Nicholas until there's nothing left if that's what it takes. Neither of us wants to lose him."

The Master paled, lips quivering around those gruesome teeth as he stared over my shoulder. I knew he was seeing the man who came to me in the night. I could smell his wine and roses, could feel the death of him like hunger pangs.

The Master nodded absentmindedly, like an old man in the home who doesn't know what he's agreeing to. It was enough for me.

"I will not become *Shinigami* for as long as my blood helps Nicholas." My voice sounded like stones dropping, final and hard, and I had no more to say. I bowed low and deep, one hand covering my fist, and waited for the Master to turn away from me before I exhaled.

I needed more strength before I turned to face the man behind me, and the presence he had inside me.

"Who are you?" I asked, my back still to the man of death. When he didn't answer me, I spun on him. I prayed he wouldn't be gone, or the feeling that came with him—that everything was about to be taken away, and I wanted it to be.

He stood in front of me across the clearing, topknotted hair whipping furiously in the wind that I barely noticed, like the storm was his alone. His bell-shaped black pants and flowing white sleeves billowed around him, but he was as solid as stone, staring back at me. Crows circled above him.

"How did you find me here?" I whispered to myself, though he'd certainly be able to hear me, even from his distance. Did I really think I could have escaped the spirit of death by leaving New Hampshire? I'd known I was coming to meet it all along. I could never leave it, and it could never leave me.

We were the same.

"I cannot find what is not lost," he said, and I jumped at the softness of his voice. Powerful and gentle. Mournful.

"Who are you?"

"I am the space between heartbeats and the breath at the end of things. I am living shadow and lamented life. Izanagi."

He burst into the space in front of me, leaving the air torn like paper behind him.

Silence echoed around us. The brown-gray sky seemed bigger suddenly, and Izanagi dwarfed me with the power of his being. Human in stature, heavenly in proportion. He was the height of mountains and just as immoveable.

"Eliza," he said, leaning close to my cheek, tendrils of his hair tickling my nose. "Take death by the reins."

And he was gone but for that scent of death. The walls of the mountains threatened to swallow me, and I ran back to Nicholas to try to stop death again.

CHAPTER 9

Nicholas was asleep when I got back to his room, the crisper version of his log cabin in Ossipee. It was warmer than my place here, not just because of the fireplace. The wide mattress on the floor ran almost the length of the wall, pillows all over it. Nothing hidden here, everything close. Zen, fresh, and of the Earth. The peace followed him into his sleep, his chest rising and falling quietly. The hollows under his eyes weren't as deep. Already, he was better. I ached to give him just a little more. Anything to bring the man back I needed.

My thoughts went to Izanagi, and what he'd meant when he said *take death by the reins*. Nicholas and I, we might have done it.

My fingernail bled where I'd been biting them with nerves. I'd been at the temple for one day, and had more questions than I did answers, and the answers I did have weren't wildly supported by the powers that be. And as much as I wanted to feed Nicholas forever, I knew it was impossible. I wouldn't outlive him as a human, and like Nicholas said—it wasn't my job.

I would become *Shinigami.* But I would do it in my time, on my terms; no one else's, fate's included.

I looked at the blood on my finger, and slowly slid it between his parted lips. Squeezing my fingertip, blood dripped into his mouth. He closed it around my finger, sucking gently. Nicholas rolled his shoulders over, and clutched my arm to his chest, sucking on my finger like a wounded animal, getting more and more intense. He groaned, making me groan in response.

His eyes popped open, heated and searching for me. Pulling my finger from his mouth, I kissed his wet lips, and for a minute we were back in New Hampshire, being just us, not afraid. It seemed now like we were always afraid.

My hands found his bare back cold underneath his shirt as I caressed his ribs and shoulders, down his spine, stopping at his waist when he moaned, but not for long.

I was tired of waiting for everything to happen *to* us.

Nicholas pulled my hips closer to his, and kissed me forcefully. "Eliza."

"Don't stop, Nicholas," I breathed in his ear, my hair falling into my face, the same color as his, our curls winding around each other, our limbs winding around each other.

He grunted, pushing his hardness against me, his rough fingers dimpling my fleshy arms. He took my hand, and lightly pierced my fingertip with one fang, making me pull back for only a second before I pushed it in further. The thin stream of blood left me, deliciously slow.

"Sorry?"

"What?" I said. Confusion scrambled me at a third voice, in my head, followed by a fast vision of a man I didn't recognize. I didn't know where he was, or why the hell he was in my head. I sure didn't love vampires in my head, and certainly not now.

"What?" Nicholas grumbled.

Then Nicholas's head snapped up as the voice sounded, out loud this time, at the door.

"Sorry?" the voice said from the other side of the door. This was déjà vu of the worst kind, where nothing made sense and I nausea bubbled in my gut.

Had I just seen the future a second before it happened?

"Shit!" I said, scrambling to straighten out my clothes under the blankets.

Nicholas was up like a bolt of lightning, pulling aside the *shoji* door as I struggled with the blankets. I grinned that he'd been so caught up in me that he hadn't heard the third person approaching.

I was still smoothing down my hair when I made eye contact with the young man at the door over Nicholas's shoulder. He smiled sweetly, his ice blue eyes piercing me.

"Sorry to interrupt," he said shyly, looking at his feet. His was the same voice I'd heard in my mind.

"Get the hell over here, kid," Nicholas said, pulling our visitor into his arms and clapping him on the back. "Eliza! This is Paolo!" like I was supposed to know who that was.

Paolo was still looking at the ground with an embarrassed grin.

"Well, great to meet you, Paolo," I said, trying not to

sound resentful or give away that I would much rather have met him another time. Almost any other time.

"I-I'm so sorry to interrupt," he said again, looking anywhere but at me. I ran my hands over my messy hair again, in case I was scaring him.

Nicholas leaned into his ear, one eye on me. "Been a while since you've seen a pretty face around here, has it?"

Paolo laughed too loud, wildly, refreshingly awkward.

"Sit, kid. Tell me what I've missed around here. It's grim as hell, like nothing any good has happened since I left." Nicholas was so much like *himself,* before he began melting into nothing. My heart swam with pleasure at it, and any resentment I had was gone. For anything. For our interruption, for the tension between us since Kat died. I only needed him to be Nicholas French.

As Nicholas sat cross-legged at the low, dark wood table with Paolo on the other side, I answered when a shadow appeared at the door.

"I asked for tea," Paolo said quietly. "The good kind."

I opened the door to a young woman. "Hi. You know, *konnichiwa.*" She bowed, averting her eyes. It was weird. I was the one who didn't look at people.

I realized she was waiting for me to ask her inside, so I moved, allowing her to glide in gracefully at human speed. Her kimono shuffled making the sweetest swishing noise. I wanted to hug her for being a person like me, but I would have given her a heart attack.

And no person was like me.

Nicholas and Paolo chatted and laughed as if they'd just seen each other last week, though the both stopped to thank the girl as she poured their tea.

"Thank you," I said as she left, head bowed.

"*Hai*," she replied before running off.

"It's funny when you scare people," Nicholas said. Paolo still hadn't looked at me for more than a second.

"I'm honored to meet you, my lady," Paolo said, an accent now clear.

"I'm happy to meet you, too," I said, eyeing Paolo. It was his scent; I'd never smelled anything so fresh and *empty.* He smelled like goodness and freedom. So calming, and Jesus Christ, did I need that. I waited for Nicholas to tell me something about him, but knew the pain in the ass was waiting to see what I could find out on my own.

"We've missed you around here, Nicholas," Paolo said, his accent getting thicker as he became more comfortable. Italian. "It has been a bit dull. *I've* missed you." He spoke so plainly, no mincing words. "I've been aching to see you fight again."

"Sure, sure. I have a little healing to do before I see myself in the ring, but you'll get front row when I do."

"Nicholas is all but a celebrity at the temple. We all wait for him," Paolo said to me with a grin.

"Some more than others," Nicholas answered, throwing a tea towel at Paolo, who caught it without movement.

"Yes, I've heard, and met a few of his *admirers*," I said, my mind needling in images of his creator, Jenniveve, the heartless bitch. And Roman, of course.

"Wait until you see him out there, Eliza," Paolo said. To hear him say my name was like the purity of churchbells. The man was extraordinary. So humble, unassuming, with this clarity about him that made him a white light of a person. Or vampire. My eyes sought Nicholas's to let him know I expected to hear more about Paolo, but Nicholas just waggled his eyebrows at me and drank his tea. Paolo watched every move he made. He was a *fan*. Nicholas had *fans*.

I wondered what that made me.

"I admit, I'm pretty anxious to see what everyone else thinks the fuss is about," I said, nudging Nicholas with my elbow.

"Oh, he's legendary," Paolo piped up, eyes wide, finally really looking at me. Excitement glittered in his eyes, lit up his young face. "What I've learned by watching him—"

"Kid, you're better than me in the ways that count, with the humanity and closeness to God and all that."

"You guys worry about being close to God?" I asked.

"You know I'm not really a God-fearing kind of guy," Nicholas said, leaning his elbow on the table.

"I was a priest in life," Paolo said with a humble smile, silencing me. "I was deemed a man of God at a very young age, and my studies began immediately," he said, sensing my questions.

Nicholas uncovered a basket of bread in the middle of the table, and leaned back with a huge piece. "Paolo was more than a priest. He was very nearly a saint," Nicholas said solemnly.

My head swung to take in Paolo. There most certainly was something about him that was *higher*. It made sense. Nicholas was right.

"A saint?"

Paolo looked down. "Many believed I was destined for sainthood, yes."

My confusion came out as irritation. "But the *Shinigami* know their destinies. *This* is our destiny, how could there be two of them?"

"Paolo was turned by mistake." Nicholas shoved bread in his mouth and raised his eyebrows at me.

"Mistake?" I whispered. "How can that be?"

"I wouldn't say *mistake*," Paolo said, shooting Nicholas an apologetic smile for disagreeing. "The Lord knows the path we must take, and fate is part of his will. I am this because it is what was meant to be, from the hands above."

Nicholas watched him intently. "You don't resent being turned at all?"

"Resentment changes nothing. *We* change everything." That was *Shinigami*-speak if I ever heard it.

"Cut it out, kid. This is me you're talking to."

The wisdom in Paolo's young face was, indeed, heavenly. "I mourned my life. But this life is eternal, and the good I can do with it is still His will. Had I been deemed a saint, would that not be another form of immortalization?"

Puke. "But, you were so devout, and now—now you kill people."

Nicholas went dead still.

"Yes. I do what the Lord asks of me."

"Or what the Master asks of you?"

Nicholas made a shocked noise and jumped to the defense of his Master. "*Unmei nashi* have no fate. The Master's just a guide for us." His eyes flashed with irritation. I didn't care. Answers didn't come easily here, and I would find them all, kicking and screaming, before my life was taken away from me, as pathetic as it may have been.

"Good talk," Nicholas said, finishing the conversation as he put down his tea cup. He stood, and looked stronger in stature than I'd seen him in weeks. "I'll make my grand appearance tomorrow, but now I need rest."

With calm fortitude, Paolo asked something that would probably be on the minds of many *Shinigami*. "Why do you need so much rest now, Nicholas?" He sipped his tea and waited.

Nicholas shrugged. "Long trip."

"That's not the rumor, my friend."

"Always listen to rumors, Paolo. They're always right."

"In this case, they are," I said. Both men looked at me. The mouth I usually shot off at home seemed to have purpose here. I went with it. "What? Why hide it, Golden Boy?" I turned my back on Nicholas and looked in Paolo's swimming blue eyes. "My best friend was his *unmei nashi*. But he couldn't do it."

"Is it true that Roman took her life?" Paolo asked with a pleasant firmness. He spoke with the certainty of a man who never doubts himself. I nodded. Silence filled the room, trapped by the paper walls.

"Nicholas, not feeding on your *unmei nashi*, it will be the end of you. It's a miracle that you're not worse off."

"Not quite a miracle, kid," Nicholas huffed, throwing a meaningful glance my way.

"What is restoring you, if I may?" I definitely thought Paolo knew the answer.

"You already know," Nicholas said.

Paolo looked at me. "This is not how things are supposed to be, my dear."

"I don't like how things are supposed to be," I said with a stiff jaw and a raised chin.

Paolo smiled, like someone would smile at a particularly strange child. "You're strong, Eliza, but we are His sheep."

"I am no one's sheep." And it was as if Izanagi were with me, his astounding power fueling my words.

"Certainly no debating that," he said with a tip of his head and a grin.

"What rumors are there about Eliza?" Nicholas asked. The room got a little colder with his question, but I was warm from his protectiveness.

The boyishness returned to Paolo's face in a huge smile. "She is an instrument of change for us all. The buzz is everywhere."

"And the Master? What does he think of it?" I said.

"The Master keeps his opinions close. He is closer to the gods than any of us," Paolo said, then laughed. "But I've got a hunch you'll have a way of getting them out in the open."

It was beginning to make sense to me why the *Shinigami* had chosen victims; their prey held something they needed, something they were missing. I wanted to dig into it more, the importance of it screeching at me to figure out the riddle. It could be the answer to making Nicholas whole again. Maybe it would give answers to a lot of the *Shinigami*. They deserved them. They deserved to know why things weren't in their control, no matter how powerful they were.

"Eliza, may I walk you back to your room?" Paolo said, since Nicholas had implied we were done talking. The snow had begun to make drifts against the bottom of the door.

"Sure," I said, but I really just wanted to crawl into bed with Nicholas and keep him strong, never be without him. There was nothing I wouldn't do to keep him strong.

If anyone had the strength to live forever, it was Nicholas French. I hoped I could keep up.

I kissed Nicholas good night as Paolo put on his wool trench coat. It made me think of Nicholas standing in the snow at home, though this trench was older, speckled with holes, and thinning. Nicholas's coat was in good shape, but at any moment Nicholas himself could be speckled with holes, thinning. I kissed him again, wrapped my arm around his waist to pull him into me, bit his bottom lip, swooped my tongue deep in his mouth, anything I could do to show him that I was all in, that I would never let go. It left his lips hot pink and puffy when I was done with him. He raised his eyebrows, swollen lips parted, and mumbled something about things done in front of a holy man.

"Quite all right," Paolo said shyly.

"See her back safely," Nicholas told him.

The night was pin-pricked with stars through the falling snow, and there was no wind for the first time I'd been out on the mountain. Paolo took my arm in his like an old fashioned gentleman, which I suppose he was.

"I'm glad we talked," I said through the silence.

"The pleasure is all mine, Eliza. I've certainly not met anyone like you in my long life."

More silence.

"So, you are romantically involved with Nicholas, yes?"

"Um. Yes, we are. Plainly." I laughed the nervous laugh Kat always hated and would kick me for if she was within range. *No longer in range.* I shook my head at my inner crassness.

"Do you not find your relationship to be a bit dangerous?" Paolo asked with not a hint of judgment.

"Everything about us is dangerous," I replied.

"Indeed. Do you think you tempt fate too much?"

"Fate can kiss my ass. Fate has done nothing except give me that man, and a reason to not be human."

He stopped. "Is this also the way you feel about God?"

"With all due respect, I have enough on my plate without worrying about God judging my choices. He lets me make them for a reason. He doesn't like them, he's the one who gave them to me, so… And then the *Shinigami* tell you that there are no choices. So, I'm inclined to do whatever I want right about now."

Paolo only blinked, slight smile on his lips. Unreadable. "I hope you find your way, Eliza. Your way will carve the path for the rest of us." He turned and began walking again.

First the crows landed in my path, and then I got the familiar jolt of him, Izanagi, near me. Through me. I couldn't see him anywhere in the woods surrounding us, but a flicker of darker than dark shadow between snowflakes.

"You have a big day tomorrow, my dear," Paolo said, putting his hands on my shoulders, like he was so much older than me, which I guess he was.

"I do?" I said.

"Tomorrow Nicholas will make his appearance, with

you by his side. Tomorrow, you begin to become." He kissed my hand, a salty ocean scent mixed with cherry blossoms folding over me as he did. And he flashed out of sight, leaving me alone.

Not entirely alone. Izanagi was there, behind the trees, I sensed him; not like the prickle on the back of my neck, but like a hand in the soul. He had something I needed, and it unnerved me to know it.

"I know you're out there," I said quietly, certain he could hear.

Something opened in me. It let me see Paolo before he got to his door. It was the beginning of a purpose. I could feel it here. And it's the thing that drove me to look for Izanagi with my vision. The presence of death I'd known all my life lurked in the woods, real and with answers for questions I couldn't put to words, that had formed my life.

I crouched down to the birds, who met me with one hop forward. I reached out and laid my hand on the one closest to me, stroking the spot between his eyes with my thumb. "Show me," I said.

It was me that zeroed in on that spot, far out into the mountainside, and it was me that reached for Izanagi's death scent of wine and roses. But it was the stream of crows that fled into my vision in a thick straight line, that led me to him.

There he was in my head, a shadow deeper than the blackest night, darker than the murder of crows. There but not quite there, a presence as light as the snow.

And he could see in my mind's eye, too.

My breath caught painfully in my throat, my knees went weak, and I got dizzy. Eyes that had seen unfathomable darkness stared into my thoughts. I would have hit the ground if he hadn't suddenly appeared in the form I knew, to catch me. I was close enough to look in those depths, and see that the Hell in his eyes didn't come from within—it was a reflection.

He'd seen things only a god could live with, but never understand.

"I'm okay now," I said while I got my feet under me. He didn't let me do it alone, putting me upright before I realized we'd moved.

"Yes, you are," he said, still locked on my face, so close I could see the lines in his lips, see where his teeth had dimpled them. He was still looking *inside* me. And he was worried about me, despite telling me I was okay.

"I am. Izanagi, don't leave me with the horrible mystery that vampires seem to love. Tell me what I need from you. You have something for me, to help me. Don't make me fight for it."

With a quick bow, he vanished like they all did, leaving the trail of death incarnate in his wake.

"Goddammit." Destroyed and revitalized all in one day, over and over. "Japan is exhausting."

The bed was on the floor, making it easy to crawl to. I dreamed of death.

CHAPTER 10

"I can't believe I let you near all those vampires alone," Nicholas said, shaking his head like a madman.

"You weren't yourself." Still wasn't. Or wasn't again. The hollows were back under his eyes. His cheeks were sunken. As quickly as my blood had revitalized him, it was used up it seemed, left him emptier than before.

"I had to be drunk. Did you get me drunk? You're a bad enough influence without getting me drunk, too."

We'd been back and forth over it since Nicholas dragged himself out of bed and realized what exactly he'd given his consent for me to do when I went to the Master. I'd wandered the temple alone, among hundreds of vampires that only wanted to kill humans, not hang out with them.

"They didn't know who you were yet. Any one or fifty of them could have attacked you and nobody would have batted an eye."

"I made sure they knew who I was quickly enough."

"Wait until they see what you can do. Who you really are under that stunning face and smart-ass mouth."

I smiled. "I think you just called me 'ass mouth,' but thanks?"

"You're better than them all. Every last one of them."

"Pretty sure you're still drunk."

He was at my side in an instant, tipping my chin up with one finger, making my heart stop, making my mind race back to the times when I was too numb to know what it meant to be so close to him. When all I could think of was how he'd taken things from me. Her from me. I was still losing him in one way or another, all the time. His fingers shook as he touched me. I hated that it was with as much physical weakness as with emotion.

"That was an incredibly brave thing you did. For me," he said, taking me by surprise with a swift kiss that lingered like a bee sting.

"Um. Sure, I guess. You would have—"

"Don't do the self-deprecating crap, it was amazing and you know it. You knew the danger you were in. You did it anyway. Thank you."

I kissed him that time, making the dryness of his thirsty lips softer with my touch. "I would do much worse for you."

He leaned his forehead on mine, hands wound through my hair. "I could test that out."

"What, make me walk on broken glass or something? Lift up a burning urn with my bare arms, Kung Fu movie style."

"Yup, that's what I was thinking. As soon as I stopped thinking of you naked." He kissed me hard, wrapping his arms around me, still stronger than life. My will flooded out of me, and I was his to do with as he wanted.

What he wanted was to tease me. This was getting painful.

He pulled away and kissed my nose. "Time to make our great appearance."

I whined like a candy-deprived fat kid. *It has been so long since I had anything but healthy food.*

Smiling, he started digging through my clothes, which were in the process of being unpacked, and probably always would be. They were currently all over the place, hanging from the screen at the back of my room, on the floor, in stacks, in the old suitcase. Unpacking sucked.

"You need layers. We'll be outside a long time." He threw gloves at me, and a hooded sweatshirt. "Put these on under your *gi* top," he said, throwing the white karate uniform at me. And socks. And another thin shirt. Then the green sweater I stole from him.

"What exactly are we doing?" I said, getting bulkier by the second as I pulled more shirts over my chest. I looked huge. Huger. My boobs were planetary. "Nicholas, do I really have to make an effort to look more like the Michelin Man?" I twisted and turned trying to loosen up my arms, but gave up fast.

"You don't look like the Michelin Man," he said, still nose-deep in my suitcase, inspecting a red bra. "Sexy Stay-Puft Marshmallow....Lady." He looked up long enough to waggle his eyebrows. "We're formally introducing you, presenting you, in fact. Watch some training. Maybe do some. But it will be cold, and my shield isn't strong enough to contain you in my pathetic weakness."

I was reminded of Nicholas encasing us in a man-made shimmering snowglobe to protect me from the wild storm, making me untouchable in the backwoods of snowy, windy New Hampshire. It was magic. He was magic. The night was a fairy tale.

Everything was real now. He was dying.

"Nicholas, feed from me."

"No." He zipped up the suitcase.

"I can already see you losing your strength. Let me help you."

"Nope. Thanks."

"Nicholas! We know it won't really hurt me. What's the harm now?"

"The harm, *Eliza,* is that you're human. And whether you're *unmei fumetsu* or not, you're still human. This isn't the Red Cross. You'll be needing your blood." He winked as he passed me into the snow.

Dressed to Nicholas's overbearing specifications, we began the walk to the clearing I'd been to the day before. My nerves fluttered at the idea of seeing the hundreds of *Shinigami* again, but they weren't going anywhere, and neither was I.

"Nicholas, I have something to tell you," I said, as we walked, my head down, his head held high.

"Shoot."

"My visions are different now."

"How?"

"They happen. Not about you."

He didn't break stride. I was, as usual, impressed by his coolness. "Have you had any before that weren't about me?"

"You know I haven't."

"Don't worry, I don't think they're like wet dreams. I won't get jealous."

My sigh was probably insulting. "I saw Paolo come to the door before he did. Seconds before, but still. *You weren't in it.*" I swallowed. "And then last night, I looked for someone with it. And it worked."

That furrow between his eyes. I wanted to kiss it. "Who were you looking for?"

"Izanagi," I blurted.

"Izanagi. The guy from before?"

"Yes."

"Stop clenching your fists. It's okay. You found him?"

I nodded, breathing in through my nose. I knew I looked guilty and nuts. Nicholas's smirk told me.

"That's really something," he said, and started walking again.

"What do you think?" I said as I ran to catch up with his too-fast feet.

He shrugged. "Probably because you're here now, where it all began. You're with *people* like you. You'll flourish even faster."

"That makes sense," I mumbled. I was looking for a little more excitement from him, and didn't know what it meant that he was brushing it off like this. But I knew one thing: when Nicholas kept secrets from me, they were important. Things I needed to know. And I didn't like having information doled out to me in rations.

I grabbed his arm and he let me turn his body toward mine. He could have stopped me if he wanted to, but he knew there was no stopping me in the long run.

"Nicholas, tell me who this man is. Izanagi."

He swallowed hard. "I'm not the man for that job."

I raised an eyebrow.

"Since when do you care whose toes you step on? I trust you, there's nobody better to tell me secrets that have to do with the rest of my damn life."

"Nope, not my story to tell." He walked ahead.

"You'll make me figure this it out on my own? Right? Initiation crap?" I caught up to him again, and we were suddenly staring down at the arena, or whatever it was. With him by my side, it seemed smaller. But it wasn't my fight down there today.

"Tell me what you know, Nicholas French. Nothing gets kept from me in the interest of sparing my fragile little mind anymore. This is my story. Tell me how it goes."

He breathed in so deep his chest rose like a balloon was inside. "Maybe you're right." He looked at his feet, cracked his knuckles, and began.

"The Japanese god who created all the other gods, who created Japan itself, is named Izanagi."

"Okay."

"Nobody knows who you're talking about. I've asked a few, and this guy who only you see, he doesn't train here, or live here, or do whatever here." He ran his fingers through his hair fast. So he was troubled. "I think you're seeing a god."

"Jesus Christ, what?"

"Yes. I'll tell you his story tonight at the ceremony—"

"Ceremony?"

"Yeah, there's always a ceremony around here. But I'll

tell you then. Right now, we have a date." He nodded toward the crowd below. "Ready? All look, no touch today."

He gave me that face that shows he's proud, but also shows he thinks he had something to do with it. "You're really not scared, are you?"

"No, really not. I'm ready for whatever." Even to find out I was seeing gods. Emotion that I'd just started to let back in took me over, and images of Kat and Roman exploded into memory. "I'm ready to not be part of *that* life anymore. I want a reason to exist. I don't want this limbo anymore. I want to put the world behind me."

He pulled my chin up to face him, and I held it there, finished with hiding. It was time to own this thing I was to become.

"Let's go, my love," I said. And I started down the stairs.

CHAPTER 11

We descended the steps to the watchful eyes of all below. Everyone stopped, the sparring in the center ceased, and a throng of vampires stood to face us. Some wore karate uniforms, billowing and black, like pictures of samurai, others in slimmer fitting and less showy white *gis* like mine. But every one looked distinctly not of this world. And of course, the Master was the most ethereal and intimidating of them all.

Nicholas walked down the steps at my side, our bodies touching with every movement. His scent was powerful, like cardamom and cloves, and I could see his chin cocked out of the corner of my eye. He was an arrogant bastard, and I loved it.

When we got to the bottom, the *Shinigami* parted to let us through. They didn't make a noise as he passed. He made eye contact with a few, all of them bowing their heads to him with respect. He was so much stronger here, no matter how frail. He was a god himself. Pride made it impossible for me not to smile, and I was cool with knowing all the vampires saw it. Pride and respect went hand in hand.

"Master," Nicholas said as we approached, and put his fist into his other hand, bowing. I did the same. All this bowing was unnatural to me, but Nicholas had told me the value of respect here. I'd read a book or two, I said, and I'd argued that not bowing didn't necessarily show my lack of respect, but I had no leg to stand on. I was being arrogant, and I knew it. Even here, totally out of my element—in theory—I didn't want to let anyone have the upper hand. I couldn't afford that attitude here; I had to let myself give in, let go of my defensiveness. The Master's haunting eyes searched me out, rather than Nicholas, and both of us noticed, acknowledging it with a glance to each other.

"Nikorasu," the old vampire breathed. "And our Eliza."

Our *Eliza is an endearment, not an insult.*

It was cold outside, and colder still with the vampires at my back.

"Thank you, Master, for having us," Nicholas said. I'd never heard him hand over authority so easily. He was always the one in charge. Ironically, it made me want to protect him from whatever dangers there might be here.

"Thank you for bringing us this gift," the Master said, fathomless eyes on me.

"Are there any other humans here, Master?" I asked, apparently out of turn.

His white eyes grew cold, and I grew colder. I knew he was doing it to me, like he'd done before when I didn't know my place. This time, I wouldn't cower, or let the frost forming between the Master and I stiffen me. Keeping my attitude in check was just too hard, and who knows—that attitude might keep me alive at this temple. I stared back, refusing to even grit my teeth against the cold he was wrapping me in, until Nicholas gently squeezed my fingers, and I relaxed. The Master loosened up as well; the lines of frost from his hands and feet to me wound their way backwards like tentacles to his body. I stood tall.

The Master didn't speak to me, but reached out fast as a whip and spun me around to face the crowd of *Shinigami*.

"Eliza is Nikorasu's *unmei fumetsu,* but she is more than that. You all sense it. You have all been speaking of it. But not a one of us knows what her great gift is." He turned his head slowly to me. "We begin to find out now."

The silence of the creatures staring back at me was unsettling, their stillness chilling. I bowed in the awkward silence, and they all answered in kind simultaneously. *Yes, got that one right.* I could feel them breathing me in, smelling me. Their scents were all jumbled and mixing, a white noise of smell. But Nicholas's cut through them like a knife.

"Sit with me," Nicholas leaned over and whispered in my ear. Simple words, but they sent a shiver down my spine.

We sat cross-legged on the small set of steps where the Master continued to stand, facing the vampires who returned to sitting as well.

Only one continued to stand. He leaned, James Dean-style against an intricately carved doorway, ankles crossed, hair mussed up, days-old stubble roughening his cheeks. He squinted like he was looking into the sun as he took a last drag off a cigarette and flicked it into the snow, burning a hole in the clean whiteness. He wore jeans and a black t-shirt, faded tattoos peeking out of the short sleeves.

"Nicholas," I whispered, leaning over. I caught him rolling his eyes but with a bit of a smile, also looking at the only man dressed like he just rolled out of a bar.

"Kieran."

"Right, am I up then, boss?" this Kieran said with an Irish brogue that made every woman in the crowd sigh. If Nicholas hadn't been next to me, I might have done the same thing.

He swaggered to the center ring, looking more bored than a derelict at the police station. As he passed, he swung his eyes at me, burning with a sultry glint, and winked. I couldn't breathe. Nicholas made a haughty noise, and I squeezed the frost off his fingers with a smile.

Kieran looked up, and pointed lazily at a raven-haired beauty with her arms around her knees.

"Blue, me and you, lass," he said, and turned his back to the crowd.

This Blue was suddenly on her feet, with that non-movement the *Shinigami* threw in my face. She was tiny perfection, a total bombshell with more strength in her petite, voluptuous body than any woman I'd ever seen. She made the loose-fitting dark blue uniform look dramatic and sexy. Black hair shimmered in waves down her back. Her eyes were wide, but piercing, and her lips were rose red, full, but not childish. She was exquisite.

I stole a glance at Nicholas, who couldn't take his eyes

off of her. My eyes took on a heat of their own when I watched her glide to the ring, to face Kieran as he stared her down, arms crossed, chin down, the tip of one thumb in his mouth. He was making me blush. He was completely focused on Blue, like he wanted her, or wanted to eat her alive.

The tiny woman and Kieran faced each other, Blue's back straight, all business; Kieran's slouched like he was just as ready to pick up a beer as fight.

"He's going to fight *her?"* I whispered to Nicholas.

"Hajime!" the Master barked, and Blue moved like the wings of a hummingbird, darting and flitting, knocking Kieran flat on his back. He sprung back up, still looking like he had somewhere better to be.

Blue was a tiny tiger circling him. Kieran's lips quirked like he was watching the best part of a porno. She moved in on him again, this time flipping over his head and kicking him from behind so that he landed on his knees halfway across the ring. He let out an *oomph*, and laughed.

"Give me more, Blue, baby," he said. It made Blue growl and run at him again, this time slowly enough that I could see her steps, and her bared teeth. She was more predictable in her anger.

The Irishman stopped her solidly with his forearm, but caught her in a dancer-like dip before she hit the ground. He kissed her with an animal ferocity that had more than one gasp coming from the crowd. Blue wasn't swayed. She pushed him off; he landed on his ass in the snow, still laughing. Blue marched back to the center of the ring, bowed to the Master, and went back to where she'd been sitting. Fury was all over her face. But when she met

Nicholas's eyes in her scan of the crowd, she smiled wide. A blazing, brilliant thing.

"She's pretty amazing," I said into Nicholas's ear.

"Sure," he said, waving to her.

"Kieran likes her."

"Kieran is the peanut butter to the jelly of every woman here."

Kieran was leaning back in the doorway again, lighting up another cigarette.

"Kieran," Nicholas said loudly. His voice carried and echoed, silencing the crowd's murmurs.

"Frenchie!" Kieran called back. "What's cracking, mate?"

"Frenchie?" I said.

"Give me a try," Nicholas said, ignoring me, and stood.

I tugged on his pants leg, and he looked down at me, knowing what I was about to say. "Eliza, don't worry about me." That Nicholas smile that made my heart stop, and told me I was in for trouble. "This'll be fun. Hair of the dog that didn't bite me."

"Wha—"

Nicholas strode to the center of the ring, forcing the Master to hide his surprise. Nobody was expecting this. *Shinigami* pointed and nudged, and if I didn't know better, I'd say they were placing bets.

He told me we were just watching today. He wasn't strong enough for this.

Kieran met him in the ring, and they did some handshake thing that looked like they'd met for a beer. So they were friendly, then? That was a relief. I didn't need him to have any other battle to focus on besides getting better.

They bowed to the Master, Nicholas deeper and with eyes down, Kieran like he'd rather be smoking.

Nicholas straightened up, still strong as hell, but not what he was. Kieran was well-muscled, lithe, as if he'd fought on the streets of Ireland his whole life. He shuffled a little, readying more than he had for Blue. The pin-up girl on his arm winked at me like she knew a secret I didn't.

Kieran moved first. He was brutish compared to the cat-like silkiness of Nicholas's movements or the darting beauty of Blue's. He was all means to an end, with the least amount of show and the most scrappiness. Nicholas didn't flinch, but met Kieran's swift punches with equal blocks and artful strikes of his own.

But he was tired.

The more Kieran came at him, all punches, no kicks, the more Nicholas backed up, moving slower, even if he was the fastest thing on two feet. My teeth hurt from gnashing them together.

When Kieran hit him with an uppercut that lifted him a foot off the ground, I jumped to my feet. Nicholas didn't recover fast, and Kieran kept on him with another blow to the gut, then one to each side of his beautiful face, the second knocking him to the ground. Nicholas spit blood.

And that son of a bitch, Kieran, looked up at me with a smirk on his face like he'd pissed on a national monument.

"He can take it, lass," he said to me. My lip curled back, and I growled out loud.

Nicholas's fingers dug into the snow from where he lay on the ground, and it froze underneath them, creating a crackling spiderweb of ice that raced across the ground toward Kieran. I'd never been so pleased to see Nicholas angry.

He was on his feet in a whirlwind of snow and ice, making the closest vampires gasp and cover their eyes. Nicholas was on his opponent, invisible in his stormy flurry of movement, but the snapping of Kieran's head and the buckling of his body made it clear what happened.

There was blood in the air, frozen droplets suspended around them.

"Yamete!" the Master yelled, banging his staff on the ground. Nicholas and Kieran both stopped to stare at the Master with wide eyes. Apparently, his anger wasn't something they were accustomed to. They both bowed low to him, to each other, and left the ring to stunned silence all around.

Nicholas fell to the ground when he reached me.

CHAPTER 12

"What the hell is wrong with you?" I shouted at Kieran, as I tried to pull Nicholas to his feet. Blood splattered the snow.

Kieran's eyes were wide with alarm, puppyish despite his roughness. He put his hands up, to tell me to back off. "Easy, love. He came after me, remember?"

Nicholas fell again to the ground, making me groan with disappointment in myself for not stopping him. I turned on Kieran as he approached us.

"Get away from him or I will end you one way or another."

The Irishman stopped in his tracks, and I couldn't look away; his thrall was working on me, a smoke that traveled through my body. Nicholas said that the thrall was unintentional, but I wasn't sure if I'd believed him. Still didn't.

The scent from Kieran wasn't enough to lure me in, but it was just dangerous enough to make me want him, ever so briefly. Campfire, smoke, burning leaves. Heat emanated from him, melting the snow under his feet, making waves in the winter air around him. Wisps of smoke drifted upwards from his hands and hair. And his eyes….. From this close I could see flames dancing in the autumn brown.

"I didn't mean to—"

"You didn't care!" I shouted at Kieran. "Now look at him."

Vampires watched us from all sides, but Blue was the one who caught my eye because she was looking at Nicholas, crumpled on the ground.

"He's mine," I hissed in a feral cavewoman voice as I hovered over him, shocking myself. But what else could I do to keep vampires away from him at his weakest? Celebrities are only loved until they're at their worst.

Nicholas struggled to his feet, and once again the crowd parted for us. We left tradition and honor behind as we climbed the steps together.

"I'm sorry," Nicholas said, his arm heavy across my shoulders.

"Don't be."

"Good, because I'm really not."

We were quiet for the rest of the walk back to his room. All I could think about was healing him, and to what extent he'd go to prevent me doing it.

He fell on the bed face first. Crashing after that short bout, where a month ago it would have him strutting around with his shoulders back...it hurt to watch. I thought of his constant battles with Lynch, how invigorated he was after. I was constantly battling not to lose

Nicholas like I had everyone else, but there was never a break, never a promise that I would ever get to stop. He was slipping through my fingers and I'd have eternity to live with it.

"What the hell got into the Irishman?" Nicholas moaned, rolling over.

I chuckled. "That's what I called him in my head, too."

"Picking off the biggest guy in the yard isn't his MO. Really excited he decided to change his mind today."

"Why did you?" I spat.

"What?"

"Why did you change your mind and fight? Today wasn't your day, it was just a meet and greet. I didn't do much meeting, since you were so amped to get your ass kicked."

He put his hands behind his head and looked at me, standing there in my absurd layers. He was still god-like to me, and he knew it.

"I don't like having my footprints stepped in."

"Stop being obscure."

"I know no other way."

Sweating under the bulk, I struggled to peel off clothes, barely able to move under them. Nicholas watched my pitiful strip tease with amusement as I grunted and pulled all the knotted layers off. I wiped my hair out of my face and turned my attention back to the weakened thing that was Nicholas.

"You can't laugh this off," I snarled, but softened up when he didn't deny it. "I think we both know what you need right now."

He groaned, and bit his lip with a sexuality that only

Nicholas French could pull off. The laugh lines around his mouth wrinkled, his swirling eyes quickening. "God, I hope you weren't thinking of waffles, or a nap."

I wouldn't let him distract me.

"Nicholas, you need to feed from me. Don't be shy. I can handle you taking more than you did before, but you can't handle not doing it."

"I'm going to live forever," he said with a regal wave of his thin arm.

"Right, you'll live forever looking like hell and feeling worse, so sick you won't be able to make bad jokes."

"Well I never!"

"Stop it, Nicholas. Do you think I'll be any better off when you're rotting away, or do you agree I could stand to lose a few pints now? I'm not exactly underfed, Nicholas."

"Trying to make me to tell you you're not fat?"

"What? No. Look. I'm healthy—"

"—Healthy is a good way to describe it," he said, looking at my chest. I sighed.

"*You're* not. If I was the one dying, you'd do anything you had to. And I'd drink from you because I trust you."

"One day, that's how it *will* be."

"When you turn me, I drink your blood? Dracula-ish?"

"Something like that. I don't have a harem. Yet."

"The rate you're going, you won't be *able* to change me. You'll have to outsource." Deep breath. "Maybe I could get Kieran to do it instead, if you'd rather put off getting back to yourself."

He pursed his lips. "Sonofabitch."

He got to his feet with a single movement; faster than human, but not his usual. He pulled his shirt over his head, revealing the still strong body of a man who you'd see chopping firewood, but bruised. I'd kill that Irish bastard.

Those shadowed eyes never left mine as he crossed the room, his confident swagger making my heart pound. Orange and cinnamon waves lapped over me, leaving me heady—and when he kissed me, the seductive richness of it was overwhelming.

His fangs pierced my bottom lip before I could even gasp, and hot, salty blood filled my mouth, making me sway. Nicholas wrapped his arms around me, and gently sucking the puncture. I tingled and writhed through the starry sensation, losing myself as he groaned and pulled me closer. I took his cheeks in my hands and pulled away just to regain my fleeting consciousness and see how he looked, what I did to him. He let me stop him, so I could see my blood drip from the corners of his mouth, down his chin. The swirling of his eyes was chaotic, and he heaved, cheeks flushed, desperate for more of me.

I wanted him to have it all, to take away all my memories, the pain and crushing responsibility. I wanted him to own every last drop of life in my body, to take my soul and make it his.

So this was the vampire thrall in action, then.

With a bear growl, he sunk his teeth into my neck without warning. My knees buckled in shock, but he caught me. He always caught me. The fight-or-flight fizzled away in that orange cinnamon sugar rush he brought with him, and I was his, never wanted to be anything again except his.

No fate, just blood.

My flesh tore. The room was a haze, the crimson streaks on Nicholas's chest, the red stains on the floor, the only color in the gray static. The crudeness of it made my head swim, and I retched. My head hit the floor with a *thunk.* Nicholas picked up my head, apologizing, as another wave of nausea rolled through me.

That was when it happened.

I saw him.

Roman.

"Eliza," Nicholas whispered.

"I'm okay." Knee-jerk answer that wasn't true. I got up on one knee and fell to my side like a jackass. Nicholas was a spinning blur. The vision of Roman was the only real thing for me then. His self-loathing throbbed in my mind like a fresh bruise. It was reflected in his eyes; glaring and animalistic. And he was alone. Alone, and full of hate at the wonderment he felt and the happiness he'd stolen.

Kat's blood popped like champagne bubbles inside him, an effervescent, energizing brilliance that he'd taken. Her goodness swam in his painfully bright eyes.

"Eliza, I don't know what to do," Nicholas said, panicked. I'd never heard him not know what to do before. I couldn't get Roman out of my sight.

"Air."

I managed to get to my feet, even if I fell into the shoji screen and heard a rip. Nicholas opened the door, letting me stumble outside, wearing karate pants and a tanktop. I shivered from nausea and the cold, and sank to a crouch on the boardwalk.

"I have to get you blood. You need blood," I heard Nicholas thinking out loud to himself.

"I'll be okay," I said through dry heaves. Roman was fading.

"What in the hell did you do to her, you nutter? I can smell the blood a mile away!" Kieran's firery scent cut through the mix of bile and blood. I was suffocated by Nicholas's too-warm smell, poisoning me with its false comfort and intent, no matter how much I'd asked for it.

Hands on me, rougher than Nicholas's, but not stronger.

"Your particular brand of salvation isn't needed here, Kieran. She's mine, and don't you forget it." Nicholas's voice was chilling, resounding. He was his old self.

My blood was bringing him back. It might kill me yet.

Kieran pulled me closer, my body burning with his touch.

"You were killing her, man!" he said in his brogue. The worry in his voice touched me; so unexpected from the jerk that basically put us in this predicament to begin with.

Nicholas was silenced, and I had to speak up for him. Shaking my head to clear it, I looked into Kieran's eyes. "I'm fine, Kieran," I said quietly. "I can pull it together now. Thanks."

The scent of ashes surrounded me as he pulled me to standing. "Anytime, love." My vision was clear enough now to see the sexy smirk on his lips as he ran his eyes down my body.

Nicholas growled like a kicked tiger, and the air began to spin with thickening hail around him. Nicholas's frigid anger mixed with Kieran's lusty fire wrapped me in another world, and I swayed, wobbly again.

"Looks to me as if this girl needs to start taking care of herself a little more, and letting you do it a little less, if you know what I mean," Kieran said, inches from Nicholas, eyes alight with a defiant blaze.

"Guys, stop," I said, sounding weak, despite my brimming power. "Kieran, I wanted him to feed from me." Nicholas groaned with irritation.

"You're just a hum—"

"I am not *just* anything," I blurted.

"My mistake," Kieran said, his voice barely a murmur, that accent making it sound like something out of a dream, the overly intimate smirk back on his lips. "You, my dear, need to look after yourself more than you look after anyone else." He said it with such a gentleness, my heart skipped. I wanted him to look out for me. There was no other way to put it.

I wanted *him.*

I backed away, to Nicholas.

"Thanks for your concern, but I think we've got it from here," Nicholas said, wrapping his arms around me from behind. The air shimmered around us, and became a solid thing, the shield that he created like a snowglobe separating us from Kieran. I breathed out, the warmth and safety of it holding me close. The cold disappeared, and Kieran's burning scent was replaced with the peppermint brownie of Nicholas's. My mind flashed to my mom in the kitchen, back when I had a home—and then to Nicholas's cabin in the woods. All of the places where I felt safe, but none as safe as in his arms. Still safe, no matter how much he took from me.

"Aye, well, I'll leave you to your destiny then," Kieran said with a pointed look at me, and turned away.

We turned back to Nicholas's room, but not before I saw Izanagi lurking in the trees.

CHAPTER 13

I'd seen Roman.

I stayed awake all night wondering how in the hell it had happened. The more blood I gave to Nicholas, the more I envisioned. If I took control of it, I could find Roman. *Something* wanted him found, something connected to me.

In the middle of the night, I dragged my exhausted limbs out of bed, threw on my puffy coat and boots, and stood outside. I couldn't lie there anymore, my mind working and reworking answers it didn't quite have. I walked, to find somewhere away from the only two rooms I knew, somewhere I wouldn't be a kept creature. My new, self-induced anemia made me colder. Shaking, I walked and thought, until I didn't know where I was or how long I'd been drifting.

"Well, this is how horror movies start," I said, looking around the woods, the night sounds making me feel small.

There were things in the night that knew better than to make noise.

Under a canopy of skeletal trees, I found the remnants of a garden, long ignored before it had been covered in snow. Instantly I was transported to the pond in Nicholas's back yard, shimmering in pinks, blues and purples in the sparkling winter night. This place was too beautiful to be wasted, in its broken down antiquity. It had to have a purpose, but it was misplaced, half-useful.

It meant something to me, at least.

I brushed off a rickety bench that had been barely visible under snow and vines, and sat, huddled into my jacket. There was so much to see; the roots of things, mosaic tiles, smashed by the wildlife growing between them. A birdbath filled with snow so high I couldn't believe it didn't topple over.

Beautiful things driven to the dark. The best kind.

"Lass, you smell more like the flames than I do."

I almost fell off the bench with surprise.

"Jesus Christ, what are you doing here?" I blurted, catching myself.

Kieran stood in the snow, same black t-shirt and jeans, same disheveled look of wrongdoings. Blood tattooed his chin, stubble and throat.

"Call of the wild, dearie," he said, running a thumb under his lip; it came off red. "I think you have a bit of the same." His eyes glittered, and could have melted the snow.

I pulled my jacket over my chest tighter, only making my boobs more of a spectacle. "I had thinking to do. It couldn't be done where I was."

He growled as he smiled, making my chest burn. "Well,

you do have a bit of the dark inside, don't you?" A new smell of heat came from him, a secret burn, something sacrificial.

"Yeah, well, darkness follows me around," I said, glaring at him. He chuckled.

"I wouldn't call your Nicholas dark. Bit of a shining light, that one." He pointed at me. "I can help with the cold," he said. His eyes narrowed and an assault of heat, like a blast from the fireplace took me in. The air bubbled around me—a shield, like Nicholas's, but different. Sheer orange, red and yellow danced across it, like glass being heated and blown into shape. To protect me from the outside.

"Oh my God," I breathed at its fiery beauty.

Kieran sat beside me, crossing one ankle over the other knee, and threw his bare, tattooed arm over the back of the bench. He motioned with one curling finger for me to come closer, looking like sitting in the freezing night was the most comfortable he'd ever been.

Maybe the cold soothed his fire.

I did it. I inched over to him, the bubble of fiery glass moving with me. I was unable to take my eyes off of the trails of smoke that rose from him where the snow touched. The bubble grew to hold him inside with me. I leaned back, eyes on his, his hot arm behind my neck.

Nothing could touch us, nothing that we were *supposed* to be.

His eyes called to me like moth to flame, their combination of doe-soft brown with thick black lashes, and the jumping silhouettes of flames you could only see up close.

There was more turmoil in him than in me, and I needed to be close to it in a selfish and mystified way.

"How does the fire not burn you?" I asked, thinking back to the time when Nicholas's foot slipped into a fire, rending it black.

He licked his lips. "I take strength from what consumes me."

Didn't expect that from him. "What's your story?"

"My story's a wee bit long, with not a lot to say, love."

"That's not a fair answer."

"You just don't want to tell me about yourself."

I kicked the snow at my feet, slushy in this bubble of warmth. "I wouldn't know where to start, and I definitely wouldn't know where to end."

He looked at me harder. "Nobody knows *your* end, dearest heart, do they?"

His riddles weren't so hard to figure out as Nicholas's. And Kieran was just so—out of the box. Different. Welcoming in a way that even Nicholas wasn't for me, in a way that I couldn't put words to. I guess it was obvious that Kieran was no stranger to slumming it, and I felt a little slum-like, with my *higher purpose,* and my trail of dead people, and my pimping out of my blood to keep my lover alive, and my running from everything I was.

"Everyone thinks I have this amazing gift to change things, some untold future here, and all I want to do is just not be this half-thing anymore. And tonight, when Nicholas fed from me, I saw—" I cut my rant off, and tried to ward off the guilt; I'd not been caught doing something wrong.

91

"What did you see?" he said, taking a strand of my hair in his fingers with assumed intimacy.

I swallowed, mentally said *screw it*, and told him. "I saw Roman."

"Aye, okay."

"We don't know where he is, he left the night he—killed my best friend. She was Nicholas's *unmei nashi...* Anyway, that's why Nicholas was so easy for you to beat," I said, elbowing him, but unable to keep up the air of amusement. "Roman was so real in my mind, and it was because Nicholas drank my blood."

He ran his hand through his hair, like Nicholas did. When Nicholas did it, he came away looking more put together; when Kieran did it, he looked like he just rolled out of bed with some girl, and was ready to drink. Leaning forward, resting his elbows on his knees, I could see all of the lean muscles in his back and shoulders. I tried not to look.

"All right then. You have visions of the vampire that drank the blood Nicholas was supposed to drink. You get them when you let Nicholas drink from you." Kieran was talking more to himself than me, but it was a relief to have someone apart from me say it out loud, try to piece it together.

"There's a connection," I said. State the obvious, why don't you.

"I don't listen often, but I don't think this has happened before." He rubbed his scruffy chin. "What do you think it means?"

"I was hoping you could tell me. What am I supposed to do?"

His smile was brilliant. "What the feck do you care what you're supposed to do, love? Do what you want with it."

For a heartbeat, a jagged saw threatened to slowly cut me in two; the pain that Nicholas and I endured when we were too far apart. *Do you feel it now, Nicholas?* Guilt overwhelmed me and I let it rather than go to him. It intrigued me a little, actually. Being here, in Japan, next to the rebel with plenty of cause, made me want to question everything. This tie between Nicholas and me, between creator and chosen, if it was so strong, why did it need to lord over us a hideous, agonizing pain to remind us we belonged together?

And the pain disappeared as quickly as it reared its ugly head. I laughed, too loud. "What are you talking about? Fate, destiny, my entire life, yours too, we're all shaped by it. This is what we're meant to do. But I don't know what *this* is yet. I don't know how these visions fit in."

"Not *these* visions, Eliza. *Your* visions. They belong to you. Don't let anyone tell you how to run your life—it's still yours."

"For now."

Kieran took me by the shoulders firmly, and I thought he would kiss me, but he just looked hard into my eyes, searching. God, I wanted him to kiss me, and hated myself for it. But the burning in him—it felt like hitting the self-destruct button. Sometimes, that was all I wanted to do.

"Eliza, do you want to become *Shinigami?*"

With him looking at me like that, the fire burning in and all around him, so full of vitality and willpower, I didn't know. I didn't know if I just wanted to run from my life, or if I really wanted to be something else forever. The *Shinigami* came for me, and I never bothered to look for another way out of the world that didn't want me.

His face was so close to mine now that I could capture the heat of his breath if I tried.

"Why did you let him drink from you? I can smell him," Kieran said, distantly.

"He needed to. He needs to. He's dying." I said it with cold calculation because saying the words brought something to the light that I didn't need to see.

"He'll never die, Eliza, no matter how much you fear it."

The flames in his eyes jumped higher, and the smell of cinders called to me until I looked away.

"Everything can be taken away. Nicholas is this way because of me. I'll never turn my back on him."

Kieran let out an irritated sigh. "Have you wondered what would happen if you just said screw it to what you were supposed to do, and just did what you want to?"

"Should I wear a t-shirt and jeans to train tomorrow? Is that what you're telling me?"

"What I'm telling you, love," he breathed into my ear, making my stomach clench in a vice grip, "is that the wolf in sheep's clothing is still a wolf. Don't turn from the wrong fangs."

"Nicholas is no last resort, and he's no wolf. He's exactly who he is, and has no impression to make," I finished, eyeing his overt sexiness.

Kieran sprang to his feet, hands in pockets to make him look disinterested. But the look in his eyes was one of such a deep intelligence and emotion that it was impossible to believe he was as laid back as he looked.

"You owe him. That's what you think."

"A little. Doesn't mean I don't love him."

"He hurt you."

"Everyone gets hurt, Kieran. That's what life is."

He belly laughed, and it echoed through the trees. "*That's* what life is to you? No wonder you're so quick to end it! But why in hell would you want to make it last forever?"

I was starting to see a little fire of my own. "Fate cornered you, too, right? Let you have nothing in life so when the *Shinigami* claimed you, you'd have nowhere else to go. That's how it happens for us." I hoped he didn't have a different answer than the one I knew.

"I always had somewhere to go," he said with a hint of mournfulness. "I have a place because I make one."

"You're braver than me, then. I know my role, I'm not looking for another." The words came out without my allowance. I was going to be a vampire, and Nicholas was going to be with me. There were doubts in everything in this world, but this... This I knew.

Was it only because I was too afraid to find my own way?

Kieran said, "I'm not brave, I'm resourceful. But I don't let anyone use me for their means, and I don't like to see it happen to a woman like yourself."

"This is just another way for someone to tell me what to do, if you look at it that way."

His dark, intent gaze was heated from inside. "I'm not one to mince words, Eliza. I find you very attractive, and I don't want to own you. Perhaps it's time you let your eyes be opened." Inches from my lips, the scent of brimstone danced between us.

"Kieran, your pick up lines are solid, but—"

"Not a pickup line. I mean it. Maybe it's a little bit of a pickup line, but you're not afraid of directness, and you're not a follower." He licked his lips. "Come with me for a while, and I'll let you take the lead."

I was short of breath. "Are we talking about the same thing?"

His lips parted, a glint of his fangs behind them. "Wouldn't you like to find out?"

CHAPTER 14

K ieran walked me back to my room. He was all the questions I hadn't known I'd wanted to ask come to life.

And if I was being honest, I liked the way life looked on him.

"Well, here we are then," Kieran said. I looked up, and indeed I was looking at my door. I'd been running over and over in my head what I was supposed to be doing with this vision of Roman and barely registered anything but snow and heat. I picked up my head too fast and got dizzy. Too little blood, too little food, too much mayhem.

"Holy hell, woman, get inside," Kieran said, and steered me by the elbow into my room. He led me to the floor in front of the fireplace, leaning close enough that the stubble of his cheek brushed my own smooth one.

"Watch this," he whispered in my ear, his voice the growl of a barely tamed animal.

His fangs emerged slowly. I braced myself for the waves of frost that I was accustomed to, but instead, a thin line of flame came from where he stood and went straight to the fireplace logs, flaring them up. He turned his head to me and grinned. "Brilliant, right?"

My mouth hung open. "How?"

"The same way the rest of them make things cold, I suppose." In a ripple of motion, he was on one knee in front of me, the devil's grin alight with the flames behind him. "The burning in me begs to be let loose," he said, and kissed me swiftly on the cheek with soft, hot lips. I thought I might pass out. "Now, my pet, you stay put. I'll be back with something to take away that death pallor."

A gust of cold wind came in as he left me to sit and wonder what in the hell I thought I was doing.

I nodded off and dreamed of Roman. I was awoken by a gentle kiss on the top of my head.

"Mmm, Nicholas."

"Not this time, love," the Irish brogue said, and I sat up, my cheeks hot.

"Sorry," I said.

"Here you go," he said, sitting cross-legged by my side. He put a bowl of bright red strawberries in front of me, and the sweet scent of them made my stomach growl. I wolfed down one after another. "I hope they bring back a little life in those cheeks," he said, and brushed a finger down the side of my face.

"Kieran—"

"I know. Your heart belongs to Nicholas French. So would mine, were I a woman." He held up another strawberry. I took it in my hand, though I think the intent was for me to eat it from his.

"Then what are you doing here, with me?" I said, eating another strawberry.

He looked at me, and no matter how much of a black sheep he was, and how tough, his eyes were just a little boy's. "I don't know, truth be told." Trouble—he sensed it, too. "But I think you're lost here, and this is where you should be found. I don't want to see your life cut short to save one of us, even Nicholas French."

"I *am* one of you." Our voices were barely above whispers, our skin so close that the heat fizzled and popped between us.

"Not yet." His breaths were shorter, his voice a rumble. "I want to watch you get there, see you play by your own rules."

"I will when the time comes."

"Eliza," he said. "I think I should go."

I didn't want him to. I sickened myself with it, and he could see it as I looked down at my lap. Nicholas and I belonged together, and here I was, running after the first hot Irishman that looked my way.

I nodded. "Thanks, Kieran." Sucking in a breath, I met his eyes. "I loved talking to someone that doesn't want me to just—I don't know—just be what they tell me. We had no choice in being this, and I don't need more people telling me what I have to do. God, that sounds juvenile."

"But right. Juvenile, but right."

We laughed, and the pleasure spread from my head to my toes, overtook me.

"Right, then," Kieran said, and ran a thumb along my

jaw. I sucked in my breath, watching him follow the trail of heat his hand left on my skin. "Sleep well now."

He pinched my chin between his fingers, longing in his eyes. With that, he was up and out the door, his smoky scent lulling me into a sleep right there on the floor.

My eyes snapped open, heat from the fire on my face. Weak and alone, I wished I didn't want Nicholas to make me stronger. Nighttime did things to me here that made me wonder if I'd run away to the wrong place.

I dragged my feet to the door, more tired from confusion than anything else. There was no shame in wanting help from the man I loved, I'd put myself entirely in his care in coming to Japan, and yet I still... I slapped my hand against the door frame and swore.

"You need something."

I screamed.

Izanagi faced me from the woods.

"Do you live in the goddamn woods? You're always hanging around me, I thought I was up here to be alone. I'm sick of being surrounded."

He didn't move, just watched me, pissing me off more. I knew why he appeared when I was alone, why nobody else saw him; he was a part of me.

"You're missing something," he said.

"Yeah, I usually am."

"We need each other."

This was too much. Too many personalities to contend

with, and me, alone with them all after spending my adult life close to only one woman, who was now dead—

No. Don't go down that road again when you're already coming apart at the seams.

"Thanks for trying to help," I said to Izanagi, not masking my sarcasm, "but I'll deal with Nicholas, and Kieran, and my visions on my own. Alone."

"I've always been there. You've never been alone."

I shivered, not from the cold.

A snap of air, and he was inches from me, wrapping me in that all too familiar wretched funeral scent. I held my chin up. I was tired of being run down by death.

"I am what you need."

"Cryptic. I never get that these days. Look, I'm so tired I could die. I've had the blood drained from me, watched Nicholas get beaten into submission, and Kieran—" What to say about Kieran? "There's too much happening, but all *I've* done is talk and get pushed around. I'm ready for action." I realized that was true as I said it. I didn't try to hide from death all those years just to turn into its puppet. I wanted power.

I'd never wanted power before.

The wind whipped Izanagi's long hair, making black slash marks against the snowscape behind. "When the visions overpower you, when you're empty and no one can help you, you will drink from me. I will calm the storm."

As if on cue, Roman materialized in my head again, a clue in a scavenger hunt given to me too slowly; I was losing the game. I got dizzy, seeing the world outside spin through my haze of people who weren't there, and the god who was.

"I have to stop talking now," I said.

"I will be close," Izanagi said, and was gone.

As sure as I knew death, I knew he would be.

CHAPTER 15

"I'm so mad you didn't tell me I was doing this today."

I was all gussied up in a black silk kimono that showed off my chubbiness really well.

Nicholas looked straight ahead. "There'll be food there, and beer."

"And the other humans. And a lot of vampires. And me in this." I tugged at the waist, envisioning myself bursting the seams when I sat down.

"You're a princess. Now shut up."

A dark wood table ran the length of the temple. It was dim, only orange lanterns lit the walls, casting a comforting glow over us all. I was anything but comfortable.

"I want to punch you so hard right now," I whispered into Nicholas's shoulder.

The Master sat at one end of the table, glaring with those awful eyes, making me want to crawl in a hole and die. At his side was Blue, a china doll in an elegant midnight blue kimono. Paolo sat beside her, smiling, laughing. He was the only one who waved to me, like I had a place at the high school lunch table and wouldn't have to huddle in the bathroom eating my meatball sub. Vampires lined the table, none attempting to welcome me, either staring at me like I was a sideshow, or ignoring me altogether. I breathed a sigh of relief to sit down so everyone wasn't staring at my chest. This was reminiscent of one of Kat's endless cocktail parties, and it hurt that I didn't miss them one bit.

"There are your new best friends," Nicholas whispered to me, nodding, giving me brief rundowns.

They were only two other humans. I don't know what I was expecting, but these two weren't it. Arthur was exactly like you would picture an Arthur. Glasses that made him look like a mole, thinning hair. Despite his soothing British accent and bookish appearance, he was actually a pompous, shallow ass. I'd been watching him as he looked Blue up and down, elbowed supernatural creatures in the ribs, and made a general monkey of himself. Nicholas watched him, bemused, forehead slightly wrinkled, eyes wide as if interested in everything he had to say, sarcasm just oozing from his pores.

I kept hoping for Kieran to appear at the table, but he didn't. He would have ripped this guy to shreds.

"I don't care that I'll have to kill people," Arthur was saying to one of the vampires that wouldn't look at me. "What have people ever done for me?" He threw back a sip from a flask, and looked around for a reaction.

His creator, his *Shugotenshi*, sat next to him, looking like some French cartoon with a thin mustache and

American-hating upturned lip. Attractive to look at, but his physical beauty was secondary to what a jerk he seemed to be. The condescending disgust for everyone around him made him the perfect nightmare match for Arthur. Jesus, I hated them both instantly.

"Do you know Arthur's *Shugotenshi?*" I asked Nicholas as quietly as I could, but of course, the vampire could hear me from across the table. He briefly glared, and I met his eyes, forcing myself to be unafraid.

"Pierre," Nicholas said. The French man's lips quivered into a sly grin full of malice and distaste. I forced my heart to slow down, determined not to let him sway me; he was working a thrall smoothly on me, I could *see* it, but for what reason I couldn't possibly discern. Nicholas's calloused fingers laced through my own under the table.

"To live for eternity without regard for life will be somewhat of an empty existence, don't you think?" Paolo asked Arthur. Pierre made a haughty noise that Paolo ignored.

Looking at Paolo like he was the kid who didn't want the candy, Arthur said, "The *Shinigami* don't need to have regard for life; a death god that sympathizes with its prey is a weak god indeed." He looked over sweet Paolo, like he was *better* than him.

"And you think there's strength in being a self-important ass?" *Why do I say this stuff?*

Arthur's paunchy cheeks reddened. "I won't hide behind humble lies, and I certainly won't deny my nature to spare my *girlfriend's* feelings," he spat, looking at Nicholas. My blood boiled until I could barely see straight through my own heat. The table fell silent. Nicholas squeezed my knee under the table.

"That's spectacular relationship advice, did you hear that advice?" Nicholas said, looking around the table, wide-eyed. "I'd deny my inner child a goddamn lollipop if it meant keeping this woman on my good side."

"And your nature means nothing if your soul is nonexistent," I said angrily.

The Master sat silently, weightless somehow, as if made of air. So powerful that he had too much presence to be distracting.

Paolo was looking at me thoughtfully. Eyes were on me from everywhere. *Way to make yourself the center of attention.* I sucked in my stomach. The other human girl smiled at me.

Her name was Leann. She had pieced-together beauty that said she'd been too many places, most of which were in her head. Thin, with long, tousled blonde waves, she was a fairy of a girl. Confident, quiet. She had these wide, but sultry eyes that gave away her cynicism, showed her damage. I'd keep my distance.

"Who's her *Shugotenshi?*" I asked Nicholas.

"It's Kieran," he said.

I took in a sharp breath. I wasn't sure if she was being quiet and observing anymore or if she was so lost she had no words. "Why isn't he here? She's alone."

Nicholas swung his eyes to me, shades of cocoa rolling over and over in them. "You know he's not one for tradition." He raised an eyebrow. "What's that? Eliza Morgan, you're blushing."

"So?" Real mature.

"He's made an impression on you, too?" The hand Nicholas held suddenly ached and tingled with cold; out in the snow with no gloves on kind of cold.

"Nicholas," I gasped. The Japanese vampire across from us grimaced. I'd been trying to ignore him due to his extreme creep factor, but when he responded with a blast of cold from his own hideously long nails that shot across the table, I jumped. I suddenly longed for sweatpants and for once, anything but horror movies. Especially *The Ring.* Or *The Grudge.*

"Sorry," Nicholas muttered, reminding me of his icy fingers. He took his hand from mine; the ache was worse that way.

The other vampires took his cue. It seemed they did that often, even the most reclusive of them. They all relaxed a bit, the chill dissipating. The Master raised his hands and the air warmed instantly.

The room breathed a sigh of relief, and Pierre ruined it. Obnoxious.

"You truly care for each other, no?" he said, gesturing to Nicholas and me. Disguised innocence made it seem harmless, but he was trying to provoke us. All eyes were on us, but Nicholas just sipped his wine, while I squirmed.

"You don't care for your *unmei fumetsu?*" Nicholas replied after a hearty mouthful. My heart faltered some when he didn't just answer that I was the woman he loved.

Pierre leaned forward, clearly happy to talk about himself. He and Arthur were a truly nauseating duo. "He is a fulfilled purpose for me, of course," he replied. "But we will both be pleased to have ourselves back, without this *need* to be near one another. It is one side effect of our relationship that we could both live without."

Arthur did nothing but stare at the vampire. It was impossible to imagine him experiencing the pain I felt for Nicholas when he wasn't with Pierre. It couldn't be. My curiosity got the better of me. "Arthur, do you have visions of Pierre when he's not with you?"

Arthur and Leann both gaped at me like I'd stepped off the mother ship. "No. He's in my personal space enough. I don't want him in my mind."

I pitied him.

CHAPTER 16

"Thank Christ that's over," I said, eyeballing Nicholas on the walk back to my room.

"That wasn't the usual fly on the wall game you play in groups," he said, glancing at me with something like pride. "What gives?"

"If ever there was a time for me to open my trap, that was it. Arthur and Leann—"

"Are dull. The both of them. I was worried how you'd react," he said, matter-of-factly. "I mean, they aren't blank canvases entirely, but I didn't want you to think that *Shinigami* were only created from the saddest of the gene pool. I knew you'd apply it to yourself and make me spend hours telling you how wonderful you are." He popped a piece of gum in his mouth from a hidden pocket.

"Is *that* why we sat so far from them? I might as well have been at the kids' table at Thanksgiving! I'm still pissed you didn't tell me what was going on tonight, by the way. A little preparation would have been nice."

"You would have argued with me to get out of it. Then you'd have freaked out, worked yourself into a frenzy and come anyway. I cut out the middle step."

"I wouldn't have argued," I said under my breath.

"Even you don't believe that."

I laughed. "No, I don't."

The room was warm, and I wanted to curl up with a book. I missed that.

"You were pretty magnificent tonight," Nicholas said, closing the door.

"I couldn't shut up." I dropped my huge coat and looked down at the black kimono, dying to get it off, and not sure where to start.

"Right, that's what I like. I like to see you becoming who you are here, in the minds of all of these vampires." He ran his fingers down my arm, raising goosebumps under the silk. Watching his hand move, he pulled the sleeve down, revealing my soft upper arm underneath. My breath quickened.

"I don't feel like anyone yet," I said, closing my eyes to his intensity, wishing my bra strap wasn't as wide as a highway. "I'm ripped in so many directions, and I have all these questions that I make up the answers to, none of them right. Arthur, Leann, they might be dull, but they know what they're here for exactly. Exactly."

"Look at me," Nicholas growled. I had no choice but to do it when that voice told me to. "Everyone else here is an extra in the movie that is you. Don't get caught up in them. They can put your fire out too easily."

The mention of fire made my cheeks flush. *Kieran.*

"Nicholas—" I started, nearly telling him about the

vision of Roman, but I stopped. It had the air of a secret, and yet Kieran knew, and Izanagi; my other secrets.

"What is it?" Nicholas said, suddenly stopping me. With his face so close, the light in his eyes so strong, I couldn't lie to him.

"Izanagi came to me again. He knew something about my visions." I still didn't say I'd seen Roman. It would hurt him, make him long for things that I couldn't give him.

Nicholas raised an eyebrow.

If only he knew I'd told Kieran all my deep darks.

"He said he could help when the visions became too much," I said, my lip quivering. I left out that he said I would drink his blood. Not that I would need to, but that I *would.*

Nicholas looked like he was waiting for me to break, or wanted to break himself. "I feel you slipping from me," he said out of nowhere.

I gulped. "I belong to you more now than I ever have, Nicholas. You're my future."

"That's it?" he said, lip curling up, a chill running down my spine. "I'm a game plan?"

"You know better. You're my fate."

He bowed his head. Once again, I'd saddened him.

"Eliza, how can I make you into a vampire when your blood is the only thing keeping me alive?"

I hadn't heard him admit it before, that we'd been backed into a corner. It was time for me to figure out what fate's next trick was before my cards got crumpled in a ball and thrown away. I needed another vision.

"Speaking of which, you're looking a little grim right about now."

His eyes went dark and still in his sadness, but he couldn't help licking his lips and looking at my chest where my heart was. He lifted his hand to touch it.

"Your heartbeat haunted me when we were apart in New Hampshire. I could hear it like a band playing. It killed me but I couldn't die. Now, I'm supposed to make that heartbeat stop forever. What a torture to endure." His eyes were so faraway, I just wanted to tether him here, with me, and yet I was doing so much to keep him away.

I swallowed hard, my emotion strangling me. "Taste it now, while you can," I whispered.

He brushed my hair aside, and without further ado, sank his teeth into my neck. Nothing more intimate, making it all the more intimate at the same time; no pretense needed.

My head swam, but I stared at the paper wall before me, forced myself to stay conscious and will the visions to come to me. They had to give me an answer, if I just looked hard enough for it.

Nicholas held nothing back, didn't try not to hurt me or take too much, giving in to his own weakness. Maybe he figured out I was strong enough to handle it, even if that wasn't altogether true.

No visions came, and so I gripped Nicholas by the back of the neck and pushed his head closer. His lips clamped down and he groaned, wrapping his arms around me. The blood came faster, and then the vision hit me. Not Roman, like I was waiting for.

Lynch.

Chris Lynch sat on his white sofa in his giant white house, with his head in his hands.

Jesus Christ, he's crying.

A wave of nausea passed over me, but I stifled it the best I could, and I watched.

Lynch stood up, looking every bit the successful, dapper attorney he was. *A ladykiller*, I thought angrily. But I forced thoughts of Kat out of my mind as the blood was forced out of my body. Just one more wall to put up, that shouldn't be too hard. Clarity was too important now for my pain to interrupt.

The attorney paced frantically, tears streaming, before flashing across the room out his front door into the night.

Nicholas pulled away from my neck, making my body buckle. The vision became a vacuum in my mind, sucked out and leaving me empty, as Nicholas heaved with exertion.

"That's enough," he growled, my blood coursing down his chin onto his chest.

"No," I growled back, and pulled him to me again. He pushed me off hard, and I landed on my back on the bed.

"What are you doing? You'll die, Eliza!"

"I need this, and I'm fine." My heart raced from blood loss, a hot flash skipped over my skin.

Nicholas cocked his head at me, swirling eyes narrowed. "What do you mean, you *need* this?"

Screw it. Man, I was saying that a lot. I sighed, running my hands through my blood-soaked hair, fingers catching in the knots. "When you feed from me, I have visions." Clenching my fists, I said the name I didn't want to say to him. "I saw Roman, Nicholas."

He became more still than I'd ever seen him while conscious. "Do you know where he is?"

I shook my head. "But I've seen Lynch, too. He's still in Ossipee. I don't know why I'm seeing either of them, but the answers are in me, and only you can draw them out. Nicholas, this is no coincidence. You have to feed from me for me to show me the way. I know it in my heart."

"And if I kill you?" he spat.

"You won't."

"You have no idea if that's true."

"So what? There's more at play here than we know, and we have to dive into it headfirst, Nicholas, or who knows what we're missing? The things I can see, the way I can *call* Izanagi to me without even trying—"

"I don't know…" he mumbled, shaking his head of ringlets and waves, droplets of blood flying.

"Well, I do. Nothing happens by accident for us, and you know it. If I die while you feed from me, that's the way it's supposed to be. But we both know that I mean something here, and things are changing all around me, *because* of me."

"You've been talking to Paolo. This sounds like his divine providence double-speak."

"No, it sounds like mine. You've drilled into me that I'm meant for more. Let me look for it."

His eyes drilled into me harder than his fangs ever could. He wanted to protect me, but there could be none of that anymore. I needed to become the thing I was meant to be, before it was too late for Nicholas.

"Okay," he grumbled. "You're more than this. I have to let you become it. But I hate taking from you selfishly this way."

"I'm the selfish one. I need you." In a wind of peppermint brownie, the first and warmest scent I knew him for, he pulled me into his arms. "We're both so weak," he said into my hair. He felt like home, smelled like belonging, sounded like my future.

"We know what we need. That's all."

He sunk his teeth into me again, and I waited for magic to happen.

CHAPTER 17

I sprang to life from a puddle of my own blood, gasping, trying to move rigor mortis-stiff limbs. I slipped in the wet thickness and fell. Sobbing, confused, I cried out for him.

"Nicholas!"

With a *whoosh* he was at my side, covered in blood himself.

"I passed out," he said apologetically, pulling me to him.

"Me too, I guess." I shook in his arms, blood everywhere.

"You're trashed. We need to get you cleaned up, not in a bucket of water," he said. He lifted me too fast, and I wished I would black out to escape the dizzy heat wave.

"Nicholas, please."

"Sorry. I'm stronger than I've been in a long time," he said. "Thanks to you. I'm high. I'm trembling."

I couldn't respond; I had no energy to do anything except be carried to wherever he was taking me.

Nicholas put up a shield around us, as strong as it should be from him. The air solidified in a glass-like arch. He carried me, safe from the elements, lulling me, until I heard a door swish open.

"What's this?" A woman's voice.

"This is my *unmei fumetsu*," Nicholas said, slapping me on the butt that was pointed in the air.

"Why is she here?"

"You have a shower."

That made me pull myself up on Nicholas's shoulder, and struggle to get down. A shower sounded to me like sex must sound to prisoners.

Once he'd set me on the ground, I was looking at Blue. Then I looked back at Nicholas. Because he knew she had a shower.

Why the hell did he know she had a shower?

Blue saw jealousy bubbling in me. Her gorgeous, wide brown eyes shot to my chest where my heart was punching like Mike Tyson. She gave me the prettiest kissy smirk, and I wanted to rip her lips off. "I have the only shower on the mountain," she said softly, with a British accent I hadn't noticed before.

"Ah," I said, putting my head down to hide my embarrassment. "You must have vampires beating your door down."

She leaned forward with a conspiratorial smile. "I also have quite the reputation for not giving it up." She turned away, Nicholas and I following.

Blue's room smelled like farm fresh apples, and felt like

her, not like a girl stuffed into a Japanese room. The rice paper walls were hung with pink silk tapestries from floor to ceiling. There were old, bound books everywhere, in piles, not a shelf to be found, like in my own room. Open CD cases littered the floor in one corner, near a stereo that had perfume bottles lined up on top, in reds, pinks, blues and purples. All color, all decadent.

Best of all, her low-lying Japanese bed, covered in a rich purple silk bedspread, had Peanut Butter Cup wrappers all over it.

I laughed, making Blue turn around, smirking like we had an inside joke. I liked her so much, it hurt. It hurt the Kat part of me.

Nicholas was looking at me like I'd just eaten a spoonful of Tabasco sauce.

"Are you all right?" he said out of the corner of his mouth. "You laughed."

"Yeah." I smiled to reassure him, or me. Blue was in front of me in a heartbeat and a burst of Red Delicious.

"You're soaked in blood. It's rather disgusting. You can use my shower this time, but don't make a habit of it, American." She winked at me and put a fluffy white towel in my dirty hands.

Turning to Nicholas, she said, "I'll make tea for us. But first, get the poor girl something decent to wear."

The water was the hottest I'd known in weeks, and it had some serious pressure. The blood pooled around me in the drain, and I just stood there in the dimness of orange lanterns.

I could hear her and Nicholas chatting in the adjoining room, only separated by a silk screen with ornate carvings in its ebony frame. Her Tinkerbell laugh was so like Kat's, tears sprang to my eyes to be washed away with the rest of the past.

When my pale skin was beet red and I was sure the rest of the residents of the mountain would need to liquefy snow if they wanted water, I forced myself out. As soon as the water shut off, a pair of karate pants and a long white jacket were thrown over the top of the screen with some panties, a t-shirt and a bra. I caught them as they flew at me.

"What time is it? Is it…the next day?" I asked Nicholas from the other side of the screen.

"Yeah, it's the next day all right."

Blue piped up, "You both have some expectations today, I believe."

"God, no, come on," I groaned to nobody in particular.

Nicholas came around the screen, making me cover my chest for a second. Then I didn't care. I pulled my shirt on over my bra, and started putting on the jacket.

"There will be training today," Nicholas said gently, holding one side of the screen and looking me over unashamedly. "But I'll make sure they go easy on you."

I fastened the jacket and lifted my head high. "No. We have to move forward, and I refuse to be treated like some spineless girl who needs special attention. I have to learn."

Nicholas glanced behind him, and leaned over to me.

Our little secret. "Eliza, what did you see last night?" he whispered.

Until he mentioned it, I hadn't remembered. But the reappearance of the vision made me cry out loud and fall back.

"Shit, Eliza!" I could hear Nicholas, could hear the screen fall over, saw my body moving wildly, but couldn't answer.

"Is she having a seizure?!" Blue screeched. Her apple smell enveloped me, fighting with Nicholas's peppermint brownie. I only know my body slowed because Nicholas's grip loosened. Gasping like I'd been drowning, I looked back and forth between the two faces over me, both so worried and terrified.

"The vision is strong with this one," I said in my best Jedi voice.

Nicholas fell back on his butt, and ruffled his hair. Fidgeting became him. "What the hell just happened?" he blurted.

Blue was still over me, looking down, her hair falling on my face. "Can you move?" she asked.

My limbs dangled, heavy and tingly, and Blue seemed noticed. With her delicate arms, she managed to pick me up like I was a child, and carried me to her bed in a blinding movement. "Maybe you should tell me what's happening in that pretty little head of yours," she said, sitting with me, tiny body not even wrinkling the comforter that all but groaned under my weight.

And without question, I did. She served me cup after cup of tea in a grandmotherly, unabashedly doting style, pairing her exotic beauty with maternal warmth. Between the blankets on her bed, Blue's comforting and Nicholas's brownie scent, I'd talked for hours before even realizing it. I'd told the whole story; *my* whole story to her. Everything from the ever-present feeling of death replacing my parents when they died, to how Izanagi was the living, breathing version of it. I talked about Roman, and Ossipee, and Kat. I talked about the pain of Nicholas and me, of not knowing how he really felt, while he watched me with glistening eyes.

Blue was a rapt listener, nodding when she needed to, sad with me when I needed her to be, hugging me when I didn't know I wanted it.

Kat would have loved her.

"God, I'm hungry," I said. I really needed a watch—for someone who couldn't be accused of missing meals, I did it a lot on the mountain. Blue rang a bell that brought a young girl to the door. They spoke quietly to each other.

"Nicholas," I said while Blue was away, "when are we supposed to train?" What a nightmare to think of doing anything physical. On my best day I wasn't running any marathons—right now I felt like The Blob, but with less conviction.

Nicholas smoothed my hair, the muscle in his bicep leaping. He looked so healthy again, and I'd have given every drop of blood to keep him that way. "I told the Master it had to wait until tomorrow."

"But—" I protested, even though hearing that was akin to hearing that I didn't have to go on one of Kat's blind dates, or watch any movie with that British romance guy in it that everyone loves. But I didn't want to be seen as weak, would have pushed through anything to prove I wasn't.

"But nothing. You've been talking a Blue streak," he said with a grin, "and still nothing about your vision. We're staying here, for as long as it takes. You needed this, and neither of us knew it. You want to talk, finally, and you found someone you can do it with."

I'd not had one of the rare long talk-about-our-feelings nights since I was falling in love with Nicholas, and Kat demanded details. It was tranquilizing and energizing at once to curl up, warm, fresh and clean, with hot drinks, the snow drifting against the door. It was wonderful to relax, to be with people who wanted me.

I nodded. "Okay. I guess it's not a terrible idea to take care of myself a little today. This is really good, actually." I smiled over at Blue, still talking politely to the servant girl. "I've missed having a friend like this."

Nicholas's face darkened. His brow wrinkled. God, I was stupid.

"I'm sorry, Nicholas, that was stupid to say."

He quickly kissed me on the forehead. "I don't expect you to avoid the subject of friendship forever just because Roman is gone. I'll be fine. Always am."

Blue joined us again. "There's food on the way," she said with a sweet smile. "Now, I hear talk of Roman. Let's hear about this vision, shall we? Let's try to fix this."

With one more glance to Nicholas, I let her rip.

"I saw Lynch," I said in a breath, my voice shaking already. "He had two girls pinned to the ground by their throats. They were young, really young, like teenagers. And he—" I stopped to breathe, "he leaned down and ripped a huge chunk out of the redheaded girl's breast, a big chunk of it came off in his mouth with her shirt—"

"Dear lord," Blue whispered.

"Then he just tore into the other girl's throat, and drank and drank, while the red-haired girl kicked and sobbed. He killed them both, I watched the whole thing."

"God, he's worse than ever," Nicholas said.

And the worst of it was still yet to come. "But before that, I saw him—*crying*. He was a wreck. He misses her so much, Nicholas, our hearts were one in the same, his was mine—" I pleaded, for what I couldn't say. I couldn't come to terms with the idea of asking for mercy for the abomination that was Lynch. "I hurt for him. With him."

"No, Eliza, you can't."

"You can't tell me how to feel, Nicholas. It never works." He smiled sadly back at me.

"So," Blue said, breaking the moment, "Lynch is back to his tricks."

"Lynch's tricks are piss poor and he's always at them," Nicholas told her, their faces close. I didn't even get jealous. Nope.

"Then what's different this time?" Blue asked.

"Well, I know he's doing it now because he's so grief-stricken," I said. "Not that the motive makes it okay, it's just he's in pain, and..." And what? He can brutally murder people because his girlfriend's gone? If I thought of it outside of Kat—no, it was still inexcusable. "I'm no psychiatrist, and it's confusing to know why he does what he does."

"Great," Nicholas muttered. "Now he's got reasons to be a unconscionable monster, and nobody's watching him.

Jesus, he has nobody keeping tabs on him." He pinched the furrow between his eyebrows.

"That's not all," I said.

"What else, then?" Blue asked.

"I know something about Roman." How to do this without hurting Nicholas more? I hated even saying Roman's name. "His depression. It's all-consuming, such heartache, sadness like I've never felt in my life, and that's saying something. I don't know where he is, but he's alone. I don't know how my visions of Lynch and him are linked, or what it means to me and you, but I intend to find out."

CHAPTER 18

G od bless Blue, she managed to get me a cheeseburger.

"You need iron," she said with a wink, and handed me the plate. I devoured the thing in three bites and looked for more. Blue was laughing hysterically, holding her stomach.

Nicholas lifted the lid on the tray with as much flourish as a magician. A half dozen more burgers were underneath.

"Eeeeee!" I squealed.

"How are you getting this food?" Nicholas asked, eyes narrowing at Blue. "Cheeseburgers don't grow on this mountain. This isn't Cheeseburger Mountain."

"Nicholas, a girl like me gets what she asks for," Blue said, biting her lip.

"You do have all the comforts of home here," I said, eyes roving over the luxurious room.

"This *is* my home," Blue said with a mournful beauty

that made her a kitten amongst lions. "I don't leave the mountain—much."

Nicholas studied her, weighing whether to open his mouth or not. Obviously, he did. "I've heard that you don't even leave to feed," he said.

Her face paled. I was so confused, I stayed quiet before I asked something dumb.

"Well," she said, chin tipped up with dignity, "you've been asking some strange questions, then, Nicholas."

"Just looking out for you, that's all," he replied.

Exactly how much was he looking out for her?

She sighed. "Don't worry, Kieran takes care of me. I'm afraid of being away from here." Her smile was apologetic, like she owed us something. "So Kieran brings me my victims. He doesn't like to see me scared."

To be so powerful, and so trapped…it had to be gut-wrenching at times.

"What happened to your home before?" I asked her. The kind of fear she spoke of I knew well; it came piggy-backed on loss.

When you lose enough of something you cling to what's left as hard as you can.

"Fire," Blue said. "I lost my whole family in a fire. And when Kieran found me, the burned-out thing that I'd become myself, he took me with him to Ireland. And a fire took our home there, too. It wasn't until then that we found out he was to be my creator."

"You were his *unmei fumetsu*, too?" I breathed, glancing at Nicholas. He shrugged. How many *unmei fumetsu* could one vampire have? How did Leann deal with that? I didn't like thinking of Nicholas being close to anyone but me in this singular way, this mystical and horribly magical way.

And it was glaringly clear to me, the one connection that nobody was mentioning: All the fire in Blue's past—it had to be indicative of the fiery vampire in her future. The very one who was to take her from life took everything around her with a stamp of his own.

Secrets were as deep as the snow in Japan.

"How long have you been a vampire?" I asked.

She smiled sadly, like she had something to be embarrassed about. "A mere fifty-two years," she said.

"So young, and so strong," Nicholas said.

Blue looked at me, a glow of knowing in her eye, a message. "The circumstances made me strong. The time it happened is inconsequential." Fate strengthened her, but she was strong to begin with.

My fate as *Shinigami* gave me the visions, but the fighter I already was had to make sense of them. That was my *choice*, not my problem to solve. I just had to choose to do it.

"Nicholas," I said, turning to him, begging him with my eyes to trust me. "Figuring out what to do next is in here," I said, tapping my temple. "I'm strong enough to survive another feeding, I know it. And you're both here to help me, take care of me." Suspicion pinched Nicholas's face, and Blue was blinking like crazy.

"What are you saying?" she asked.

"I know this seizure and the blood loss is scary for you guys, but I'm okay. I want to keep pushing to discover what my visions mean; how they can help Nicholas. I know I have the answer, and the blood-letting is when I find the pieces of it."

"No way. You think I'm going to drink from you again tonight? You're crazier than you look."

"Izanagi won't let me die."

Nicholas's jaw clenched, and the familiar cold shook down his limbs, spreading across the carpeted floor at the mention of the god's name.

"Nicholas, stop it. Izanagi only wants to help me."

Closing his eyes and cracking his neck, he said, "I just don't know him, and I don't like him near you when I don't know him. No strangers allowed."

With a tight-lipped smile I went to him, standing for the first time in hours. I willed myself not to look as dizzy as I felt. Touching Nicholas's arm gently, I looked into those eyes that exuded something unearthly that wanted me for its own.

"Izanagi's not a stranger to me, Nicholas. He's death to me, *my* death, the death that always hung out and made me different." Nicholas gave me a look that I deserved, because nobody wants death to hang out. "I didn't know what I was when my parents died, when my grandmother died. I hated death, but it was constant at least, the only thing that was. Izanagi is what being *Shinigami* means to me. He's good, I promise you. And he'll be there for me when I need him. When we need him."

Nicholas pulled my head to his chest with one hand, and kissed my hair with a lingering love, wrapping his arms around me.

"Seeing you suffer for the sake of helping me sucks.

But you trying so hard to become what you're supposed to be is the most beautiful thing I've ever seen."

"If you're going to feed from her, do it here. I have better resources," Blue said, waving her hand around. I nodded and smiled. Then I did something I barely recognized as my own action.

I hugged her.

She was warm, and smelled so much different from Kat that it made me hug her harder to escape the loneliness and help me blink back the tears that came with the memory.

"Thank you," I whispered in Blue's ear.

She pulled back some, still holding me with the strength of a large man, a funny smile on her rosebud lips. "My pleasure. Have another cheeseburger," she said. "You're going to need it."

CHAPTER 19

"I need to go outside," I said to them both, shocked that they listened to me so readily. There was a desperation in Nicholas's eyes, but they were letting me call the shots. *I really am something special to the* Shinigami. *They listen to me.*

Standing out there in the cold, tiny snowflakes flurrying around me, I was able to breathe, to be me. Me, who'd eaten too fast, whose head was swimming. I closed my eyes, and imagined this to be my home in Ossipee, facing the mountainside full of trees, Nicholas and a friend just a step away.

And I reached out to find him.

"Izanagi," I whispered as I called him into my mind's eye. There a drunken pressure in my head, but I pushed further. The flutter of wings against both my palms at my sides didn't come as a surprise. I didn't need to look to know that a pair of crows were loitering with me.

Faster than last time, he was there.

"Izanagi," I said again. There, in front of me, but not quite real. Hair blowing as always, black streaks in the night, his head tipped down in a slight bow so only his eyelids were visible. *Gi* jacket and pants flapping in time with the gusts of wind. A vision of black and white on a background of the same, part of the world, yet removed from it.

"Eliza," he said, his voice ethereal, like death breathing down my neck in the most comforting way. Inevitable, we were. Tied forever.

With one shaking hand, I reached out and touched his arm. Lifelike, but like a carved thing as well. A being of another place and time.

"Fate has given me a way to carve the fates of others," I said, images of Roman, Lynch, the girls he killed, and Nicholas, coming to me in rapid bursts. "It will take a lot from me." I raised my hands to his cheeks, smooth and soft, and I tilted his face up to look at me. "You will help me when I need you?"

His dark eyes bore into me, as soulful as the Master's were chilling. He put his hands on mine where they held his face.

"By all the devils of Yomi, I would destroy this world to help you."

I pulled my hands down slowly, the crow feathers brushing my fingertips again. "What are you doing here? What can I give you?" I knew he needed something, as much as I did. We were one in the same.

"Salvation from this place. I created this place, and it

has become something different. You can free me, all of us."

"I don't understand."

The air stilled, bowing to his words. Words that held a weight of centuries, and words that came to me simply, without riddle. "My wife, Izanami became a thing of Yomi, that shadowy land of the dead. My beautiful wife..." His dark eyes glinted with a swordlike edge. "A coward, I left her there to decay and rot, abandoning my honor and my love in my fear of the devils of Yomi. Izanami was a creature of great passion, sharp intent, and with pride as deep as Yomi itself. In her rage over my betrayal, my beloved vowed to destroy one thousand people every day in this world that we created together. And so, I vowed to give life to fifteen hundred."

"You," I breathed, heart skipping madly. "You created the *Shinigami*."

Mournfully, he continued. "I created the *Shinigami*. Bound to this mountain, I create beings to never die by her hand, a new god to balance what we had done to fate. And now, we need saving once again."

"I am no god to help—"

He put his finger to my lips. Such a human thing to do. "You have just begun to cast pebbles on this path. All becomes clear with blood."

Izanagi looked over my shoulder, and I turned to look with him. Nicholas and Blue stood, watching us. They could see him this time.

Their mouths hung slack with his magnificence, and he was a part of *me* somehow.

"Go," he whispered over my shoulder, and without a look back, I went to drain myself again.

∾

"He was there. I mean, barely, but there," Blue said, eyes wide, staring out into the night.

"That was Lord Izanagi," Nicholas said in a haze. "He rang through my bones."

"Told you," I said, as I picked up a burger, still warm from the chafing dish, and waggled my eyebrows at Nicholas. With a roll of his eyes, he turned to Blue.

"You're sure you want to be here for this? There's blood," he said simply.

She batted her lashes without a thought to how stunningly feminine it made her. "I'm fine. Kieran just paid me a visit." Thoughts of Kieran throwing an unconscious body on the bed and Blue attacking it made me blink extra hard and refocus on the task at hand.

"Izanagi chose *you* to speak to," Blue said, shaking her head, one hand on my shoulder. "It's a miracle."

I bit my burger and thought about whether or not I should tell them the things he said. More secrets.

"We should tell the Master," Nicholas said.

"No!" I yelled without meaning to, startling them both.

"Why not?" Nicholas asked.

"Because if Izanagi wanted to involve him, he would have," I said. I realized that the Master could see Izanagi. Memories of that day at the sparring arena came to me; the Master was afraid because of what he saw behind me. Of *who* he saw.

My suspicion of the Master grew. I glanced to Nicholas, who was watching me eat with a little smile, but his eyes were sadder than they should be. It left a bitter taste, to tell the man I loved to keep secrets from his the man he thought of as a father. But this was not my secret to let go of.

I felt Izanagi breathe a sigh of relief from the woods outside.

I finished off the burger, thankful that I wasn't wearing jeans, and straightened my spine. I had work to do.

"Now," I said, clapping my hands to rid them of crumbs. "Drink from me, Nicholas, before I get too tired. We have training tomorrow, and a long night ahead."

CHAPTER 20

The visions swarmed me like angry bees trying to get inside, and fill the emptiness I'd known for too long. Nicholas sucked long and hard at my throat, and when that puckered and pained, he went to my wrists. Blue stayed close, holding my hand sometimes when I whimpered or let a cry out, or slipped away.

And there were many times I could have slipped away to unconsciousness, but I didn't want to go to the place the visions were taking me.

Not even if it was once my home.

I saw New Hampshire, Lynch again, and so many images of the women he'd killed that it angered me through my stupor. The metallic scent of my own oozing blood kept me present, and I forced myself to make sense of what I was seeing, and why. Izanagi was out there, in the woods, urging me on. Urging Nicholas on.

Why am I seeing all of these murders?! I shouted in my head.

Light flashed in my mind, blinding me. And just like that, I knew what needed to be done; and I knew what would be asked of Nicholas the following day.

"The Master is going to ask you to return to Ossipee, Nicholas," I heard myself say. I felt nothing.

"He's going to what?" Nicholas's voice was an echo in my bloodstream, reverberating through every cell, not heard, but breathed inside me.

"To take care of Lynch. He needs handling."

"I won't leave you," he growled into my soul.

"Lynch needs watching more than me. I can't see past you enough to know what to do next." My heart pounded. "My mind needs to be clear of you."

It was an arrow through my sluggish euphoria to say such a thing. Nicholas's hurt wove into my own blood before he pulled his mouth away, air flooding my skin; it felt like the agony between Izanagi and Izanami.

"You want me to leave?" he whispered. Blue left the room, though I was certain she hadn't heard any of the words that passed between us; it was all through my blood. My eyes fought to regain clarity.

"Nicholas, of course I don't want you to go. Do you think these are my *feelings* driving me to do this?"

"Your *feelings* are why you give me your blood. Now this, this is something else."

I swallowed, and clung to the bed for stability. "Something is in me, struggling to get out, and the *Shinigami* need it. You need it for me to restore you completely. I need it, to find out why the hell I'm alive, why I have to die to be someone! I need you to trust me. This is me finding my way. Let me be *Shinigami.*" What had begun as a way to soothe Nicholas ended with me struggling for my identity. That escalated quickly.

"This is you having other options."

I almost fell on the floor with that one. "Excuse me? You think I want you out of the picture so I can play college freshman with some vampires?"

"Don't be ridiculous, you didn't go to college."

"Your sarcasm sucks." The thinning blood in my body was boiling. I closed my eyes and called to Izanagi. It had become that easy. With every drop of blood I lost, we were closer and closer.

He appeared next to me with no time lost, the door left wide open.

"I need your blood," I said to him.

Blue had returned, shifting foot to foot in my peripheral vision. The room became that level of cold only Nicholas could inflict upon it in so short a time. I tried to soften up when I said, "You've made me want to be more than what I was. What I have to do—"

"—is drink Izanagi's blood," Nicholas finished for me.

My heart ached for Nicholas, angry or not. I had done this to him, was always doing something to him. I took his face in my hands; his cheeks were ice, his eyes the cold chill of old coffee.

"Tell yourself you have to do this for me, because that's what I'm doing." His voice broke, and my heart with it. "I'm not angry," he added. "I'm just not ready to kick you out of the nest."

I pulled his face to mine, and kissed him hard enough to show him he belonged to me. Resting my nose on his, I said, "We're building a new nest."

∼

"Do you have fangs?" I asked Izanagi.

He smiled serenely, and shook his head. He was human in so many ways, just a man, who'd been thrown into a vacuum because of being afraid, being in love, having choices that weren't really choices, more fated occurrences. He was *human*.

And one day I would become as inhuman as he had become.

"You're not a vampire, you just make them," I said with a grin. He cocked his head at me like a child trying to understand.

A rush of intoxicated air, and his body was so close it could have been as much a part of me as his heart was.

It was time.

He held up his hand, and looked at his wrist. A gash opened up on it out of thin air, making me cry out. The god looked at me slowly, willing me to calm down, and I did. "This pain," he said, corner of his mouth twitching at the gushing wound, "is nothing compared to what I live each day with my wife a shadow that I can never touch and would leave me colder if I did. This pain is nothing compared to waiting for you to come."

Trembling, I put my lips to the wound, knowing that I was about to drink *blood.* Knowing that something was about to happen that was written in stars, knowing that this choice would change my life into something it hadn't been.

"This won't make me *Shinigami,*" I murmured against his pouring blood. Not a question, something I knew. This wasn't how I became a vampire; Nicholas would do that. Only Nicholas.

"You have always been *Shinigami*," the god whispered, loud as thunder.

I drank, and it tasted nothing like when you instinctively put your finger to your mouth when you cut it with a pizza slicer once a week. This blood was tingling, alive, the taste of constellations and oceans. It didn't fill me, but *replenished* me, revitalizing every sensation, every memory, every dream as it coursed through me with dizzying speed. His potent mix of wine and roses enveloped me, death mixed with life mixed with death. One in the same.

The visions lost their aggression, and became more cohesive, until they melted away entirely, leaving me feeling stronger. So much stronger. *Haunted* by strength, like it was the remnant of someone else, inhabiting me.

"My god," I said, wiping my clean chin. I didn't miss a drop of that ecstasy.

"How did it taste?" he said simply.

My eyes let me see what wasn't there yet.

I sucked on my lip for one last hope of a drop. "Like a world of death at my fingertips."

CHAPTER 21

I tried to stand still in the cold break of day, mind whirring like an engine, my body bursting with an inhuman energy.

The sleep I'd had after drinking Izanagi's blood was more peaceful than Sleeping Beauty's, despite being filled with dreams of things I didn't understand; demons, devils, spirits of Yomi. And her face—Izanami.

The peppermint brownie essence fanned across me before Nicholas was in sight. My vision told me he was coming, even while I slept. I woke up and put on fighting clothes, ready to go before the sun rose. I would face a vampire, I knew it like I knew my own name. It was supposed to intimidate me, toughen me up Navy Seal-style, but the Master didn't know what I had now: the blood of a god.

I'd touched death with my lips, and nothing scared me.

"You're up? Not like you," Nicholas said, appearing in front of me. With my heightened senses, he was even more irresistible. I grabbed him by the arms and pulled him into a kiss that would have bruised a human man.

Nicholas drifted away after, licking his lips to savor the taste of me and said, "That stuff is good." I smiled while he looked me up and down. "You look different, too. Oh, I know, you're dressed like you're going to the Vampire Human Resources Barbecue. Aren't you cold?"

I looked down at the lightweight white cotton *gi* top and thin, loose pants that matched. They did look brand spanking new compared to the worn-in ones that the other *Shinigami* lived in. My bare feet were invisible under the newfallen snow, and only then did I realize how crazy that was.

"I guess the blood warms me up."

"Pretty sure you can still get frostbite."

"Maybe." I looked at him, to see what I could see. What he'd done the rest of the night while I was with Izanagi.

"I'm okay, stop worrying. Jealous of another man touching you, sure. But he doesn't touch you the way I do. And it wasn't your choice."

"Nicholas, don't think I'm some victim. I decided to drink his blood. I'm not a puppet."

"You're telling me he didn't mean anything to you?" he said.

"I'm telling you that it isn't a tie like you and I have. And I'm also telling you that we didn't touch any other way except for me to drink from his wrist. I don't want anyone that way except you." A flame of Kieran flickered into my head, and I just as quickly snuffed him out.

He sighed and smiled the winning, egotistical smile

that I loved. We were okay. "How do you feel today?" he asked.

Grinning, I said, "Like nothing can stop me."

"Frostbite can stop you. You're barefoot, you lunatic. Go put socks and shoes on, I'll wait." He put his hands in the pockets of his hoodie and stared at me as I pulled my frozen, bluish feet out of the snow and wiggled the toes.

"Ha. They still move," I said. I looked at everything in a dream state, like I was stoned. "How did you know I was barefoot?"

"I smelled your feet. No, you're boots are by the door."

I bypassed the boots and put on socks and the wooden nightmare shoes I'd been given, highly impractical for snow, and sparked the vision of Nicholas the night before. Like snapping my fingers, as easy as blinking. I saw a fraction of a moment of Blue and Nicholas sitting on her bed, talking low, and I thought steam would come out of my ears. Their fingers were nearly touching, their eyes trained on each other. I didn't know what they were saying, and I was glad not to. It would have boiled my heart inside me.

I willed my hands not to shake, and my voice to remain even. "All right, let's go," I said, tottering with as much dignity as I could muster in these shoes on the boardwalk ahead of him, toward the sparring ring.

I was becoming used to the order of the sparring ring. Hundreds of *Shinigami* in a crowd around the open center, with the Master standing at the head on his little stone step, just always that much more important than everyone else. I spotted Blue where she'd been the last time, on the ground cross-legged with a few other female vampires. They all watched her, listened to her. I still liked her, despite my vision. It was then that I became aware I could *feel* the air between her and Nicholas, how powerful their connection was, the both of them. My heart warmed, oddly more toward her than it did toward Nicholas, who held my hand firmly at the top of the stairs.

"I know what's going to happen today," I said, my voice hollow, borrowed, as I stared down at the *Shinigami*.

"What?"

"I'm fighting a vampire. That one," I said, pointing to a young man in the crowd that sat motionless, staring at the empty center like it had his favorite toy and he wanted to take it back with the most violent means possible.

"Him?" Nicholas said, incredulous. "Wait, how do you know this? You know you're fighting today? And who— because of what happened last night?"

I merely nodded, unable to put words to the experience of having not new senses, not heightened ones, but different layers of understanding, new dimensions.

Nicholas shook his head. "He looks a little mental, that one. I don't like this. Do you know what happens?"

Relaxed, I shrugged and shook my head, Izanagi's blood a drum beating in my bones. "No, but I want to find out. Let's go."

"I mentioned I don't like this?"

The Master watched every step I took, and I didn't take my eyes off of his. The blank cloudiness of them didn't bother me.

Nicholas started towards a spot at the inner edge of the circle, with vampires making way for him fast and excitedly. Some were saying, "Hi Nicholas," like he was the quarterback of the football team and they were the Mathletes. Nicholas smiled at them all, the perfect class president.

I took my hand from his. "Nicholas, I'm going that way," I said, motioning to the Master whose eyes were still trained on me. He wiggled his long-nailed fingers at his sides, like he was trying to cast a spell.

I was making the Master nervous.

"Okay," Nicholas said, confused.

The vampires at my feet bowed their heads when I walked by, without willing themselves to, a magnetism from Izanagi's blood. As if the obscure promise of what I was to become to their race wasn't enough. As if being Nicholas French's *unmei fumetsu* wasn't enough. My chin lifted higher, my back straightened. I didn't need to suck in my stomach or fiddle with my hair.

I couldn't wipe the smirk off my lips when I bowed low to the Master. I was totally out of line with my sense of superiority over this *Shinigami* god, but I couldn't lie to myself as much as I could to Nicholas; there was something about the Master I didn't trust, and that Izanagi trusted less. Something about the man that Nicholas all but worshipped that I thought had ulterior motives.

When the Master tangibly relaxed in response to my show of respect, his momentary ease tingling down my spine like a drip of warm water, I sensed that he *did* trust me. He didn't want Nicholas to choose between us and knew he one day would. Thank you, all-knowing blood of Izanagi.

"You have changed, Eliza," the old man said.

I stood to face him. "I have. And you know who's touched me this way. Don't you?"

The eyes of hundreds of vampires were on my back, and of course, they could hear every word I said, no matter how far away they were. It was okay. If the Master was all Nicholas said he was, then he'd welcome a little effrontery. Maybe it would remind him fondly of taking Nicholas under his wing, but I didn't necessarily care. For once, I didn't need to hide behind the fear that I might get called out on being strong.

The Master didn't answer the question, but he didn't need to. He felt my power. It was juvenile and robust; growing, waiting. The Master's fear of me was a blanket upon it, willing me to go forward and become more.

I leaned forward to his ear, watching the anxious clench of his jaw, and I whispered, "Wait until I'm a vampire."

With a short bow, I walked unhurriedly back to Nicholas's side in the circle, every set of eyes on me. I caught Kieran's as I sat down, and he gave me a wide, defiant smile that warmed me like the campfire. Nicholas's hand chilled me to the bone when he put it on my knee.

"What was that?" he said.

"What was what?"

"All that with the Master? It's like you were calling him out or something."

"He can probably hear you."

"He's not listening, and if he were, he'd be glad I asked you what the hell you were doing."

My grin disappeared as I turned on Nicholas. "Sorry, I didn't realize he was so untouchable that he couldn't be spoken to. Is he not supposed to be a mentor? And you were the one who wanted to tell him about Izanagi. Think of it this way; I just did."

Nicholas got colder, but it didn't touch me. "He's like a father to me," he said, full of hurt.

Pursing my lips, I took his icy hand. "Nicholas, I know you love him, and that's important to me, really. I want to love him, too. But I can't give up *me*."

"This isn't you," he said with a mirthless laugh and not a little condescension. "This is Izanagi talking, and maybe a little too much Kieran."

Kieran heard it, and noticed my head snap in his direction, if he'd ever looked away from me at all. And leave it to the troublemaking bastard, he winked and smiled. My hand froze stiff in Nicholas's.

I'd had enough of the pettiness. A volcano of unease boiled in me, and I needed to *do* something. At that very moment, the Master pointed his staff at the vampire I'd spotted earlier, the one I knew I would be fighting. And knowledge hit me, hard, with unfaltering certainty.

I was the one who decided to fight the vampire. Nobody chose for me. Nobody made me do it, not even fate itself.

I stood fast, turning the heads of every vampire around me. "I would like to spar with him," I said solidly.

"Sit down, Eliza," Nicholas hissed.

I looked down at him and smiled, a happy smile, not an angry, defensive one. "I want this."

"You've never done anything like this in your life. You've never even thrown a punch, have you?"

"Sure I have, and don't worry about me. You won't let me die or anything. You think my super wonderful purpose here is to die in the ring? I don't think so."

A heavy sigh from him made me smile more, but he was freaking out.

"This is the worst idea I could never have come up with," he said. "This is Kieran-worthy of a bad idea. Don't think I don't see it."

There was the anger I needed.

I stalked to the center circle, more self-assured than I had any right to be. This was madness, and I had not an ounce of panic in me. Standing there, with hundreds of vampires judging me, I wasn't scared.

I wasn't even scared when the wiry vampire with too-wide eyes began bouncing around the ring like a meth addict ready for his next score. I swear, he was salivating. What purpose could *this* creature serve? Fate chose *him*? I immediately felt like a jerk for thinking it. Just because he looked like a disaster, didn't mean he was useless among a fleet of nearly perfect vampire peers.

Maybe we weren't so different.

The Master barked, *"Hajime!"* and I threw Nicholas a reassuring smile.

A second of hesitation too long.

The vampire struck me in the jaw with the back of his skeletal fist, and I hurtled across the ring, falling into a snow mound.

I expected to hear noise, besides the ringing in my head. Noises like you'd hear at a chicken fight or something, hollering and whooping. I heard nothing. But the blood inside me sensed something—concern. From several of the *Shinigami*, not just Nicholas, Blue, Kieran and Paolo. From ones I'd never spoken to. From strangers.

They wanted me to win.

I righted myself, pulled myself up and went back to the ring, one foot in front of the other, just like I'd gotten there to begin with. Blue and all her following were smiling wide at me from behind my opponent. It gave me strength, more than the considerable amount I already had.

The Master didn't look at me with the questioning eyes of a referee in a boxing match. He just signaled for us to go again. Without thinking, I lunged at the vampire, hitting him with a girly punch to the chin; artless, but with strength behind it. In dreams, I thought of punching people I was afraid of over and over, but my fist had the impact of feathers on their face. This punch had impact. His head snapped back. I hit him again, both fists at once, one to the face, one to the stomach, with all of my might, surprising myself. He stumbled backwards. I threw a kick like I'd watched Nicholas practice, landing it in his belly as he fell back, propelling him backward faster. Nicholas yelled encouragingly from out of my vision.

This was happening. I had power.

The vampire came at me fast, but inspired by my own tenacity, I rushed at him too, throwing a flurry of kicks that I had no idea I knew. I landed almost all of them somehow, as he spun and flitted like a sickly humming-bird around the ring. It wasn't until I knocked him down that I was too overcome with exhaustion to continue anyway. I swayed on my feet, and in that instant the vampire had a new light of anger in his wild eyes, and he swung back like a wrecking ball, hitting me on the top of the head with a hammer of a fist.

I felt Nicholas suck in his breath. The Master showed no sign of concern. Kieran was burning inside, and Paolo had stilled like fetid water. All of these things I felt in my core as the world spun.

Eyes closed to the maelstrom of color outside, I struggled to get up. When I opened my eyes, the vampire was in front of me, slack-jawed. Shaking his head, he put his hand up and said in a remarkably normal voice for such a wretch, "I give up. This one's yours."

I heard Nicholas breathe a barely audible word: "Amazing."

CHAPTER 22

I huddled against Nicholas's chest, drifting in and out of sleep before the sun set. My bone-crushing aches were all too human, but easily forgotten in the safety of his arms—arms that were back to the hulking, wood-chopping things I knew before his emaciation set in. I'd done that for him. Now, his cinnamon and springtime scent drugged and healed me to a perfect state of pleasure, and I smiled to think of what I'd done.

With his lips on my hair he mumbled, "I can't believe what you did out there today."

"Me either," I said, slurring with heavy, comfortable exhaustion.

"It was stupid."

"Totally."

"It was eerie. That was nothing a human being could do, stand up to one of us like that."

"Are you talking about the meth-head vampire or the Master?"

He snickered. "Both. What are you trying to do to him, anyway?"

"Nothing, I don't want to give him more meth, if that's what you mean."

"You know what and who I mean."

I sat up with great difficulty. "Come on, I didn't really do anything. If he's who you say he is, as a person, he won't mind. He's not a dictator."

"What difference does it make to you, though?" he said, bristly.

"It needs to be done. Part of it's for me, part of it's for the rest of the *Shinigami*. And part of it is for Izanagi." Nicholas stiffened, but didn't get cold, so I went on. "There's something between the Master and Izanagi. Something old, more important than us, but a part of us somehow? Standing up to the Master is something I can do for Izanagi. I want to."

I expected Nicholas to get a little irritated by this, but he softened, his eyes running over me, the warmth of them matching the scent that rolled off him like a newly opened oven. I loved this man for all of these things; he brought my heart to life. He ran his hand through my hair, his touch instantly making me want to fall asleep, and my body slackened more.

"It's okay to go to sleep," Nicholas murmured. "I might do the same, actually. I'm tired. This day has been—a little more than I was expecting."

I'd exhausted him and given a breath of life to him, as usual. My blood churned in a half-dream state, and another sense told me there was one more thing to do that day.

"Nicholas, drink. Just a little. Let me dream my visions."

"El…"

"Do what I say, I'm right."

"You're an obstinate bitch, too."

I smiled, even if he meant it. And I smiled again when he opened the vein.

Known only to me, Izanagi hovered outside as I fell asleep, a deeper calm than I'd known in a long time. Nicholas was drinking from me slow, slow, and it was actually *relaxing*, even as the visions of Lynch appeared.

Half-conscious, I saw the Master. He was outside the door, looking in with his blank eyes. I was too exhausted to open my eyes and see if it were true, but the presence of such a man was overwhelming, even in my sleep. Nicholas got out of bed with barely a movement, and I knew what would happen next.

I saw the scene in the room as if I were wide awake and watching. Nicholas flashed to the door in a burst of baking scents, and the Master hovered there, cold and ghostlike, a presence that filled the room before he entered it.

"You have a duty to perform," he said in Japanese, but I understood.

Nicholas bowed. I disliked seeing him in supplication to the Master, even if he did create their race.

Wait.

Nicholas thought the Master was the creator of the

Shinigami. It was common knowledge among them all. It only occurred to me in this vision that it wasn't true. Izanagi created the vampire race, and the Master made everyone believe otherwise. It had to be part of his thrall. He was so incredibly old and strong, he could make them all believe whatever he wished.

I connected with Izanagi in the woods, saw him as plain as I was seeing this scene, all at once. He felt me, too, and the realization I'd come to. And I was right.

How could I tell Nicholas? I couldn't, I just couldn't.

"So Eliza was right," Nicholas said, moving aside so the Master could enter.

The Master gave my sleeping body that frighteningly empty glare, full of anger and judgment. "Yes. It seems she is right frequently. You know what I'm going to ask of you, then?"

Nicholas sat, sprawled out on the floor, leaning lazily against the table. It was comforting to know he was still this much himself with the Master, reminded me that they were family. We expect family to disappoint us, in the end. But it wouldn't make it easier to tell him that their history was a lie.

"Eliza had a vision of you asking me to go to New Hampshire." He looked over at me with love-filled eyes, and I drifted more comfortably into my deep sleep.

"She's correct. You know why, then. What else does she see?"

"Lynch is on a killing spree. He's hurting over Kat." The simplicity of his words cut through me with their obviousness. It was still hard to think of Lynch as capable of love, a serial killer dubbed "the Abomination" by the *Shinigami.*

"Roman needs you to repay the favor he did for you."

"Favor," Nicholas said quietly, eyes downcast. I'd said to him so many times how hurtful it was that Kat's murder was a *favor* between Roman and Nicholas. Killing my only friend brought them closer together, even if Roman was nowhere to be seen. And I was alone, without her.

"You alone can keep the Abomination in line. It is only you that he's afraid of."

Nicholas nodded. "What of Eliza? What happens to her while I'm gone?" They both looked at me, and I saw myself through their eyes, my side rising and falling where I lay curled in a ball like a sleeping cat.

"She'll become what she must. Then everything will change."

Nicholas looked at him sharply. "Master. Nobody else can turn her. It has to be me." He breathed in through his nose, eyes drilling into the old vampire. "Nobody else can have her that way."

Both reacting to the other's anxiety, the two vampires put up glassy shields, which immediately crystallized around them in domes of ice. Two grim smiles showed through the shields like fun house mirrors. The Master's fell away like it had been in my imagination the whole time, while Nicholas's exploded into millions of fragments and disappeared. So like the men themselves; one a complete illusion.

"Of course nobody else will touch her, my boy. Do you

think she would allow it?" For the first time, I agreed with him.

But Nicholas's neck twitched, and I knew he thought of Kieran, and maybe a little of Izanagi. He stared at me in the bed, shoulders stiff. "I want to change her before I leave."

I was awake.

In the woods, Izanagi clenched his fists.

CHAPTER 23

"Stop pretending to be asleep," Nicholas said as he slid into bed.

I rolled over and slid my hands over his shoulders and back. So robust again. After feeding from me the solid jaw and cheekbones under the five o'clock shadow didn't look fragile.

"I heard everything, saw everything," I said.

"In a vision?"

"Yes."

He released a troubled, sad sigh. "I was hoping you were wrong and he wouldn't have me leave."

"We've been over this," I said. "What I'm more afraid of is what happens to *you* when you leave. I won't be with you to feed from me."

He didn't want to admit that worried him, or that he would just plain miss the taste, and the intimacy. He swallowed hard. "You're overlooking that I want to change you before I go."

I had no words. Nicholas had to leave, it was part of fate's plan, *my* plan to save him, and I was terrified to become a vampire before he was cured. The idea of taking away the one thing that made him whole again chilled me. The time between me deciphering the visions and Nicholas withering away without my blood couldn't be avoided. As certain as the death that owned us.

Nicholas wiped tears from my cheeks with his thumb. "Trust yourself, Eliza. You're afraid of what will happen to me, but you're doing it *for me.* I don't doubt you, and if this is the end, if we're wrong, you have given me Heaven here and I'm ready for Hell."

Only one question remained. "How soon do we do it?"

His eyes bore ferociously into mine. "Speaking of things we've already talked about, are you absolutely certain the way you feel about me isn't just the pull of being my *unmei fumetsu?* This thrall thing, and the scent... Once you've been turned, the illusion is gone, all that goes away—"

"Don't."

"You may never remember what you saw in me." His jaw tightened, and he went still, the way people do if they are very, very afraid and don't know what to do. "You could be so disgusted by this existence when you see me through eyes like my own, that you'll feel you could never love anything again." My soul ripped when he tore his eyes from mine.

"First of all, you're in love with me and I accept it. Why can't you do the same?"

In that nonchalant way he had, he said, "Oh, I regret

every day the time I spent denying that I was hopelessly in love with you."

"No regrets. And we don't question it again. End of story."

"The problem is, it's only the beginning of our story."

"Sorry, that's a problem how?"

Fear of what unknown thing he might say next chilled me to the bone the way the icy woods of New Hampshire or Japan could never do. He ran his fingers through my hair. "Because, beautiful girl. I could *ruin* you. Make you something you're not, damn you for all eternity. Loveless, cold, trapped seeing the world and me too clearly through superhuman eyes."

I grabbed his hand in my hair, angered by his ridiculous despair. "Is there going to be a time you don't think I'm a moron? This *thrall* you still think you have me in, well, people do it all the time. They fall for someone and can't explain it, because of the way they smell, or some look they can give. You're not so special." His lips puckered, and I was encouraged that maybe he understood my logic. "I can explain exactly why I'm drawn to you, Nicholas. It's that you're *you* no matter what human residue gets left behind in there. It's *your* emotional walls, *your* sarcasm, *your* generosity and your laugh, and the way you're just so good at everything." I choked back some of my own emotion. "Those things and so many more things that I see in you is why I'm forever in love with every curl on your head, and every pain in your heart. Can't you trust that the more clearly I see you, the more I'll know how worth loving you are?"

His eyes glistened. "We can be like this forever," he said.

"As long as you don't think eternity is too long to have the same girlfriend."

He propped up on one elbow. "No. I think probably everything—slows down. Takes on new meaning. Not just once, but over and over. Probably all the things I saw before will become clearer when I look in your immortal eyes, so I'll think maybe I never *really* saw anything. And I think those times when nothing matters, when time is my enemy because it won't stop, I bet that doesn't happen anymore. I bet time is on my side again, when I never have to turn from you. I bet I'll be glad that time won't end. I bet I wouldn't be able to stand it if it did. Not that I've put any thought into it."

Through hazy grins, we dreamed of when eternity would start.

My visions followed me into sleep, where I was dumbfounded to see Leann. Of all people, the other *unmei fumetsu* was the last person I expected to see, so little an impression she made on me. I woke up eager to get training, though from the aches and pains, I knew I wouldn't be volunteering to fight that day.

"Nicholas, wake up," I whispered, shaking him hard.

"Why are you whispering when you're shaking me like the human earthquake?" he groaned, his face in the pillow.

"We need to get ready to training. Right now."

"Right now?"

"That's what I said."

"Bossy." He got up with a dancer's ease, his bare back rippling, his thigh muscles flexing, revealed by only boxer shorts.

I literally rolled out of bed to a crouch on the floor. Jesus, I was sore. And covered in bruises. I'd put on a long sleeved black t-shirt and sweatpants, and the bruises still peeked out from under the sleeves and cuffs. I couldn't let Nicholas see. He wasn't looking, but stepping into his karate pants and grabbing a Star Wars tee with Japanese writing on it.

"Cool new shirt."

"One of the young ones gave it to me," he said, smoothing his hair fruitlessly after pulling the shirt on. God, they showered him with gifts.

Was that going to be me one day?

After rubbing his eyes and grimacing either at the taste in his mouth or his breath, he really looked at me.

"Holy shit."

He crossed the room in one motion to touch my cheeks with tentative fingertips.

"How bad is it?" I asked him. "Is it like, G.I. Jane bad?"

He pursed his lips, with a pained frown. "Yeah."

I smiled, the skin tightening around my eyes where they must be bruised. "Progress. Outside hurts heal, it's the inside ones you have to worry about."

"That's a heroic thing to say."

"It's how I feel."

He kissed me with featherweight lips on the cheek, and it still stung. I pulled my hair into a ponytail, stifling a sharp breath when I touched the top of my head. "Hero turned vampire. That will be perfect. But we knew that. Now we have training to attend to. I guess? It's what the boss says."

I kissed his lips hard, not caring that I had bruises around mine. "Thank you for blindly listening to me."

"Your eyes are fresher than mine, and your mind knows more. I'm dying to see what kind of ride you take me on today."

"Something is happening with Leann today, but I can't see what."

He looked faraway for a minute. "You can see her now, too?"

I shook my head. "She just popped up. It wasn't as clear as my other visions, but it's definitely a real thing that's going to happen."

"Should you tell her?"

"What could I possibly say?"

Nicholas made me lie down while we waited for breakfast to arrive. He just watched as I devoured eggs and fruit, and looked for more.

"Still think it's sexy when I eat?" I said through a mouthful.

He curled his lip back, animal-like. "I could devour you."

I choked, and pictured myself black, blue and yellow, food on my face, chewing like a goat. He smoldered looking at me, and I tried not to get distracted. We had to go.

The walk seemed shorter all the time, even being all banged up and in awful wooden shoes. It wasn't long before I'd planted myself next to Leann on the outside of the circle, hoping not to be pointed at. I could've used a day without being the center of attention.

"That was pretty ballsy of you yesterday," Leann said, hugging her knees, not looking at me.

"Or pretty dumb. Look at me." I said it, but didn't mean it. I felt goddamn good. I could take on the world, and all it could do was bruise me.

"Did you train before that at all? Like, at all?" Her face was full of unhidden skepticism.

"Not so much."

"Then why did you volunteer to fight a vampire?" She smirked, like she was talking to someone stupider than her.

She wasn't the one who had visions so clear she could taste the air in them. She wasn't the one that had Izanagi's blood bubbling in her veins. She wasn't the one who had Nicholas French in her bed and in her future.

This superiority wasn't like me, but it was. It was like the new me. *Shinigami* ran deeper than the rest of me. Leann may be on her way to becoming a vampire, but I was something more.

"I wanted to do it. What have I got to lose?"

She squinted, sizing me up. I didn't like it. *This is my place.*

"Where do you come from? What's your story?" she said, not really asking me, more wondering out loud.

"New Hampshire. Story is death took over and all that. You?"

"Pretty much the same."

"You're from New Hampshire and death followed you,

took the world from you so as to make you its slave for eternity?" God, what a bitch I could be.

She laughed, eased by my unease. "Yeah, something like that. From Ohio. An orphan. Never had anyone, so nobody I cared about died. We're not so different."

I sniffed at her. She was nothing like me. I was a jerk for looking down on her, but I did. I just did.

"Are you afraid?" I asked her, without intending to. They were words from within me, from that place that gave me visions. Maybe they came in part from the place where I was misinterpreted and alone, too. Possibly I just wanted to hear someone like me say out loud that yes, she was afraid, and that she didn't have everything under control.

But Leann's malicious sneer didn't offer me any comaraderie. "Of course I am," she spat at me, like I was a complete imbecile for asking.

But I was the one who knew she was becoming a vampire that day, not her.

"Do you know how it's done?" I asked her, because I didn't know *everything*. Kieran was alone, smoking. She shrugged and looked away. "My—Nicholas—only told me it's very personal, and hard to explain, because he's never made a vampire before." But Kieran had, with Blue.

A bolt of lightning-filled jealousy shot through me as an unsolicited vision of Kieran's naked silhouette came to me.

With *her.*

I stared at Leann, forcing the image of her nudity beside Kieran's out of my mind, and she looked back at me with actual fear in her eyes.

"What's your problem?" she said.

"What's yours? I'm a useful one to have on your side, seeing as Kieran clearly isn't interested." Izanagi buzzed inside me.

"What is it with you and your *Shugotenshi?* You two are so attached," she said, like it disgusted her.

"And you and Kieran aren't. Sucks to be you, huh?" I snapped back.

"Nicholas is nothing like you. Kieran is nothing like me. We aren't meant to be together."

"You don't have the attachment we do?" Genuine curiosity. Kieran paid her hardly any mind at all. The pain would have slaughtered me in every way.

For the first time she looked at me like a person, like someone with actual emotions who wanted to trust and be trusted. I just think she didn't know how. "I hurt all the time," she said, voice cracking. "I couldn't take it if we were *together*, like Nicholas and you are."

I'd never thought of it that way. Like it was harder to care for each other. I'd never had the choice. And from the look on her face, I don't think Leann did either. She blistered with emotion so much that it was nearly invisible until you knew what to look for.

"What makes you think Nicholas will stick around after you turn vamp?"

Gulping, I had to fight off every cell in my body that wondered the same thing. Would I be the same for him when vampire blood roared through my veins, or when I took on my victims' traits after draining them? When I acted more like a dead person than myself? I had to believe it when he said it wouldn't change anything.

"We were meant to be together, it's there, every time he looks at me," I said.

Leann's eyes narrowed. "Yeah, good luck with that," she muttered.

In the center of us all, Kieran and Nicholas ignored us to good-naturedly batter each other with fire and ice.

～

"Tonight?"

Nicholas was sweaty, something I found amazing when it occurred. He swatted my hand away when I put a finger on a burn mark on his arm.

"Holy crap, is that from Kieran touching you?"

"It will go away soon enough," he said, pulling his arm away. "So, tonight. I don't know if she's ready."

Leann would have to be ready. Our training was different, every one of us. She'd been at the temple for months. Sometimes it took years. Arthur had just barely arrived when I did.

Nicholas was deep in thought, cracking his knuckles as we walked. "The Master asking me to leave, Izanagi showing up, all this centers around you. I wish to Christ I knew why."

As if he'd heard the Lord's name used in vain, there was Paolo, keeping pace with us.

"Eliza," he said, nodding quickly with a smile for Nicholas. "Eliza, there's a haze all around you. Do you need to talk?"

I was so taken aback by this, I stopped completely, and so did Nicholas. Paolo kept going. "Realizing your higher purpose requires a lot of soul searching. Your soul is troubled. Do you need to talk?" he repeated.

I looked at Nicholas, who looked back at me, bemused.

"Eliza's not really a woman of God," Nicholas said.

But the idea of having someone to talk to about the conflicts in my heart had certain appeal. Paolo noticed me considering it. His peacefulness flowed over me like beach waves.

"When you need me, I will be ready to listen," he said.

"Th—thank you, Paolo," I stuttered. I was uncomfortable, not because Paolo could see my soul changing, but because Nicholas could not.

"Nicholas, a true pleasure to watch you and Kieran today. You're such an artist," Paolo said, bowing his head in reverence.

Nicholas bowed back. "Thanks, Paolo. Now come have a drink. We could all use a stiff drink."

"Oh, I don't know about that."

"Luckily, I do," Nicholas said, cuffing the younger man round the back of the neck. "Come with us. Loosen up."

CHAPTER 24

P aolo's skin was flush from attending the sparring matches in the bright sun. That meant he'd fed on a good person, someone with a good soul. And he, a man of God.

He caught me looking at him as Nicholas poured sake. It was barely noon.

"What wracks your lightning-quick brain, Eliza?" Paolo said.

My cheeks got hot. "Sorry. I just was thinking of all the vampires out in daytime."

"I fed last night," he said, with the hint of a smile. "As all God's creatures do."

"We're drinking, this is no place for God," Nicholas said, downing his sake. We sat around the table once again. Like a family.

Kat and Roman would have loved it.

Blue appeared at the door. Dragonfly presence; shimmering blue kimono top against black hair, a tiny stature that didn't threaten, but was fearful all the same. Dark beauty. "I want in," she said, grinning. Her presence made me lighter. She sat next to Nicholas with a decided plop and looked at us all. "What are we talking about?"

Paolo smiled wide at her, as charmed by her as the rest of the world.

Nicholas answered first in the way only he could. "Talking about how a man of God consumes the blood of the innocent and walks in their daylight and still considers himself holy." He grinned at Paolo, who grinned back.

"I fulfill a purpose, and I'm happy to do His work. I'm more concerned how Eliza is feeling about coming into her own." He pinned his eyes on me.

May as well be honest. "I'm feeling a little pompous about it, actually. Weird."

"You've been hanging around me just the right amount, then," Nicholas said.

"The visions are stronger, aren't they?" Blue said in a whisper, turning it into a secret between friends.

I nodded. "I can call them up, and sometimes now I get these…premonitions, I guess." I glanced at Paolo and Nicholas. "I know Leann is becoming a vampire tonight." Paolo smiled, but Blue paled.

"Kieran will change her tonight?" she asked, voice thick.

"What's wrong?" I asked. Nicholas didn't look at me, only at Blue, wordlessly showing disturbance.

"I—I, um, just wasn't expecting it. But I should have. She's his. Too," she said, sentences broken, eyes on her hands as they twisted in her lap. I wanted to hug her. I couldn't imagine how hard it must be to see your *Shugotenshi* sharing that intimacy with another.

"There's nothing between them, you know," Nicholas said quietly, meant only for her.

"There is and there isn't. Nothing…lasting. But it's still not easy to think of."

"It doesn't mean Kieran's going to have sex—" Nicholas started, but Blue gave him a withering look.

You only had to take one look at the Irishman to know he most certainly would be having sex with the girl. All the girls. Nicholas put his hand on Blue's back, and she smiled at him sadly.

"That means there will be a ceremony tomorrow night," Paolo said.

"So many *ceremonies…*" Nicholas moaned, rolling his head back. Great. Dressing up was imminent.

"We celebrate our own," Paolo said.

"It's beautiful," Blue said, cheering up a bit. "You'll love it."

"It's a lovely thing to see someone who was mere flesh and blood become one with their destiny," Paolo went on.

I wondered what it would be like for me. It wouldn't be long before I found out.

"Pour me some sake," I said to Nicholas.

Nicholas and Paolo went off to practice *katas* together, a prospect Paolo was absolutely giddy about. It was still funny to see Nicholas treated like such a celebrity. The *Shinigami* were starstruck by him so often, it threw me, but I was equally happy to see that everyone recognized his splendor the way I did.

Blue stayed with me to drink more sake. It was probably a bad idea, but slurring and laughing about the room being so blurry made me not care that much. Blue was an open book, so willing to talk about her feelings for Kieran. She didn't think she was in love with him, but she didn't know, and she was sure he wasn't in love with her, or anyone.

"Nicholas denied we were in love for a long time, too. Thrall this and that. Chosen ties, blah, blah."

"They're still men under it all, aren't they?" Blue said softly.

I reached out and held her little hand. "I wish there was something I could say to make this better for you."

She looked into my eyes, and asked, "Is it happening right now?"

"Not yet. It will be dark."

"Thanks for telling me. It makes it easier, just a little."

We sat quietly, leaning against each other, watching snow squall in circles.

"I can see them outside in this weather, right now," I said, closing my eyes and smiling. "The snow is wild, and Paolo and Nicholas are fighting in it."

"Is it hard for you to be human and see what he is? Are you afraid of killing?" Hearing her talk about it in her singsong voice was surreal. To remember her fighting, and to think of her ripping someone's throat open, it was somehow *beautiful* to me.

"It shouldn't be so easy for me to think of people being killed. Of being the one to do it."

"No," Blue said, looking desperately into my eyes. "I felt like I was becoming a monster. I wasted too much time thinking how awful I was. Maybe that's why Kieran doesn't love me—he knows what I thought of him then."

"It's not your fault. Kieran feels how he feels, nobody has to be at fault for it."

She threw her arms around my neck without warning. "How are you so wise about things that are so terribly simple, and so terribly complicated?"

I laughed. "Because I'm something—else."

CHAPTER 25

Darkness brought the return of Nicholas, and my own dark with him. A bleak sense of overwhelm writhed in me and I was alone in it. Blue wanted to cope with Kieran's next move by herself. Thank God she didn't have the visions I did of their naked bodies.

"You drank like a drunk, didn't you?" Nicholas said. "Impressive. Manly."

"Sssshhh."

"Headache already?" He put his cold fingers on my temples. It nearly lulled me off to sleep standing up, and I would have welcomed it. Too much was happening too fast, and yet not fast enough for me to react to it. I wanted out for just a while.

"Paolo's a big fan of yours," Nicholas said, leading me to bed by the hand. "You may be the new icon around here."

"That bother you?" I sounded drunk.

"I'm your biggest fan."

"Creep."

"The worst kind."

He covered me up as I lay on my side, and moved in behind me. Sweat and cinnamon overtook my senses. His hands ran up and down my arms, his nose nuzzled into my neck, and if I hadn't been so comfortable, I would have turned to kiss him.

I sat bolt upright when the heat in the pitch dark reached me. A sudden blast of inexplicable warmth, waking me out of a sound sleep. Nicholas slept like a porcelain god next to me, hands folded on his chest, sleep-puffed lips parted. A vision was skirting the edges of my mind, but couldn't quite find its way in, fogging my thoughts up. I almost woke the peaceful beauty at my side to have him drink from me, so that I could let in the images that wanted to be mine.

I was becoming an addict.

Frustrated and groggy, I got up, throwing on my heavy coat and Nicholas's boots by the door; old things of habit. It warmed me to think that he missed the place where we'd trudged through the snow together. He missed New Hampshire.

The blustering wind hit me hard when I opened the door, and I looked around for the source of the heat that was warming me when I should have been freezing.

The Irishman sat on a rock only feet away, his head in his hands. I rushed to him, wanting nothing more than to make help, his despair was so evident. Waves of heat shimmered the air around him, regardless of the icy wind. He was boiling inside.

"Kieran," I said, putting my hand on his shoulder. How

the heat emitting from him didn't burn the black tee right off his body, I didn't know.

He didn't lift his head. "Leann's a vampire now," he said.

I gulped. "I know."

"Right," he nodded. "What if she wants more from me?"

"That, I don't know."

He looked up, smoldering tears in his eyes, the remnants of earlier ones smoking on his cheeks. I gasped, not expecting to see such emotion in him. I'd thought he bottled it all up to let it out in every self-destructive way he could.

"Kieran," I breathed, dropping to my knees in the snow next to him, the cold a welcome change next to his incessant burning. "Why are you so upset about this? She's your *unmei fumetsu.*"

"Aye, but I don't want her."

I blinked dumbly over and over.

"Does she want you?"

He looked at me with those sweet brown eyes, eyes that betrayed hurt that he so successfully hid from everyone. "Not like Blue does. And I don't know what to do with either of them."

It strangled me to see him so conflicted. It hurt like when Nicholas was hurting, or when Kat was crying. It hurt like I cared a frightening amount.

"You must be freezing, love," he said, that accent melting me more than the fire in his eyes and heart.

"Not next to you," I said. God, did that sound like I think it sounded? I glanced back at the doorway, where

Nicholas slept not so far inside. A disgusting guilt overcame me, and vanished when Kieran put his hand on mine.

"It looks like you've got as much trouble as I do. I could see it from you a mile away. I wanted to be near you."

This close to him, the simplicity of those words, I felt stripped. My eyes tore from his. "There's a lot going on in my head. And—" Should I tell him this? Catching myself mid-sentence, I looked at him, scared. But I had nothing to be scared of.

"And what?"

"And Nicholas is leaving."

"Leaving?"

My throat tightened inside an invisible fist. "He has to go back home, but nobody knows yet."

"Except you. You knew first." I nodded, and he added, "Our Mr. French is leaving you with no one? Hardly seems right."

"I'll be a vampire before he goes, and I can take care of myself. You made Leann one, what, twenty minutes ago?"

"You're a hell of a lot different from Leann."

"Different, but still afraid."

The sweltering heat of him wrapped around me in cuddly bear hug. I'd never felt anything so soft and warm in my life, and he hadn't even touched me.

Then he *was* touching me, his tattooed hands holding mine against his chest. "Don't be afraid. I'll make sure nothing hurts you."

My heart crumbled. Part of me wanted to be weak and taken care of, was so tired and bored of being different.

There was no end to how strong I had to be, and sometimes it was just easier to fail.

He pulled me to his chest, wrapping his arms around me tight. No one had ever made me feel as understood as he did at that moment. We were alike in that moment. It hurt like rubbing a bruise.

I swore I could hear Nicholas breathing from inside.

"Kieran, I don't think I should be out here."

He let me go, and the wound I didn't know was there opened up again.

"What do you *want* to do?" He held a strand of my hair up to his nose. The slight tip of his head bared the dark stubble on his throat, its straining tendons, intensely sexual. His voice was guttural, lustful. I couldn't move, the burn of him holding me captive there. "What Nicholas gives you is part of the vampire package, love. Don't let it tell you what you want."

That sent a chill through me, and I leaned away. "Nicholas and I are in love, and we would be whether I was his chosen or not. He's what I want."

Eyes on mine, Kieran put a cigarette coolly in his mouth and lit it with the touch of his fingertip.

"Then it shouldn't be such a distraction to come with me for a while?"

CHAPTER 26

In Nicholas's boots, my pajamas under my big mess of a coat, still tipsy, I went with Kieran. Maybe he was right, maybe I just wanted to do something that wasn't expected of me. He was the devil on my shoulder and I found myself all too willing to listen.

"I didn't know about this place," I said as we walked into a dark, decadent tea room. Smoky under purple lantern light, I saw vampires lounged on black pillows around cherrywood tables. Their shadows on the walls seemed more real than they did.

"We don't talk about it in polite conversation, love," Kieran said.

"Like you know polite conversation," I muttered, looking around. I wondered if Nicholas knew of this decadent, dirty little hideaway.

All the vampires here were alone, even if they were together. The secrecy simmered in a haze of saccharine-sweet smelling booze and whispers, hid in violet-hued corners, flaunted in glimpses of skin and teeth.

The serenity of Japan was becoming unsettling to me, and I welcomed this place that hid a little rebellion. Zen gardens and gently tinkling music, cool, calm colors and meditation areas; all for us killers. It didn't always sit well.

Walking with a derelict grace, Kieran grabbed pillows from every empty table and threw them all on the floor against a floor to ceiling window. He sprawled across them, hands behind his head against the glass, and I sunk down with him. The air around him tasted like flames.

When the serving girl brought us tea, Kieran gave her a wink, making her giggle into her hand. My eyes rolled of their own volition.

"Is there a woman here you that isn't hot for you?"

He swigged the tea, and then bucked his hips forward to pull a flask out of his back pocket. "I can't get the deaf and blind girl to touch my biceps."

I drank my tea, but pretended it was something stronger. The hour approached when the shit would hit the fan, and my buzz was wearing off. I needed some desensitizing to this intuition telling me that too much was about to be revealed, too much would occur in one day. I wasn't ready for morning and drinking would help.

I took the flask out of his hand and tossed it back, as he watched with a surprised grin.

"Feel the burn, baby," he said.

I winced. "Jack is no gentleman."

"Gentlemen are no fun. Now tell me why you're here."

"You made me come?"

With raised eyebrows, he gave me a chastising finger point. "You need to stop doing what everyone tells you."

"Including you?"

He leaned forward to take the flask back, and finished it off. "I'll never tell you what to do, even if you beg."

I thunked my head against the window behind us. "I'm still a little drunk and I want to drink more. I agree with you, it's time I had some fun. This ceremony tomorrow's gonna get ugly, and booze makes the ugly go away."

"Eh, not always. What's that brain of yours showing you now, Miss Morgan? Is it Leann?"

I blinked, and she flashed in my head. A femme fatale of a vampire, on the temple steps. Visions of red. The sting of betrayal and surprise and lust for blood. It disappeared as fast as it came.

"Eliza!" Kieran was crouched over me, holding my back off the ground. "Eliza, what just happened?"

"Whaaa—" I couldn't speak for the mouthful of my own saliva, and it was running down my chin. A seizure.

"Christ, Eliza, this is how visions treat you now?"

"I sure as hell hope not," I said, rubbing my eyes.

"Your body is kicking out the human," he said under his breath. "Only *Shinigami* could handle a power like this."

He signaled to Giggly Girl, who was quick enough to know we wanted alcohol, not tea. My body buzzed with aftershocks, my ears rang, the room was too loud. Kieran waited for me to drink a hearty mouthful before he did the same, his concerned eyes helping to slow my heart as it pounded an arhythmical beat. Kieran's strong, working hands were on my cheeks and he was looking hard into my face, too close, full of worry.

"You keep me on my toes, woman," he said, rolling back on to the pillows against the window.

"Good thing, looks like I'll be falling down a lot."

He took the shaking cup out of my hand, our fingers touching for a pulsing moment. "You need water, a clear head. Whatever you just saw knocked you on your arse."

I put my head in my hands to slow the whirring room down. "These visions are too strong for me, they're coming faster and harder. And when they don't, they still want in and the only thing that makes them come is letting Nicholas drink from me, and that makes me weak and—"

"Sssshhh," he crooned, lifting my head gently. My hair hung in my face as usual, and he brushed it aside. "I don't know how to help you, but I'll be here. I'll hold your hand tomorrow if you need."

"Something big is going to happen. More than one big thing. Lots of big things. They're like ants crawling in my brain."

"Tomorrow will come soon enough. Then some of it will stop. I think." He ran his hands up and down my arms, every movement the smell of a freshly snuffed flame. My mane of hair hid us from what little light there was, and we were alone. Two things that weren't what they were supposed to be. "Why do you feel so much like mine, Eliza?" he breathed in that small space, his breath as heated as his words.

I tried to object, but my lungs collapsed and my heart

stopped working. My brain screamed and everything in me stopped doing what it was supposed to.

"I won't kiss you if you don't want me to," he said.

I moaned, not the kind he was probably looking for, but one of crushing defeat. Flashes of Kieran and Blue, Kieran and Leann, Leann in red, Nicholas and Izanagi, Roman, Lynch, blood. And Nicholas again. But so much blood.

Kieran leaned his forehead on mine like Nicholas had done so many times, relaxing me the same way. "I won't pretend that I don't want you, Kieran. I do. But I'm his."

"For once, do what you want, Eliza."

I pushed him off as nicely as I could, and the subtle darkness of the room filtered in again.

"Jesus, what am I doing to ya?" He rubbed his hand over his jaw. "I'm sorry, acting without thinking. Truth of it is I don't know what I want, either."

"What sent you my way tonight?" I asked. "What about Leann? Blue?"

"Ah, those two," he said with a grim laugh. "I don't know how I got blessed with two *unmei fumetsu*. I don't deserve them. They sure as hell don't deserve me."

"You mean well," I said, touching his arm soothingly against my better judgment. God, could I please drink more now?

"Intentions will be the end of the world one day."

The fire was all around him. He couldn't survive without it. The fire reminded him of the bad thing he was, even if he wasn't.

"Kieran, I don't believe you're a bad man because of all this," I said, waving my hand at his fading tattoos, faded t-shirt, faded jeans, faded conviction. "There's something so much more real about you than the rest of them. You've got more fight in you."

"Only because I'm a walking mistake. Once you're one of us, my unique flavor wears off."

"It hasn't for Blue."

He winced, stung, but I didn't regret saying it.

"Blue lets her fears turn her into something she's not. That woman doesn't need me."

"Seems to me you two are kind of perfect together."

"Perfect isn't perfect for me." His voice was becoming more agitated. He squinted, taking the last drag off his cigarette and putting it out in the cup in his hand. "Tell me you don't ever feel a little less than perfect with Nicholas French by your side."

"I don't need to be perfect to be right for him." Nicholas never made me feel like I wasn't good enough— maybe just not right for a lot of things. But Nicholas did feel right, so right that I often wondered how I survived so long without him.

And yet here I was. With another man.

"I think I'd better get back, Kieran. Got to sleep this off, be ready for Leann's ceremony, whatever in the hell's in store tomorrow." Disappointment spread across his face. "Where is Leann, anyway?"

He looked out the window, like he might see her there. "Dying, being reborn. Forgetting the world she never really knew."

CHAPTER 27

L ight woke Nicholas and I at the same time. Having him next to me in bed never lost its shine.

"Where'd you go?"

No good morning, just wondering where I went while wearing his shoes.

"Just outside," I said. Then I realized that wasn't true, and I hated myself for going on, but I had to. "Then I went with Kieran for a drink." Shit, that sounded bad.

"Oh. Of course. That's exactly what I expected to hear."

My eyes shot open to see Nicholas making that face, where I couldn't tell if he was serious or just a lot more fluent in sarcasm than I was.

"R-really?"

"No. No, it's not. That's what I'd expect to hear from a homeschooled teenybopper with daddy issues. Not from you."

"Well, if you'd let me go out once in a while, I wouldn't have to rebel, Dad."

With a gasp and a hand to his chest as if to say he was mortally offended, he burst out, "*Dad? Let* you? I didn't realize I held the reins too tight. Or at all." Then, more seriously, "You're right, I'll back off."

"No, no. You're right. I snuck out like I was grounded. I didn't want to wake you, and me and Kieran just—talked." I knew I was blushing. I wanted to cover my head in the blankets, but Nicholas would feel my heart beating fast from under them.

"Kieran doesn't ever just talk. Nobody with an Irish brogue does. They entrance and take advantage. It's fascinating, really."

"Nicholas, I was born at night, but not last night. However, I know someone who was."

Leann was a vampire now. Meaning this was the day of the ceremony, and all the *other* things that I could sense, but not quite see.

His lips darted onto mine, and were gone. "I don't ever want you to feel like I own you. You're stronger than me, I'm a fraction of a thing without you." He smelled like dreams feel; billowy, marshmallow and cookies, not quite real. Like what I wanted for us. Soft, easy, cloud-filled days.

I put my hand on his face, the five o'clock shadow he always had, different from Kieran's leftover stubble from forgotten nights. Nicholas was rugged and in control, strong. I wanted him to stay that way, and I knew I could help.

"I love you for all of it. You have your possessive side, Nicholas, but so do I. I want to belong to you, so it works just fine."

He kissed me without hesitation or seduction, a full, growing thing. Like the world would burst with the strength of it.

"I know the best way you can possess me," I said, closing the inches between us.

"Frisky minx. We have things to do, places to be," he said.

"That's not *exactly* what I meant, though I wouldn't turn you down."

His pupils dilated, and he stared at my chest, heaving with heavy heartbeats. He wanted it as much as I wanted to give it to him.

"Are you ready for me to drink?"

"Do I look like some fragile little flower? I know what I can take." What I couldn't take was the fringes of these visions that wouldn't quite come to me, but lingered and tickled and scratched at my consciousness. He could help me as much as I could help him.

"I want to drink you dry, but I'll settle for your taste." A growl of darkest intent. I bared my throat to him, brushing my hair over my shoulders, waiting for the pinch and sting.

He licked a long lap up the length of my throat to my ear, biting my lobe ever so slightly, letting the stab of his fang linger. Blood beat through every inch of me.

"I crave every part of you to the point of insanity," he whispered. "Stop me when I go too far."

"Impossible." I was panting, squirming, a wild animal with his slightest touch.

With light kisses to my collarbone and behind my ears, he teased the blood to the surface, and when I didn't think

I could take another minute without his hands on me, he plunged his fangs into my neck, making me squeal. Then groan. Then go black for a moment, a moment filled with stars and the sweet sensation of becoming lighter in an all-too heavy world.

"Nicholas," I breathed, wanting to pull my shirt off, pull his shirt off, have only the heat between us.

Heat. Kieran.

As if he'd read my thoughts, he wrenched my body just enough to remind me who was stronger.

Digging in further, the visions trickled in, filled with too much power. Nicholas's sucking grew painful with them, and I found myself just trying to suffer the moments to see what would happen next.

Try as I might to call it, the ceremony wouldn't appear. Instead I got Roman, brooding Roman, and I *tasted* how he missed his only brother. Roman had just fed. I tried to sort through the foreign blood in his veins, to see where it had come from, but the distraction of the barbs in my throat and my desperation overtook me.

"Eliza, oh God," Nicholas said, frantically patting at my neck with his fingers while I tried to hold my eyes open. Hot flashes soaked my clothes, making me nauseous. How much had I bled?

"I need to sit up," I said, not actually knowing what I needed. "Wow, I'm getting tired of passing out and stuff." He helped me to a sitting position, and the movement made a stream of blood squirt from my neck onto the blankets. My hand flew to my throat—more gushing there.

"Nicholas," I said, and then I was out.

~

My limbs ached with cold. I woke up to see Nicholas standing over me, and next to him, the god himself.

Izanagi.

"Leave us alone," Izanagi commanded Nicholas. Pink tears stained Nicholas's cheeks. If I'd had the strength to speak, I would have told him it was my fault, that I hadn't almost died, and that it wouldn't matter if I had, as long as he was okay.

But none of that was true.

Nicholas bowed his head, and with the most defeat I'd ever seen in him, he walked into the snow with nowhere to go.

I knew he would go to the Master. He needed his god like I needed mine.

Izanagi knelt at my side, a gesture I didn't want him to make. He smiled, of course knowing my thoughts. "Gods are but men," he said.

My body began to shake, convulsing with a primitive need for Izanagi's blood. I tried as hard as I could to stay still, but my throat swelled for the life in him.

I grabbed and clung to his wrist for dear life. Exactly like I remembered, the very essence of life rippled into me in a scarlet gush. I tasted oceans and Heaven, ancient things and things the world had never seen. I laughed as it ran down my chin and the warm thickness of it drenched my neck.

The intake of air when I'd had enough gave me something.

Not a vision. Knowledge. A lead weight of something

that was so true it was a presence like me, like Izanagi. A thing that could not be argued or doubted. Real.

Tears mixed with the blood on my face as I gazed at the god. The missing piece had been revealed to me because of what he'd done for me.

"Izanagi," I sputtered, my voice thick with blood. "I know what has to be done."

Izanagi stood, larger than anything I could imagine, reaching Heaven and Hell at once.

"Tell him what he must do," was all he said. And he was gone.

Every organ buzzed with an electric life, making it hard to settle enough to clean myself up. I wiped the blood off my face, neck and chest with shaking hands, and tried not to laugh at the knowledge I had, and the promise of the beginning of things, a new leaf on an old bud. Knowledge that belonged to me, and to all *Shinigami*.

But it started with only one *Shinigami*.

"Nicholas!" I shouted into the woods.

He was at my side in a blinding snap of air and light. "Christ, tell me you're all right. Please tell me you've never been better than you are right this second or I'll find a way to end this life of mine." His teeth were clenched, his eyes blood red.

I pulled him to me. He was so weak, limp, and yet I was tethered to the strength I'd infused him with, waiting for its time.

"Nicholas, baby, I'm fine. I swear. I know I wasn't,

but I am now. I promise." I kissed him over and over on his face and lips, wanting nothing more than for him to feel the roots of all life growing inside me through the blood of a god. "And Nicholas." I pushed him back to hold him at arm's length, half holding up his body. God, I was strong now. "I know what to do for you."

"You don't have to do anything for me. You have nothing else to do. What are you talking about?" The rattle of confused words made me laugh, confusing him even more.

I said the words that I hoped he would understand as deeply as they ran in every molecule of my body. "Nicholas, if you feed from Roman, you'll be back to normal. Never weak. You'll never need to drink from me again."

His mouth opened and closed, and he fell back against the screen that I feared would break under the weight of him. "Jesus, why didn't we see it before?"

"How could we? We don't know if this has ever happened before." And right away, I wondered if it had, We'd never questioned it since coming to Japan. With another surge of pure knowing, I could see the Master's thrall and just how far it extended. But why?

"We have to tell the Master," Nicholas said, upright and frantic.

"He'll find out. Relax." I rubbed the contours of his arms, and hoped I looked as relaxed as I was telling him to be. "I see so clearly, Nicholas, like a world on top of a world. You have to go to New Hampshire. I can find Roman and get him to you." Everything was so simple.

How thick was the cloud the Master had created? What was he hiding?

Could Nicholas bear to hear?

"We make you a vampire before I leave."

"Yes." Not an agreement, something I knew.

"How soon do I leave you?"

Something about those words and the undercurrent of things I *knew* made me sick to my stomach.

"You. Don't. Leave *me*. You just leave." The scent of wine and roses took shape encircling me, a burgundy shadow that wasn't just in my mind. Nicholas's eyes grew to saucer-sized, scanning the air red mist that billowed around me. Wisps of scarlet smoke circled my body in a translucent shield of funeral scents.

"Okay," Nicholas shrugged. "Maybe you should just breathe for a minute, and stop scaring the piss out of me."

I blinked madly, trying to unsee what I'd created, and it was gone. This cloud I'd surrounded myself in felt like a connection between Izanagi and I that I'd harbored all along. Ours. It poured out of me like a part of my breath and aura.

I cleared my throat. "You've got your little Mr. Freeze trick. I guess I have this."

He swallowed hard, his Adam's apple plummeting down, and pointed at me accusingly. "That. That felt like death walked in the door and wasn't leaving."

I thought of Izanagi and the ever-presence of death, the shadow that never left me and drove everything else away. It hadn't been just my companion; it had been inside me waiting to be released.

Nicholas reached out to me tentatively, as if to pat a

mythological beast he wasn't sure would bite him or not, and touched his fingertips to my throat, to my collarbone, to my heart. His eyes followed his hand, carefully averting my face. "What kind of vampire will you become? What sort of thing that we've never seen before, and what will you do?" The words came out like he questioned a prophecy—with a tinge of fear.

I covered his hand with mine, and counted my own slow heartbeats through them. Steady. Unafraid. "I'll be me, no matter what," I said softly, and hoped I meant it.

He sighed and bit his lip thoughtfully, making me shiver. "You're going to change everything, Eliza Morgan. Things we didn't know even needed changing. There's so much hope here," he said, his hand still on my heart. His forehead wrinkled as he debated with himself whether or not to go on, but Nicholas didn't debate with himself for long. He knew he was going to say what he wanted, whether anyone wanted to hear it or not.

"There were times," he said, low, fearfully, "that I thought I would never see anything except ache and emptiness behind those eyes ever again. When I looked at you, I saw a ghost of the woman you were meant to be. Kat was always in your eyes. And the lost choices you never really had—they tortured the life out of you." His hand moved, lost, over my shoulders and arms, slow and circling. "I thought I broke you without even trying."

I couldn't answer. He was right; I *was* broken. I'd been put together poorly to begin with.

"A phoenix from ashes, you are. You're brilliant, more glorious than even I saw you could be." Tears glistened in his eyes, and I was never so happy to see it. His voice thick with everything he wanted to express when I wouldn't listen, all that time I could do nothing but mourn, he said, "You will make *Shinigami* a name that the most wretched of us will be proud of."

Lynch. The word *wretched* brought his miserably handsome face into my mind.

There was so little I could say. "I'm sorry that I—was gone. Knowing that I'm going to be something special isn't enough of a reward for enduring the isolation fate slapped me with. Getting the grand prize in the end isn't good enough consolation for taking everyone from me, or for making me a placeless thing half my life. I'll never have peace about what happened with Kat, or Roman, even if it was to better the entire race of *Shinigami*, or the entire world. It isn't fair that there should be such a price to pay for something I never asked for."

He licked his lips. "But I know you. You wouldn't give it back if you could. You wouldn't want to be a regular person, no matter what it cost you."

Goddammit, he was right. I hung my head in shame.

CHAPTER 28

A red silk tube laid on the bed next to a package wrapped in light pink tissue. Beautiful things that filled me with dread.

Opening the soft package, I knew what I was in for. Nicholas thought of everything. Here we were, on the top of a mountain that the world didn't know existed, and he'd gotten me a gift. I'd worked at a gift shop back home and still knew nothing about buying gifts.

Folds of rippling pink silk unrolled in my hands, the same as the package it came from. So this was handmade, I figured. God, he knew what to do. A kimono the color of my cheeks in the cold. He loved that color on me, said it made me look like Snow White. The gray trim grew into black towards the bottom, like dusk turning into night. The white silhouette of a winter treeline embroidered against the black hem instantly transported me to the dark, wintry nights in New Hampshire, standing in the snow with Nicholas. Japanese words were sewn on the inner draping sleeves of the beautiful gown, and I could read them, like Izanagi could read Japanese characters. *Unmei shinsei* on one sleeve. *Unmei wo seisu* on the other.

Chosen for new life.

I control my destiny.

I held the cool fabric to my chest. I was pretty easily impressed with gifts, given my thoughtless nature when it came to giving them, but this was stunning no matter who you were. I cringed inside when I thought how beautiful Kat looked in pink with her red hair, and how she would have jumped up and down to see this.

Night was creeping up on us. I looked at the elaborate invitation again, all beautiful Japanese symbols written in blood red. And at the top, *"The Shinigami Grow."*

Time to get dressed. In an hour we'd see what growth meant.

I could barely take my eyes off Nicholas long enough to walk. We were completely absorbed in each other dressed like this. My kimono fit—well, like it was made for me. For once, I didn't need to pull at it to cover up my chest, or wiggle in the fabric to mask my fuller curves that weren't so much curves as little rolls in a lot of places.

Actually, I was more comfortable dressed like this than I would have been a month ago. Oh, right, when I ate pizza and cake all the time and considered myself a decent eater because Golden Grahams has iron in it.

"Let the record show that I'll stare at you all I want," Nicholas said.

"Well, me too," I said. Nicholas looked incredible in traditional *hakama* pants, black, with a white silk kimono trimmed in smoke gray. He needed nothing extra. The silken shimmer made his skin glow like a pearl, and his smile was so radiant it was hard to look at.

"How did you figure out the right size?" I asked, tucking my hair behind my ear. It knocked some of the flowers out of it that Blue pinned at the crown of my head. "Crap."

Nicholas laughed. "How did I know? By this." He stopped walking and put his hands on my waist, looking into my eyes, full of mischief and intent that I wanted to make reality. "And this," he continued huskily, his hands running up my body to graze the sides of my breasts. "And this," he growled, putting his hand on my lower back, and running it down, cupping me in it. I was riveted there, trying to breathe. It was fruitless when he nipped my ear. "Your blood isn't the only delicious part of you, and you're mine forever to taste, *saisai*." Beloved.

"*Mugen ai*," I whispered to him, winding my fingers through his hair. Infinite love.

"Party time, lovebirds!"

I jumped at Blue's intrusion, but Nicholas merely lifted his head slowly, as if he planned to anyway. "We *were* having a party."

Blue was a vision in a bright red kimono with gold phoenixes on each side. She was pure fire, and I wondered if she did it for Kieran.

"You fed from Izanagi again," Blue said. I didn't ask what tipped her off. I checked the vicinity for my red gas or whatever, but there was none. The god's blood was written on me like ink on parchment. "Let's go," Blue said, taking my hand, Nicholas trailing behind.

The great entryway to the temple which was always sparse and holy-feeling was glowingly elaborate. Hundreds of white candles lined the long walk to the altar, showcasing dozens of goth-lipstick-maroon roses scattered all over, turning the rice paper runner a carpet of soft red. More red roses hung in bunches from the eaves, but the scent of them didn't make me grit my teeth as it once did. This didn't feel like a funeral, and the kinship with Izanagi had...changed me. Scarlet paper lanterns hung from the high ceiling, showing dozens of black paper crows that would have been otherwise invisible in the moody, macabre beauty. Crows were *mine* more than Leann's; I felt possessive of them, rather than haunted by them now. The sound of drums and chimes was more eerie in the gothic elegance in the temple, and I'd fallen in love with it instantly.

"This is unbelievable," I said, taking in the decorations while I taking in as many of the guests as possible. Every resident of the temple would be here. The invitation was more a command than anything else.

I was fully aware that Arthur and I were the only beings with living blood among hundreds of vampires.

"I didn't want to scare you," Nicholas whispered out of the corner of his mouth, looking around, "so I didn't tell you how this ceremony can get a little—well, office party out of control."

Both of us still looking and smiling at his adoring onlookers as we walked through the crowd, I said, "Will you ever tire of holding information from me until it's nightmarishly too late?"

"Maybe. Depends what else I can hold of yours," he said through his golden boy smile.

Some of the *Shinigami* clearly hadn't fed in far too long from their gauntness and sunken eyes. Others were robust with the blood they'd feasted on. It was like looking at a swimming pool full of sharks and diving right in.

"Anything I should be doing? Not doing? Running from in particular?" All said through my best politician smile.

"Never leave my side," he growled. His arm around my waist tightened like a corset.

"Easy enough," I said, turning my eyes to him. He wasn't looking back, however. My eyes followed his menacing stare to a gangly vampire with bone-chillingly pale skin and something to prove. The wraith stared at me with such intrinsic animalism that it sent a chill down my spine even before the wave of frigidity radiated from Nicholas, leaving my teeth chattering. A grizzly bear growl rumbled from Nicholas's belly. The emaciated vampire sensed it too, a good twenty feet away, but he didn't look away fast enough for Nicholas.

I gulped down my frozen fear and leaned into Nicholas, putting my hand on his cold chest. Tomb-like waves of cold shivered up my arm.

"Nicholas, I'm okay. You're here. He won't do anything."

"Goddamn right he won't."

"Don't make a scene if you don't have to, Captain

Dramatic. These vampires will be my—family, I guess, and I can handle them. To a point."

The vampire took Nicholas's endless stare and my words as a challenge, and I had to wonder just how stupid he was. In the short time it took me to make my little speech, the ghoulish vampire had closed the distance, and stood face to face with us. He grinned at me, showing decaying teeth and a lack of self-preservation.

Nicholas didn't need to move; Izanagi's blood surged through me like whitewater rapids.

I hissed long and low, releasing from the red, hazy swirl of smoke from inside. It curled around the lanterns and crows above. I leaned forward, my face inches from his, radiating Izanagi's wine and roses scent, now my own, overpowering his acrid decay.

"Run while you can," I spat at the creature through clenched teeth.

I wasn't surprised when he did just that.

Nicholas was angry. It was clear in the way his shoulders were thrown back, his head angled away from me, lips tight, churning coffee eyes slow and deliberate.

"You. Are still. Human," he said.

Shaking with violence, fangs bared, Nicholas flashed across the room where the vampire had escaped to. They were yards away, but with a blink I was next to them in my mind's eye, my vision showing me what transpired as though Nicholas was still close enough to breathe in my ear.

Mad with fury, he growled, "You take your thoughts and eyes off of her forever, or I will tear out your throat like the jaws of Hell itself."

My breath was prisoner. The vampire, who'd thought he was in the clear when he fled from me, made the idiot mistake of turning, wide-eyed with fear, to look over his shoulder at me. While I took this as a question of *what the hell is it with you two*, Nicholas took it as his threat not being quite powerful enough.

He twitched forward, grabbing the vampire by the throat.

I didn't realize I'd whimpered out loud, but all the nearby vampires did. All around me were things that spoke like humans, dressed like humans, but they wanted to consume me. Countless predatory eyes bore through me. The earth stood still.

A flare of hungry heat screeched to my side, a venomous burst of fire that had every vampire in its path crying out, hands shielding their eyes. Kieran, of course. I already knew. I knew by the licking flames at my feet and the inner sigh I breathed, filled with the ashes of guilt.

He glared around him in a quickly widening circle, as *Shinigami* fell back to get away from him. Every muscle in his body was taut, veins straining like he might burst, and the only way he could relieve the pressure was to let out a deafening roar that sent everyone into terrified silence. The air crackled with the electric heat he wrought.

Nicholas glared at him from where he stood, arm shaking with the wriggling vampire in his hand, its feet dangling midair, and I swear I could see more fire in his eyes than in the fire spirit next to me.

And in an instant that would never end, the most compassionate, thoughtful and genuine man I'd ever met snapped the neck of the vampire he held.

All the dead eyes turned to the delicate snapping noise. The tension didn't leave, just shifted.

And grew.

"She's not yours to protect," Nicholas growled at Kieran, his voice an earthquake.

"She's not anybody's," Kieran said with a coolness that defied his fire. But I knew he felt different.

Why do you feel so much like mine, Eliza?

"This party's turning out awesome, right guys?" I said loudly to them both.

To add to, or detract from the flurry of activity that made me want to crawl in a hole and die and take everyone with me, another figure weighed in.

Leann appeared at the head of the room on the altar platform, scanning the crowd of immortals while they measured her up; the youngest pack member. What certainly would have been fear shivering through her yesterday was nothing but curiosity this night.

Physically, she looked the same. It was the fluidity of every small motion that set her apart. Her timidity and utter indifference that made her forgettable in life, made her superior in death. The appearance of boredom transformed into a quiet pensiveness, allowing her to take in her new world at her leisure, rather than shun it.

Vampirism suited her.

The throng of *Shinigami* drank her in, as I did. It seemed like hours ticked by, the lack of thrum from undead hearts unsettling mine, alone among them.

Alone.

I pushed my vision to the surface easily, searching for the only other heartbeat in the crowd, terrified that I had to look so hard. Then I found it; slowing, faltering. The rhythm of it peaked and jumped, and was sickly, stolen. My head tilted to the sound, a dog to a whistle, a sound I ought not be able to hear.

Arthur.

"Nicholas," I yelped, my head on a swivel, dizzy with the scents all around me, but not one of them of human flesh, not one. Nicholas flashed to me without question.

"What is it?" He bent at the knees to meet my eyes, to bring me back.

"Nicholas, where is Arthur?" I said as levelly as I could manage.

Ghoulish laughs, hisses, rumblings around me.

A frenzy was beginning.

Nicholas's nostrils flared. His pupils dilated. His head swiveling frantically. He didn't have to say it; I smelled it, too, with Izanagi's infused senses.

Blood. The faintest whiff of blood, winding like a snake in the ripe evening air.

Leann's head snapped to the side demonically fast, painful-looking. I could *feel* her need for that first taste of blood, the emptiness behind it. She had no *unmei nashi* yet, nobody waiting for her to finish their life of "no fate." And anything else she drank would leave her craving more; a mirage.

I couldn't help but look at Nicholas with a deep pang of sorrow and guilt. He was half empty.

Eyes focused where Leann's were, Nicholas grabbed my arms, and propelled us both with sickening speed to a spot hidden by a pillar, where a blonde vampire woman sucked on Arthur's fleshy neck. The scene, the odor of newly gushing blood made me go blank, seeing only flash-backs of the huddled vulture that was Nicholas's friend, my friend, Roman, murdering Kat. The sound of flesh tearing, the darkening of his eyes, the river of blood down his neck when we surprised him, drinking the life out of her gorgeous, rosy face.

Nicholas pulled the vampire woman off of Arthur, her blonde hair whipping back. She'd been looking up at me as she drank from Arthur's neck, just like Roman had. I couldn't stop seeing Kat on the ground, her face pale, disbelief the last look in her eyes. I saw Kat, but it was only Arthur there, and he was just as dead.

"He's dead," I said, but it was clear. I peeled my eyes from the body that had been one third of my peers, and looked to Nicholas at my side, unsure of what I'd see there.

A mixture of fury, shock and shame clouded his swirling eyes. "I'm so sorry, Eliza," he said.

"For what?" My voice sounded too tinny, too much like it had in all the time I mourned Kat and pushed Nicholas away. Too much like me when all my softness died with that red-haired beauty. I was afraid to ever be that thing again, to fear the crows circling overhead.

"I'm getting you back to your room—now." He swept me up into his arms as if to carry me across the threshold, and belted like a subway train from the celebration, across boardwalks and through courtyards and gardens to my room.

The last thing I saw before leaving the gathering was Leann's too-bright eyes searching wildly for the blood source. Her desire was so desperate it felt alive.

Nicholas set me down fast and smoothly on my bed. "The Master needs my help at the temple, I'll be back soon," he said, his worry unmasked. He glanced behind him to the open door. "Can you sense Izanagi out there?"

I tried, but I didn't. And I was a little more afraid than I had before.

Nicholas held my arms and looked into my eyes. "Right. Back."

"Hurry," I said.

He nodded and dashed out the door, taking my breath with him.

CHAPTER 29

My mind raced, waiting for Nicholas to return. What was he doing? Was Kieran okay? Blue, Paolo? Was everybody—else—besides Arthur—okay?

When it was my turn, would I be blood-crazed and dying to hunt like Leann was?

Would images of Kat's death haunt me in spasms every time I took a life? For the rest of my impending immortality?

The prophetic dream I'd had of becoming a vampire back in Ossipee sprang to memory; another Eliza Morgan, teeth barbed into a man's throat, blood pounding like bass drums through my every pore, until it deafened me and made me see a blanket of red cover the moon above. Blood intoxicating, overtaking. Becoming.

My heart quickened at the thought. I swallowed back a panicky excitement. I understood the desire for the succulence of human blood. Being human, I should have been sickened by it.

If I were, in fact, only human.

If I hadn't drank blood before and reveled in it.

I paced the floor madly waiting for Nicholas. What the hell was going on at the temple? I imagined vampire bats flying through the night, searching out blood like monsters, not like chosen heroes, the Master yelling after them to stop and wait for the call of their *unmei nashi* as they screeched in the sky.

My vision begged to be let out to watch Nicholas trying to help control the frenzy, but I would not. I would not. I could picture what he'd say: "*I* don't even want to see what's happening out there. You've got plenty of time to be traumatized. Immortality loves trauma," he would have said. "A vampire riot sounds cool, but it's probably not."

The crowd of vampires had become just that: a riot, a mob. Any pretense of my importance to the grand scheme of things, any fear and love of Nicholas they had wouldn't make them spare me. Put a steak in front of a wild dog and he's going to eat it. Thinking of myself as meat made the air on the back of my neck bristle.

Or was that the hair-raising feeling of being watched?

My vision blasted into my consciousness, but I didn't need it. In the corner shadows, I could saw a pair of cold, cruel eyes.

"He won't miss you for long," a rich, familiar voice said. "He'll understand I needed it."

"Jenniveve," I gasped.

"Don't!" she yelled, and my bed didn't creak or move under her added, unearthly weight. "Don't beg for your life like a fool!" The dead chill in her eyes had been replaced with a madness for blood. She was a reptilian thing, and there would be no reasoning with her. I cringed, like it would do something to help me.

She bared her teeth at me, a primitive monster with Victorian beauty. I closed my eyes.

But when I did, I saw myself in the courtyard, defeating that vampire.

I leaned back as she lunged at me, and met her chest with a powerful kick, throwing her backward. She shook her head, as if she could make what happened disappear, and in that moment, I leaped at her and connected both fists, one to her belly, one to her sculpted, exotic face.

She flung me back with brutal force, a dragon growl behind it. I hit the wall, hearing it rip and splinter. Blood trickled into my eye from my scalp, and she was on me again, and God help me, she was *laughing.*

That was more than I could take. The red vapor rose from my body, the unexpected appearance of it making her cry out with fear. No, more than fear— *it burned her.* Blazing pinpricks all over her face that she clawed at, shrieking, making them worse. I shuddered to watch it, but I did watch, thrilled. Because this fiend had done everything she could to ruin Nicholas. The mist lashed out at her, but stayed close to me, a fearsome protector.

The mist swaddled me instantly when I yelled in surprise: the Master was hovering, terrifyingly silent and ghostlike, behind Jenn, his long, yellow fangs bared. Milky eyes full of rage, he grabbed Jenn in one hand by the back of the neck. Her feet kicked at the air as she continued to scream, writhing, though I couldn't say if it was from the burning of my scarlet mist or if she was trying to see what held her, dangling in midair.

I scrambled to my feet and held the Master's gaze, to tell him I was fine, if he cared. Slowly, he pulled the struggling mess that was Jenn to face him, lifting her effortlessly to eye level while she whimpered and cried. My mist had let her go, and she could see the Master now. I think he horrified her more than the unknown attacking substance from me.

"Give me a reason not to destroy you for your—indiscretion," he said.

Gasping, she whispered, "Please, Master, I was drunk with the scent of her." She managed to roll her eyes to me, veins popping in the whites. "And she's come between me and Nicholas."

The Master shook her once, making her yelp, apologizing over and over. I loved seeing the volatile thing so terrified, as she'd terrified me so many times.

I stepped forward until I was inches from her, and the Master made no attempt to move her away. Her eyes focused on me when she said her next apology; but even now, so helpless, her hatred was deep.

"You're only sorry you didn't get the chance to kill me," I said quietly, "and you're sorry I'm going to be one of you."

The Master snarled, his eyes on her trembling face.

"She," he said, nodding toward me, "is more important than you."

The simplicity of that statement shocked us both. Jenn's eyes darted to me, fearful and plotting.

But, in the flicker of an eye, the Master held only Jenn's head.

~

I didn't even make a noise at the unimaginable thing I'd seen. My heart didn't even speed up. She was dead, and I was glad.

Nicholas crackled into the room like an electric current, mouth agape, eyes flitting from one of us to the other.

The Master turned to him, lowering Jenn's decapitated head to his side.

"Wow," Nicholas said. Always the wordsmith, that one.

"I imagine you settled the others with less finality," the Master said to him.

"Yeah, that's pretty final," Nicholas said, snickering and stealing a glance at me. Jenn's body was crumpled on the floor underneath the dripping head. Nicholas cleared his throat for dramatic gesture, and smiled. "Yes, I calmed down the rest of them with a myriad of interesting threats. Then I sent off a hunting party with Leann. They were controlled, and she needed it."

The Master dropped Jenn's head on top of her body and lowered himself to the ground, Superman-style. "I'm disappointed in them all. The last time such an outbreak occurred, all the *Shinigami* ceased to exist not long after." With blank eyes on me, he continued. "The blood of the *unmei fumetsu* is pungent. You are very lucky that Nicholas didn't seem to notice Arthur's."

"No, I didn't," Nicholas said quietly, looking at me. "But you did."

"Yup. Where was Pierre? Why wasn't he with Arthur?" I asked.

"He had a calling," Nicholas said with a roll of his eyes.

"Ridiculous," the Master spat. "Unacceptable. Selfish. There is no excuse not to accompany your *unmei fumetsu* to an event with so much meaning for them both. He will be dealt with." The air throbbed around him with his angry energy, and the room was quiet.

Nicholas, of course, broke the silence. "I didn't know Jenniveve was here," he said, staring at the body in pieces.

The Master seemed taken aback, his energy dissipating and returning like a lightbulb flicker. "Jenniveve has always wanted to be near you. She may not have loved you the way you love Eliza but she didn't know how to do anything the right way."

I blushed to hear the Master speak of our love for each other.

"Ah, morbid curiosity about my girlfriend choices. Jenn always loved making a spectacle of herself, and hated having anything taken from her," Nicholas said.

"Eliza, I'm sorry you were in fear for your life last night." the Master said, voice filled with more emotion than I thought he was capable of, at least for me. Sure enough, the sun had risen and I'd not noticed. "Rest now. You have training this afternoon."

And he was gone, leaving Nicholas and I holding hands, staring at the dead vampire staining the floor.

CHAPTER 30

B efore I could ask how we were to dispose of Jenn's dismembered body, two mild-mannered vampires arrived and gathered her up on a bamboo stretcher.

"Thank you," I said cheerily as they left. Nicholas gave me a mocking smile. "What? It's only polite."

A moment of pregnant silence rested between us.

"I'm sorry she's dead. She meant something to you," I said.

His lips turned down in that way that dismissive way. "You're not sorry, and I don't blame you," he said, still looking at the bloody spot on the floor. "She created me, and I think I thank her for it. But she was a pitiless thing besides." He turned to me, jaw clenched. "But to give me immortality only to gouge out the part of me that I live for —" It took me a second to realize he was talking about me. "The Master killed her quickly. I wouldn't have."

He pulled my face to his roughly and kissed me with a force that took my breath away. Groaning, he stole his lips from mine, leaving them stinging with their absence. He looked *different,* stronger and weaker at the same time.

"Nobody has ever loved anyone as much as I love you," he whispered huskily.

"I know an exception," I managed to say through my own short breath.

His eyes were wild pools of chocolate mousse and melting fudge. He was panting, bearlike, lustful and fearful together at once. The powerful blood inside me vibrated, a volcano ready to erupt. The small space between us thrummed before filling with my red mist.

"So that doesn't just happen when you're threatened?" Nicholas panted, mouth running all over my cheeks and lips, down my neck.

"I dunno." Red deathly desire swarmed me and I couldn't think.

"You're ready," he said, his fingers a whirr of motion.

"Always am."

He pulled back, revealing his fangs.

"Oh. Oh, you mean for—"

He nodded.

If the world exploded then, it would have been less dazzling than the heat between us. My blood grew hot in return, my body quivering with need for his.

And there was something else. A black energy that spoiled the air, a crackling lightning that shoved us together, leaving trails of steam. We collided in a burst of sparkling darkness, terrifying and pure. My lips flamed upon his, swollen, ready for all he could give me. Static electricity stung my fingertips as I ripped his t-shirt over his head, my breasts skimming the hair on his chest, my nipples screaming. His flavor overwhelmed me, his tongue caressing mine with vanilla and spices I never knew. His hair in my fingers was too soft to endure. I needed solid strength, everything hard, able to handle the power budding in me.

Nicholas groaned, grabbing my waist with one powerful hand, my breast cupped in the other. I leaned into it, squirming out of my top, breaking the snaps on my bra to wrestle free into his frantic hands. Swirls of a new, black mist swam around us, glittering, glinting, magic come alive. The air whispered and bit when he bent to pull down his pants unfalteringly fast. His nose brushed my navel, my hips arched to touch his face.

There was a chasm, a void we were the midnight center of, howling with primitive desire. A wild thing drove us, our connection as *unmei fumetsu* and *shugotenshi*, bursting to life, begging for death. The same presence that followed me my entire life, that death that was alive, that death that was waiting to have me alone.

The dark stirred in me. I grabbed the back of Nicholas's head, yanking him forward into the pulsing between my legs. His fangs pierced the skin of my thigh without warning, and I screamed. I screamed in pain, and I screamed for more.

I wanted blood. Dripping, squirting, oozing.

His.

When I couldn't take anymore wanting, I pulled him up to my face, so he could see how desperately I needed the essence of him, what lied beneath.

"Blood," I moaned through the rich scents and

sparklingly poisonous colors flurrying around me, and through me.

I was becoming something new.

"Give it to me," I hissed, my entirety screaming for his touch, the taste of him.

Nicholas threw his head back as if ready to howl at the moon, then dove into my throat, and sucked hard, pulling my skin viciously. He squeezed the flesh of my upper arm, another hand on the back of my neck to keep me close, letting not a drop escape. Black torrents of liquid air rushed around us in this not-quite-real reality, and for just a second, I was jealous that Nicholas was tasting Izanagi's blood through me.

That power was mine.

With a violent efflux of strength, I laced my fingers through the decadent dark curls on Nicholas's head, making him moan with need. I pulled his head back, exposing the pulsing vein in his throat, and plunged my own, still-human teeth into it.

He bellowed an indistinguishable word, causing the magical stars around us to scatter, and simultaneously held my naked body against his own. Fear and desire, clutching power and letting it go.

My body heaved against his while his blood invaded me, blending with Izanagi's, with my own that was some-thing *more.* The world belonged to me. All the isolation, the loneliness, the fear and resentment became something I owned, became an iron thing in my core that blood wrapped around and fed.

It still hurt. But now it was mine.

Seishi. Keieiichinyo. Izanagi's voice in my mind: Life and death. Inseparable as form and shadow.

"El—" Nicholas started, but his voice was gone. Then *he* was gone, but still there, invisible to me. A blinding black flash swallowed the stars and mist, swallowed *us.* We'd been absorbed in each other in every way, and now the world was absorbing us, too.

There was nothing except the blood racing in me, sending me quivering with pleasure and rage, power and consumption.

When I did feel someone else again, it wasn't Nicholas; it was Izanagi. He wasn't there in the room, but he was close by, and he knew what I knew.

That when the dark let me go, I wouldn't quite let it. I would be *Shinigami.*

CHAPTER 31

"She's reacting...differently," I heard through the darkness. The stars still swam, and Nicholas's blood tingled on my tongue. That flavor was all that mattered.

And the power. Raw. Power that begged to *take.* Power like mountains, power like fairy tale monsters, power of agony and ecstasy and everything in between. God almighty, it tasted like dreams.

"She's not like the rest of us," Nicholas said. I couldn't feel him, couldn't see him. Even my visions had deserted me.

He felt so *gone.*

"No, I suppose she's not," Paolo answered. I knew that he was leaning over me, inspecting me, I sensed it, but I couldn't smell his oceany saltiness, or get the tingle of his non-breath. I was swimming in the world, a bodiless thing.

Trying to envision Nicholas through my blind haze brought up a different sort of energy.

Blood came together in my veins like the most perfect puzzle: mine, Nicholas's, and Izanagi's. Not enough was Izanagi's. The god didn't take well to his blood being second best, his blood told me so.

With a full body roar, I exploded back to this plane, with an anger not all my own. My inner vision returned first, and it was Nicholas's face I saw. I cooled to see it, but Izanagi grew angrier outside, and inside me. My eyes fluttered open, and the world met them with brutal light and life.

I was floating near the ceiling, looking down at Nicholas and Paolo.

Nicholas looked up at me, unblinking, hint of a smile as he tossed popcorn into his mouth. He twitched his eyebrows at me.

"That's new."

Paolo was slack-jawed, eyes bulging. "Only the Master does that," he whispered.

"Nope," Nicholas said; popcorn tossed in the mouth.

Anger swelled in me at the mention of the Master. My red mist surged, swarmed the air, darkening the room.

I was glad I wasn't on the ground. I wanted to be high, where I was strong.

Nicholas and Paolo looked around themselves, unnerved, and moved closer together, as if a gang was closing in on them from all sides.

"Hey, Eliza?" Nicholas said, eyes still sweeping the room. "Maybe you could come down from there, and you know. Cut that out?"

I was scaring them. The shroud of blood-red mist surrounded me, my arms stretched to either side in a Jesus

Christ pose, my hair floating around my head and brushing my cheeks like some evil mermaid. Yeah, that was a little weird.

They watched as I slowly lowered myself to the ground, becoming more like a regular person with every inch I came closer to them. Aside from the *sounds* of everything; the wind outside that had a voice, the singing of the *tatami* floor, the hush of the mountains, the rushing of the blood in their veins.

And the sound of a million fates all around me and nowhere near me, watching me and waiting for what I'd do next. *Waiting for what I would see.*

I'd never be alone again.

This was what being a vampire was? This uber-aware-ness of everything, even things that weren't there?

"Eliza," Paolo whispered. "Are you all right?" He'd forced himself to look into my eyes, his waves of calm barely touching me. He needed more settling down than I did.

I smiled, and even I could tell how creepy it was. He took his hand away.

Nicholas breathed in deep through his nose. "Well, glad that's done with," he said with a dramatic grin. "You freaked us the hell out there, El. Nice vampire thing you've got there," he added, waving his hand around at me.

"What did I do." It was the first thing I'd said since I came to. It sounded like bricks moving.

Nicholas shook his head at me quickly, eyes bulging, and looked at Paolo like *can you believe?* "You have no idea," he said, running his hands through his hair.

Eyes moving, taking it all in, their movements under their movements and what they meant, the hum of motions so miniscule they didn't matter. But they did, everything did.

"What did I do," I said again. I was asking, but it didn't come out as a question, I was too solid, too controlled. I could tell I was unnaturally still, my hands at my sides, my eyes trained on them when they weren't darting to see the next thing to see.

Nicholas sniffed, with impressed shock. It was Paolo who spoke. He said softly, "You made us feel so alone."

"Like we'd been abandoned and nobody would ever come for us again," Nicholas said, his self-assured light-heartedness disappearing.

"You both experienced it," I said. Not a question. They nodded.

I take strength from what consumes me.

"What was that?" Paolo said.

"I didn't mean to say it out loud."

I looked Nicholas in the eyes, and he twitched. "I once asked Kieran how his fire didn't destroy him. And he told me it was the thing that consumes him, and the thing that gives him strength." But it was so much more than that. Kieran's burning was alive, assaulting me where I stood. It pained him constantly, and it was a force more powerful than fear.

Nicholas ran a hand over his stubbly chin. "Makes sense."

"How do you mean?" Paolo asked him.

"The thing that consumed Eliza now gives her strength," Nicholas said, shrugging, unfaltering stare on me, ready to catch me if I fell. Ready to stay with me when everyone ran.

"And that is?" Paolo asked.

"Isolation," I said quietly.

As I said it, the room became *void* again. Vacuous. The darkness in the witch's woods.

How I'd felt most of my life.

Nicholas held me. I wasn't sure I was ready for that, but I gave in because I didn't want isolation to consume me anymore.

Not when I could turn it on the world.

"Eliza, you're doing it again," Nicholas said into my ear, and kissed me quickly on the cheek.

"Sorry."

"You okay? Are you hungry? Do you want to be alone?" Paolo asked me in a flurry. It wasn't stifling, because his concern was so real.

Concern, and something else.

"Stop cocking your head at Paolo, it's weird. You can't eat Paolo."

My laugh rang high and strong, dissipating the oppressive aloneness of the room. So, I had the power to take the aloneness away, too. That was a new thing for me—to be the one the party started with. I'd always left that up to Kat. I smothered the red mist of my anger and solitude this time.

"Where's Blue?" I asked.

Nicholas blinked rapidly. "I can find her."

"Please," I said. "Paolo, go with him. I need to be alone." My voice was so different now, and not just my voice, but the person behind it.

Paolo gave me a reassuring, sweet smile. "Very good," he said. "We won't be long."

Nicholas kissed me with supernatural swiftness, but I saw every single move now. My eyes could detect the flexing of the muscles before they moved.

"Say you love me," I said. Monotone.

"I. Love. You."

With a nod from them both, they were out the door, and I was alone with myself, the only feeling I recognized. When they were gone from my consciousness, I looked to the door with a slow, measured movement. Everything I did was that way in this form.

But I wasn't really alone anymore.

"Izanagi."

CHAPTER 32

I wasn't surprised that now, more than ever, Izanagi and I were one artery, and the blood had nowhere to go until we were together.

What did surprise me was his wide, brilliant smile and boisterous laugh.

"You've arrived," he said, like I finally showed up to a family reunion that I blew off every year.

He threw his arms around me, making me gasp first from the gesture, and next from the onslaught of *everything*. Visions crowded for space in my mind, but I wasn't overwhelmed by them. I could see anyone I wanted, if I wanted. Their lives were there for me to pluck like cherries.

And I could see myself, the way he saw me.

My curly dark hair had an inhuman vitality. My skin was the same, smooth and fair, but my eyes—the green had a fury in it, the way Nicholas's had a warmth. They were bursting with it, like the reflection of light off of a rough emerald. Like the aurora borealis. They positively glowed.

And underneath what he saw on the outside, he saw promise, layered under a glimmering ferocity. He saw death incarnate. A fearsome, wild supremacy that he, himself possessed in my own eyes.

He saw the future of the *Shinigami*.

"Please, let me drink from you, Izanagi," I whispered.

The god *wanted* it, but he didn't need it. He wanted my blood to swim with his own. It was vanity.

Taking my hands in his, he looked into my eyes, quelling my restlessness. "You do not need it now, nor do I. But you will, as will I. I will be there then. Every time."

"But I don't understand these feelings, I need help." My throat constricted. "I'm too strong, and *evil*—"

"Not evil. This is not a world of right and wrong, it is a world of harmony and power. You will find yours and use it the way it must be used. Do not let your beliefs about good and evil follow you here."

I trusted his words, and though I wanted to taste his power, I knew I had enough of my own. It would drive me insane to have more so fast, the narcotic that he was.

"You have an *unmei nashi*," he continued. "Tonight."

"Already?"

"Yes. It's why you sent for Blue."

I hadn't known why I needed her, but now it was crystal clear.

"I'll be waiting for them," I said.

Blue looked at me from the doorway with a fear that didn't become her. Or me.

"I don't want people to be afraid of me," I whispered to no one.

Nicholas brushed past her into the room, eyes lingering on me. "Sorry, doll, but fear is your middle name now."

Blue pushed him away from me. "Oh, shut up, Nicholas."

"I always wanted to say that. *Fear is my middle name,*" he grumbled.

"You mean *my* middle name," I said.

"Nope. It's my middle name now. You're too pretty for it." Nicholas leaned against the wall.

"Miss me, did you?" Blue said, in such a Kat-like way it was like arsenic in my heart.

I held her arms, looking hard into her eyes. "I can't explain it, but I need you here."

"You all right?"

"I—well, you know how I am. Nobody's made words for it yet, but we'll live long enough to see the day they might."

She smiled wryly at me, and turned to Paolo and Nicholas. "I'm glad to have this woman on my side. Can you imagine having a brain like that against you?"

"I don't want any brain against me. But I bet hers would be even grosser." Nicholas smiled at me, and as usual, I just shook my head at him. He narrowed his eyes in response.

"Izanagi was here, wasn't he?" Nicholas said, and all the vampire eyes in the room looked to me.

"Yes."

"Did you drink from him?"

"Does it seem like I did?"

"No."

"Well, there's your answer, then."

Blue cleared her throat. Paolo stood silent. There was too much stillness here; it was murdering me.

"What do we do next?" I asked the group. "I imagine we should tell the Master I'm changed."

"Already done," Nicholas said.

"Of course." And as much as I resented the ancient vampire, I was still hurt that he hadn't come to see me.

Nicholas reached out to brush a strand of my hair. "He knows you'll send for him when you want him. He knows you're taken care of and need time to yourself." He smirked. "And he knows you probably won't want him here at all."

I was surprised how smug that made me. That the man believed to be the creator of the *Shinigami* gave a crap about what I thought, or that he would listen at all. It made me even more suspicious.

Was he too afraid to see how powerful I'd become?

"So, that's the thing you're talking about," I heard Blue whisper to Nicholas. I'd zoned out, and they were all three staring at me, Blue bent to Nicholas slightly, their arms touching.

"What are you whispering about?" I said in that dead voice I now had.

"You're getting misty, my love," Nicholas said.

And sure enough, there was the red mist curling in tendrils around the vampires in front of me.

"I can stop it," I said, emotionless. I looked about me, at each tendril of the red cloud, truly seeing it, and must have looked like I was trying to communicate with vapor, but hey, clearly I was weird now. *Stop now*, I thought at it, but the mist stayed.

And it began to take a shape.

"You guys see that, right?" I said, but they were dumbfounded.

The mist formed the silhouette of a woman, and though she was made of smoke, she looked to me as real, as defined as Nicholas. I knew her. So much of my life was smoke and mirrors, it was recognizable to me now.

"Crikey, what is that bottomless pit I have in my stomach? Is that—*you*—Eliza?" Blue asked with shivering words.

"Mmmhmm. That's our girl," Nicholas said, eyes on me, fascinated.

"Quiet," I said, as I watched the shadow woman move. She was washing dishes. It was the silliest thing to see in such an unnatural medium. Her name was Clara, I knew it like I knew my own. I was watching a life in progress, in a red puppet show. She was whistling, though only I could hear. She was so happy to just do dishes, because they belonged to her, and she'd had so little.

"What's happening to her?" I heard Paolo say, but I couldn't take my eyes off of the sheer burgundy image.

Nicholas would want to understand what I was going through, but I couldn't tear my eyes away to tell him. The magnetism between Clara and myself entranced me.

"Nicholas, she isn't moving."

"I know, I know."

"What's happening?"

Voices melded together as Clara dried the dishes, ran a hand through her hair, wondering why she hadn't washed it that morning.

"This happens to me, sometimes. Something like this. Scares the shit out of Roman." Nicholas.

"Roman." That was Blue's voice. It struck me in the head, as if she shouldn't be allowed to say the name.

"Nicholas, how long do you believe this will last? She's shaking, it's very worrisome."

"Should I get the Master?"

"No."

"No." My own voice that time.

The mist vanished, but the thread that tied me to Clara remained, singing with tension, a tightrope dying to be cut.

"What happened, El?" Nicholas said, searching my face.

"I have my first *unmei nashi.*"

CHAPTER 33

"I don't need a hunting party."

Paolo insisted I wait on the *unmei nashi* until the Master assembled a hunting party. Goddamn tradition.

Paolo put his hand on my shoulder, his eyes lingering on it. If I hadn't known of his commitment to God better, I'd have thought he had intention of letting it wander.

"It's too difficult a task to undertake on your own, so new at this as you are. The emotion, the sheer distance you may need to cover. Do you know where she is, your Clara?"

"London."

Paolo smiled, such a sweet smile he had. "And she already knows," he said with wonder in his blue eyes. "We will help you get there. It can be rather exhausting, and you need guidance to comprehend it when so young. This world is very different now, your place in it, very different."

Paolo and I sat on a high wall overlooking a snowy

garden. I could see the sun-colored koi under the pond's frozen surface. I was trapped like they were, waiting for feeding time.

"Fine. Then we leave. Me, you, Nicholas, Blue and Kieran. That's it."

"I thought you may want Leann to come along."

"Why?"

"She's a newborn like yourself."

I had no reason to take offense. Doesn't change the fact that I did. "We aren't alike in any other way. We'd not be any comfort to each other."

The saltwater scent of Paolo washed over me.

"Getting ready to impart some wisdom, are you?" I said through a smile. He returned it.

"Eliza, all I mean to say is that you don't have to be alone anymore. There's no need to keep yourself apart. You've arrived, my dear. God has taken enough from you, and now you've been rewarded with eternal companions. Enjoy them."

My fingers curled into the stone underneath me, shocking me when they dug right into it. I struggled not to let my new signature red death mist scare Paolo off in my annoyance. "Just because some mystical fatal force has decided that I've been *good* enough to be granted friends doesn't mean I'm ready to embrace the goddamn world. I have a heart of my own, it can't be made soft again just because I got the cheese at the end of the rat maze I was thrown into."

"I didn't mean to imply—"

"No, please, don't apologize. I know what you mean. But I think I've been scarred too much to start looking for playmates now. I can't *work* at it, and Leann, well, she's too much work. I have you," I said, trying as hard as I could to give him the peacefulness that he gave me. "I have Kieran, and Blue. And I have Nicholas. I don't need more."

A dismal look simmered in his eyes, one I couldn't understand.

"What about Izanagi?" he asked.

Suspicion. I hated it. Hated having it, hated being on the receiving end of it. "What about him?"

"What does he mean to you?"

I cleared my throat, nerves propelling me into an answer that I wasn't ready to give.

"Maybe he's a bit of what God is to you. He saves me when I need saving."

"And what do you give to him?"

I narrowed my eyes. "What do you give your God?"

His bright smile wasn't the guarded kind of a man under attack. It was full of admiration and enjoyment, and made me smile along with him.

"Eliza Morgan, I can't decide if you're a rebel or unrelentingly loyal."

I laughed, my laugh, not the creepy, flat vampire one I'd picked up. "I guess depending on whose side you're on, I can be both."

With his gentle hand, he took mine, making me smile still. "There doesn't have to be sides, you know," he said, a mournfulness lacing the waters of his calm.

Sadness crept in. "I'm learning."

"Nope, no hand holding," Nicholas said, edging between us, making Paolo chuckle. "Whatcha doin'?"

"Just talking God. God talk, with Paolo and Eliza," I said.

"So sorry I missed it."

Paolo laughed, and the snow seemed warm afterwards. "You are not, Nicholas. He can see you, you know."

"I make myself known, He doesn't even have to try."

After we all had a good laugh, I dove right in. "What's the Master have to say about Clara? I want to be free to make my own hunting party choices."

The same kind of piousness that I saw in Paolo's eyes came alight in Nicholas's. "The Master thinks you should wait to feed until after your ceremony tomorrow night."

"Woah, woah, woah. He still wants to have a ceremony for me? After what happened to Arthur?"

Nicholas glanced at Paolo, the sarcasm just screeching to come out. "But—we all hated him."

"It doesn't matter, he was supposed to be one of us. I can't believe you don't see it. There's a reason he was supposed to be *Shinigami*, now we'll never know what it was, what he might have done."

Nicholas wasn't giving in that easily. "How do we know Arthur's fate wasn't to be killed here? Maybe he was going to turn out like Lynch. Maybe he was going to irritate us eternally. What happened, happened, and there's no way to know what might have been."

"I'm not comfortable with taking the cards dealt us. It isn't an excuse to do what we want, that we had no choice. That vampire, all of them had a choice. Just like Jenn did. Just like Roman."

"And just like me, right?" Nicholas said.

Paolo stood, sparkling blue eyes riveted on me.

"There's nothing here to argue about, my friends. A higher power gives us paths, and we take the best one we can. Right now, my path is to get a good workout in. I can't take being so sedentary."

We said our goodbyes, and Nicholas and I were alone. The first time we'd been alone since I was changed. I was scared.

All of Nicholas's sarcasm and egotism was gone as soon as he had no one to perform for. His concern for me was all I could see when I looked at him, even though I'd been so spiteful. It was so reassuring I wanted to cry those watery blood tears.

"You know that what Jenn said isn't true, right? That I'm not finished with you now because you're a vampire?"

I hung my head, embarrassed by my show of weakness. "Leann said it, lots of people say it. And sure, it scares me." I picked my head back up, desperate to prove myself wrong in his eyes. "They say there's no connection anymore, but that's not how it is for me. I can still have visions of you. And I don't feel like you've kicked me out of the nest, I don't feel like you don't love me. But—" My throat constricted, and emotion tore through me. Impossible, to hold this much feeling back, it had color and teeth in my vampire form. "But, I don't feel like the person I was anymore. I mean, I feel *good*, like I have a reason to be someone, anyone at all, but I'm not the same person you saw at Birch Tree Books that day."

He turned to me more, so I couldn't get away from his gaze. As if I'd ever want to, especially now when I could see the invisible flecks in his eyes, the life inside them. I touched the stubble on his jaw, and he took my hand.

"What you are now is unlike anything I've ever seen. What you were before was unlike anything I'd ever seen, too. I want to see what's next with you until the end of time, do you understand that?"

I tried to nod, but the emotion in my throat was too thick to let me move. He took my chin between his thumb and index finger, a gesture so familiar from him that my shoulders relaxed and everything in me heaved a sigh.

"As Ellie Morgan, gift shop employee and sarcastic, passive-aggressive—"

"Nicholas, tell me this is going somewhere good."

Heartbreakingly charming smile. "When I learned who you were under that, you made me think of abandoned castles you see in documentaries. Gloriously beautiful, but cold, empty. Waiting for something to fill it and make it as magnificent as it was created to be. Stunning in its emptiness…" He stared dreamily at my lips, my forehead, anywhere but my eyes. "I always want some dying billionaire to buy those places for a bunch of orphans or a huge, poor family, then fill it with all the incredible things it once held. Think of how much more heavenly that castle would be, renewed with such purpose. Reborn."

Finally, his eyes met mine, and my haze of blood-tinged tears blurred him. "I understand," I choked out, and threw my arms around his neck. His warmth even in just his thermal shirt in the falling snow, was Christmas all over again. Every bit of comfort I ever wanted, mine for eternity.

"Nicholas?" I said into his ear, his arms holding me until my wild heart slowed down.

"Yes?"

"I know we don't need it, but could you make your snowglobe for us now?"

The shimmering bubble softly came into being, enclosing us inside, sheltered from the flurries of snow.

"Our castle," I said, and sunk against his chest.

My world had transformed. A light was in everything, and a life to everything. The world was aflame to welcome me. Thank God for that. I needed something to distract me from the constant waiting.

When Kieran showed up at my door, I jumped.

"Jesus, get in here, I'm so restless and bored I could die."

The smoldering fire that was Kieran stood in front of me, the smell of cigarette smoke lingering behind him. "Hello, love. Look at what the afterlife has done for you," he said, his arms crossed, the tip of one thumb between his teeth as he sized me up.

"Ah, cut it out, Kieran."

"Can't. Look at ya."

He was a welcome distraction. All I could see was Clara, the sweet, but not simple thing she was. The life that bubbled in her, the hardships she'd endured.

I wanted to kill her like I'd never wanted anything in my entire life. It fed from me like a leech.

"Kieran, I have to get out of here. I need to tell the Master that there isn't going to be a ceremony."

"It's on for tomorrow, yeah?"

I nodded. "I don't want one. As if it isn't bad enough

that I have to get dressed up for a bunch of vampires to stare at me, we were just *at* one, and Arthur was killed there. It's horrible. I think he deserves a *little* respect."

"And you have to feed."

I studied his face. "How did you know?"

"I can smell the need off of you," he growled. I flushed so hot, I thought I would burn like he did.

"The Master won't let me hunt until after the ceremony." The whiniest thing I ever heard.

"Won't let you?" Kieran said through a grin. "Immortal, the savior of us all, and taking orders from an old man." He tutted at me, and without warning, wound his fingers through mine with one hand, then the other. "Time to start making your own rules, love," he said with a conspiratorial smirk. "I'll be the first in line to play along."

My mind hurt from seeing Clara, drenched in my scarlet mist, smelling of life and the impending loss of it. I was her deliverance. Chess pieces ready to make their moves.

I was hungry for her.

"Fine. We go. Just you and I."

Kieran blinked several times, and I smiled wickedly at him.

"You're sure about this?"

"No. But I know I didn't become a vampire to have a leash put on me. I won't have my fate given to me in rations."

I may have meant the Master, but having Nicholas hold out on me when it damn well suited him, I let it hurt for once. Emotion as *Shinigami...* it had fingertips, blood, a will of its own. It couldn't be denied, forgotten about in my brain's attic corners.

"You have to know our Mr. French certainly won't like us sneaking off into the night together."

"This choice is all mine, and Nicholas will have to understand. Now, how do we get to London?"

CHAPTER 34

Clara was the lighthouse in the middle of my ocean. I was lost between my heightened senses and the infiltrating voices begging to be heard in my head, but she glowed and drew me to her.

"Wait till you try this," Kieran said with a glint in his eye. He stood in the snow, snakes of smoke rising from his feet, and then there was nothing but black ashes where he'd been.

I closed my eyes and pulled him up in my vision, opening the file of Kieran Coughlin. He stared into the darkness, eyes a fury of flames, waiting for me in a thicket of trees. I wanted to be there with him. And then, I was.

"You found me," he said. He simmered around me with a magical heat, enveloping me as I appeared in front of him.

"I wanted to."

His heat was too much, the buzz of moving in this

world without moving was too much, the urge to drink from her, too much.

I grabbed the back of his head with brutal need, and kissed him so hard, I thought I'd break his teeth. He met it, unsurprised, pushing back, wrapping his fingers in my hair. His tongue burned with passion. If I never left that moment, there in the dark snowy woods, I would have been happy.

If only there was blood.

"I'd like to say I'm sorry, lass, but—"

"You're not," I said. I swallowed down my guilt, and tried not to see my Nicholas in the back of my mind. "I don't want to be either." Eternity would be unbearable if I held myself back. I was not made immortal to hold back.

Briefly, I wondered if Lynch felt that way when he murdered.

Kieran's arms around me, fingers splayed on my back, darkly warm, had a different strength than Nicholas's. I don't know that I'd notice the difference of if I was still human. It held me up, and let me go all at once.

"Let's go," he said in his gravelly voice.

I let the red glow of Clara take over Kieran's cinders. Arms still around each other, we flashed again, and left that moment behind us.

"You don't pull punches," Kieran said.

We stood in pitch black, staring up at the Bethlem Royal Hospital of London. It was enormous, and cruel-looking. It may have had a makeover, but its horror was a steaming cloud hovering over it.

Pure evil.

"I know about this place," I said, reaching for his hand. I'd read a lot of everything, looking for reasons to go to Birch Tree Books to see Nicholas.

If you wanted to lose your soul, the Bethlem Royal Hospital was where you would never find it again. Where the rich once made side shows of the mentally challenged and the poor for the sake of tourism. Where people were chained to walls, sleeping on straw under holey roofs, bared to the elements, hungry, wondering whether the next torture would come at the hands of the staff or the other patients.

The moans and screams lingered, looking for a way out that they'd never find. They were dead and gone, but their cries were as loud as the crows cawing overhead.

My Clara was in the middle of it all, washing dishes even as we spoke.

"She's in there, and she doesn't know I'm coming," I said.

Kieran turned to look at me, eyes searching me for any sign of emotion. I didn't have any. I only had need.

"Are you ready?"

The words may have been gone, but the blazing light of them was a ghost over the gaping mouth of a door, written there decades ago by someone who never escaped. *WELCOME TO HELL.*

I didn't have to nod. This was all I'd ever been ready for.

~

It was as dark inside as out, perhaps darker with the fluorescent lights casting a sickly glow on the halls.

I wished Izanagi had come for a moment, but his kind of death didn't belong here. There was no poetry to the death in this place.

"Jesus Christ, this is horrible," Kieran said, cringing from a passing orderly. I remained fixed on the hallway in front of us, so I wouldn't see anything else, but it was hard to miss the wandering patients in pain of one kind or another, or the staff in white uniforms that only showed how decayed everything else was. Bethlem was a place that nursed pain only so it would be promised more.

We were getting ever nearer to Clara, and my blood burned to take over hers, and be free of it all.

"Eliza, dearest, put your teeth away," Kieran whispered in my ear as we walked. I hadn't noticed the little barbs because my mouth was open. Holy hell, I was panting like a tiger in the sun.

"Oh my God," I said with a little laugh I was sort of ashamed of. "I didn't know. I'm glad the mist didn't come out."

"You're a Stephen King book waiting to be written, woman," he said out of the corner of his mouth, nodding at a matronly nurse who looked like she could use a little mental help herself. "I'm impressed with how you're holding yourself together."

I tore my eyes away from the doors at the end of the hall, suddenly curious about him. "What was it like for you the first time you fed?"

The scent of old smoke from him. I wondered if it was consuming him or giving him strength.

"I didn't want to do it, the man I killed wasn't ready. He didn't want to die." He was quiet, but the fire in him blazed so much I thought it might singe me, too. I couldn't believe the expressionless people around us were oblivious.

With a droning, foreboding buzzing noise, the double doors at the end of the hallway opened to a battered and bent sign for the kitchen. It was all I could do not to run there, leaving every questioning staff member and Kieran behind. I wanted Clara more than anything in the world.

"You knew the man," I said before I realized I'd said it. I was transfixed on the kitchen doors, my fangs impossible to retract.

"I did. How did you know that?"

"I just know things now. I'm sorry you had to do that to your friend. It should never happen that way."

The kitchen loomed ever closer.

"You're creeping me out, love," he said, but I couldn't look at him to see how much he was kidding.

We'd arrived at the dingy white kitchen doors.

"Do you want me to go in there with you?" he whispered.

Clara was whistling from the other side. I put my hand on the door, and fought back tears.

"Yes, please."

The door creaked when I pushed it open, Kieran at my side.

The hospital kitchen was a jail cell in itself. Water-stained walls brought shadows of metal pipes to life, industrial puppets clanking and banging from within. Cracks littered every ceramic tile on the walls. The sink and stove were as discolored and rusty like the slop basins and trash barrels around them. The cabinets would never be white again, the window never quite clear. One wall was cement, blackened in spots with age. Every corner beneath the rusty metal work surfaces was brown with leakage and dirt that could never be hidden, with grunge seeping onto the floor. It was vacant of scent, like no kitchen should be; no soup was boiling, no cooking meat wafting through the air, certainly not cleaning fluid. A sadly spinning metal fan was in the window high near the ceiling over the sink. Too high to cool the room or shed any light; high enough that an inmate couldn't reach it to escape.

And under that streaked window that looked out to nowhere, a gleaming presence in the yellowing disease of this place. Clara's back faced us as her body shook with the scrubbing of dishes. She was humming. Stacks had already been done, stacks more waited for the same. And still, she hummed, amid the hopelessness and filth.

"Clara," I said, not with a whisper. There was nothing to hide from her.

She spun on us, the whites of her eyes the brightest thing I'd seen in London.

"Oh," she said, with a welcoming smile. She dried her hands as she walked towards us, her shapeless skirt swishing around her, and wiped a tendril of orange-ish frizz out of her eye. "I wasn't expecting any visitors. Can I help you find your way?" Her simple happiness was too good for the hospital, and yet so desperately necessary.

I hated what I was going to do, and wanted it even still.

"We aren't really here to visit, Clara," I said, looking as hard into her eyes as I could while her heart still beat. "And I have found my way."

Her eyes slid between me and Kieran. Panic set in, and she backed away. God only knew the dangers she'd faced herself in this place, just delivering meals to the patients. But I would be the last danger she met.

"What do you want? I don't have anything," she pleaded. Kieran was shuffling his feet in my peripheral vision, rubbing his fingers together, surely wishing for a cigarette. Her fear should have repulsed me, but it made my breath quicken.

"Don't be afraid," Kieran said. She laughed at him. She may be sweet, but she wasn't stupid. Kieran himself was afraid.

But within a beat of her heart, her shoulders relaxed, and she stopped backing away. Her eyes landed on me, lessening in fear until there was none at all. In a puff of red smoke I was at her side. Even Kieran gasped, but Clara's eyes remained steady.

"That smell—" she muttered.

"What do you smell?" I asked. So, this was my first thrall. Designed especially for the future dead.

She breathed in deep, momentarily closing her eyes. "Peonies."

I went cold at the mention of Kat's favorite scent, the perfume she wore no matter what the season or event. Clara reminded me of her; the decided obliviousness to the cruelties around them. That light they embodied, creating happiness wherever they went. Tears sprung to my eyes, and I touched Clara's hair, remembering Kat's red locks, and thought Clara's might be that beautiful if she had the mind to bother with it.

"Clara, I'm so sorry for what I'm about to do."

Her eyes welled with tears, and I wanted her blood more for it.

"My mother wore peony perfume," she murmured. It was hard to say who was more mesmerized, her or me. "And when she smelled just like that," she said, pointing her finger at me, "a mix of lemon pie and peonies, I knew she had something bad to tell me. It didn't happen often, but when it did, she put on a squirt of her perfume, and made me a lemon pie. She hated that pie, said it wasn't sweet enough. I told her I had all the sweet I needed when I smelled her perfume and saw her smile. We were alone, and she was so sick. I loved her more than anything. Even when she had to tell me bad things."

I couldn't bear to shed the tears that strangled me for her. I wanted to hold her, and kill her.

"You have bad things to tell me right now, don't you?" she asked, entranced.

I closed my eyes ever so briefly, and hoped she had wonderful love in life. I hoped she wouldn't remember how awful I was in her last breath. I wished it wasn't all my fault. *Kat, I wish it wasn't all my fault.*

"I forgive you," she said.

And with a roar that deafened only me, I plunged my fangs into her neck.

CHAPTER 35

Blood is something so familiar, and so alien all at once. It's not meant to be stolen, but when it is—it smooths out all of the heart's rough edges; the things that don't make sense, all the wrongs that need righting, they each fit neatly into the slots they're supposed to. That first taste of human blood, when it slid down my throat, was the last glimpse of an ugly world, and a new vision of one that I would make my own, one death at a time.

This was what being a vampire meant to me, when I sunk my teeth into Clara Borden.

I tasted the love she had for her mother, the way she smiled at the staff when they brought her dishes to wash; the way one old man smiled at her when she snuck him an extra grilled cheese. She desperately craved strawberry ice cream, and stopped on her way home from the hospital twice a week or more for it. There was a flavor to the way she sang along with the radio, when she didn't know the words.

When I was done drinking her, I would carry that away with me. I would sing along with every song I heard, even if I didn't know it. Her residue. And I would carry away her forgiveness.

I was buried in her in a million ways.

When I thought I'd disappear in her blood, I tore my mouth from her, breathing in the second-long difference in taste of her blood as it hit the air. There was a crimson haze over the kitchen, over Kieran.

"I dreamed this once," I gasped, still heaving with the imaginary need for breath.

"Don't talk," Kieran said calmly. He leaned against the work counter, arms crossed, watching me. I was fixated on how surreal he looked, doused in red, until Clara twitched in my arms. In *my* arms the way Kat had hung from Roman's as he bled her dry.

"Alive," I moaned. Once again I sunk my teeth in, eliciting the smallest squeal from her.

My knees buckled and our bodies hit the floor. I consumed, drinking the last beat of her heart, wanting it so that she wouldn't have to endure a fate worse than death at my hands.

With this rush of blood, I saw things. Not the things she'd done, or the person she was, but something much more painful and powerful. I wanted to scream until my throat was dead and gone like she would be.

Visions unveiled themselves to me as I drank my *unmei nashi*'s blood. I struggled to be aware of the floor beneath my knees, to keep me present while I saw the other end that had awaited her.

The vision showed Clara screaming and screaming,

here in the kitchen, back against the floor, with a monster doing exactly what I was doing to her now— drinking her life away. A flop of dirty blond hair hung over her attacker's face, thin arms pinning her to the ground. A hospital gown fell open at the back, revealing his every vertebrae.

I pulled my mouth away from her long enough to scream, the same sound I'd made when Roman held Kat's dying body in his arms.

Now, I was seeing him kill again.

Clara fell to the floor when Roman's face appeared in my vision; gaunt, empty, sad, needing, more alone than I ever thought a person could be. Not a drop of blood pooled around Clara's head on the grimy kitchen floor. There was none left. My tears hit her shirt. Confusion roiled in me, but only at what I knew could have been.

Kieran knelt at my side, and pulled my head to his chest. "Sssshh," he said, rocking me. He smoothed my hair, and lifted my face to look at his. His eyes burned me, they were too much. "You're okay, Eliza. In through the nose, out through the mouth. It's over now, whether you want it to be or not."

I swallowed hard, the last taste of Clara Borden's blood washing down my throat, and with it, the last piece of undeniable knowledge that only I knew. My head pulsed wildly.

"Kieran. I know too many things. It hurts."

"I know how it is. You know everything about her now, don't you?" he said, a rhetorical question, as he kissed my forehead. I wished that kiss could take away what I'd learned.

My eyes rolled upwards to the stained ceiling, focusing again, dripping water as we spoke.

"Roman is in the hospital."

We left her there. It disgusted me to do it, but we left her there, on the floor.

We raced down the hallways, through double doors, into elevators, looking, but never knowing where to look.

"I saw him, but it was *her*. I saw the other death she would have had if she wasn't my *unmei nashi*."

"Roman killed her?"

"Right there, where we were."

We bolted through door after door, aimlessly rushing around the hospital, as it crushed us with its oppressive sadness, Kieran following my pointless lead.

"But—but—that's the same thing— She wouldn't be any worse off if Roman killed her in that kitchen."

"I know. I was confused for a second, too." The other end a chosen victim would meet if the *Shinigami* didn't take their life was always fated to be a horrible one, something that could never be repaired. We were the better option.

"She couldn't have been chosen for more than one vampire? Or he just killed her, no call to do so. Wait a minute, wait a minute." Kieran stopped, mouth gaping. *"You can see her other fate?"*

I stopped, but hated it. My head was moving too fast to want to stop. "Yes, yes. I saw it, plain as day, but then…."

"Then what?"

"Sorry, I'm a little—lost in my mind right now. I realized that first I saw *her* fate, but she was a—supporting actor. It was Roman's story, she was just a part."

"Dear God," Kieran whispered, falling back to lean limply against the wall. "Dear God." He looked so small then, like a little kid afraid of his first day at school.

"Don't be afraid of me. I don't like it."

"Not exactly afraid…"

"Convincing."

"Eliza Morgan, do you realize what you're saying?" He crossed that space without moving and held me by the arms, shaking me a little. "You can see what no *Shinigami* has ever seen, no one at all has ever seen. You can tell us what might have been."

If I could see what the alternative was, I could decide whether or not to feed on the victims fated to me. I would have choice.

And for all their power, the *Shinigami* had never possessed choice.

"Why would you want to know what might have been?" I asked him.

"You can be the first of us to decide on their own who—"

"To kill? Why would we want the power to choose who to kill? Sure seems a hell of a lot simpler on the conscience to let fate pick for you."

He was smoldering, a delicate smoke rising off of him as he struggled with it. "I'd want to be in charge of my own choices. If I could. You have that power, Eliza. One sip, and you can decide if you want to finish their lives for them, or give them another chance."

"I can play God."

His fire nearly burned out with that. "You don't have to play at all if you don't decide to. The rules are gone now."

"But it was Roman I saw, too. If I wanted, I could have seen what his fate holds for him."

"No more guessing at what our purposes are," Kieran said, eyes glazed over. "Everything is different now."

Orderlies were gawking, so we moved on. More pointless searching.

"Should we ask one of them where we can find Roman?" Kieran said.

"No, I can find him."

"Maybe—"

I stopped again and spun on him. I knew what he was going to say.

"Maybe what, Kieran?"

"Woah, slow down, gorgeous. I know you're bright enough to have thought that if Roman ran away, he doesn't want to be found. Maybe."

"He can cure Nicholas, and he's here. This is Nicholas's chance to be whole again without me."

Something gray passed over Kieran, a ghost of a feeling. "Remember, just because you know these things now, doesn't change the fact that Roman left you both. Your knowledge doesn't change that."

I kissed his lips quickly for the things he didn't say then. But this was Nicholas's life, and I wasn't about to give Roman the option of leaving him for dead.

"Kiss me again," Kieran said, his breath hot.

I pulled him to me by his shirt, and kissed him, longer this time, vampiric emotion and strength and sensitivity to every breath fueling me. I lived every second of it like reading about someone else's life in a book I couldn't put down.

When I pulled away, my determination was even stronger. "We have to find him right now. Enough of this running. I can see him if I let myself."

Kieran held my hands, while smiling at a pretty nurse walking by. I closed my eyes, and without even having to try, Roman popped into my mind. He felt so alone every time I saw him, my heart cried out to him, despite what he'd done. What he'd taken from me.

"He's in the attic."

"Christ almighty, woman, could you make this creepier if you tried?"

We had to backtrack, and it pissed me off that I'd wasted time running, afraid to see something I didn't want to see. My entire life was about seeing things I didn't want to see.

What consumes me gives me strength.

I'd been made for this, to shape my own world using what fate had given me. This was my purpose.

Pulling open a door where no orderlies bothered to look, down a hallway that nobody bothered to walk, I paused, and made a choice again. I put my hand on Kieran's shoulder, and turned him toward me. I let everything be slow for a moment, so I could kiss him as deeply as I cared for him, my hands squeezing his bare arms, breathing in his fire.

"Well," he said, licking his lips when I pulled away. "That was a wee bit like a goodbye." His eyes took on that puppy quality again, too vulnerable to resist.

"It's not. It's a thank you."

He grabbed me by the waist with one hand and yanked me into another fast kiss. "You don't owe me anything."

"You helped me make my own way. But that isn't why I —it isn't exactly why I feel like this about you."

He looked at the floor, giving me a view of his messy, spiky dark hair. "What do you feel for me?"

"I can't give it a name, Kieran, but I need you with me. You ignite something in me that nobody else can."

"Not even Nicholas?" he said, looking up at me again. Beautiful. Rebellious and strong.

"Not even Nicholas." I shriveled inside to say it.

Kieran saw my reaction to my own words. "Don't worry, Eliza, I won't turn you against him. I won't tear you away."

My eyes welled, a pink cloud over them. "I'm already torn." My voice cracked. I looked away, and put my hand on the door handle, taking myself out of Kieran's grasp. The door squeaked. Nobody even tried to make it look like this part of the hospital was taken care of.

We would find more of that in the attic.

CHAPTER 36

Cobwebs hung like ghosts from the ceiling, threatening to descend upon us. The wind roared through the loose boards and decrepit roof. The remote parts of this hospital that the public didn't see were ignored to decay, left to die like so many of its patients.

Like Roman was trying to do.

His despair stabbed me as I drew closer to him. It was no fresh vampire sense, only the utter silence and darkness of the air that told me he wanted to die.

I'd poked my head through the opening at the top of the stairs before Kieran. It was enormous, and ice cold. Bats flew from rafter to rafter. Snow blew in from a broken octagonal window at the far end of the cluttered area. A single crow waited for me on the sill.

Kieran came up behind me on the stairs, and let out a low whistle as he looked around. "Ah, for fuck's sake, woman," he mutters.

"Sorry, we had to."

As agile as we were, our footsteps echoed. Silent, heads spinning, we walked through paths of rusty metal tables, outdated medical equipment, chairs with restraints and ripped seats, and something that looked like a cage. Jesus Christ, I prayed it was something else. Spiders skittered when Kieran picked up a tool that looked suspiciously like a cattle prod.

The attic was a graveyard, the space proof of the mental hospital's history of depravity.

"I hate that Roman's here," I whispered, kicking aside an open trunk filled with what looked like gas masks.

We turned a corner, and I cried out when I saw him.

Roman, hunched like a beaten animal, on a yellow-stained naked mattress, his forehead against the wall.

He was trying not to see anything.

"Ro-Roman?" I said, my voice creaking like the floorboards.

He didn't move. I glanced at Kieran, whose eyes were wide like a twelve-year old's breaking into an abandoned house. With raised eyebrows, he motioned with his head for me to go to Roman.

If Nicholas's life didn't depend on it, if it wasn't so *wrong* to let Roman suffer this way, I would have remembered that this was the bastard that killed sunshine for me the day he drank Kat's blood.

My feet were in quicksand, but I dragged them to Roman's side. The closer I got, the clearer was his deterioration. His golden blond hair was stringy, bedraggled, greasy. His body shook, sending whiffs of filth to my oversensitive nose. And he was mumbling to himself. *"Walking death, walking death, walking death...."*

It may have been Nicholas that was withering away, but Roman disappeared when Kat died.

"Roman," I said, my hand on his shoulder. I don't know which of us was shaking harder.

He jolted away from me, slamming violently into the corner. I screamed at the speed of it. Once again, I said his name.

And when I did, I remembered the humble quietness of him, the liquid warmth of his scent, the way he never complained about lording over Lynch's sick obsessions, his face when reminded of his family in life, his eye rolling at Nicholas's terrible jokes and egotistical witticism.

I remembered how much he loved Nicholas.

I remembered how much he loved me. And how much he loved Kat.

"God, Roman, what have I done to you?" I hung my head, ashamed. "Why would you come here?"

I can't bear to see the hatred in Eliza's eyes. He'd said it himself in a letter to Nicholas. The last we'd heard from him.

"The ghosts here are louder than mine," he whispered.

I was punishing him, stealing his life away. Walking death. That was me, not him.

"Roman, Jesus Christ, I'm so sorry," I said, tears of diluted blood splashing on my arm.

His shaking slowed, then stopped. With painful slowness, he turned his head, forehead scraping along the wall, making me wince. The blue of his eyes was a sad storm; more empty, lonely ocean on a cold day than the warming, lifegiving one that I once saw in him.

"Eliza?" he croaked.

I threw my arms around him, completely aware of the filth he was coated in. It was my fault. His decay, was all my fault.

"Roman, I can't let you stay here, you need to come with me. We'll make you better—"

"No," he said, clearly and with backbone. "I stay here."

"No, no, you can't. You can't! This place will kill you!" And the vision I'd had as Clara's blood flooded my own slammed into mind with a destructive brutality. I fell back, and Roman caught me.

"Eliza Morgan, why have you come here?" he said.

My tears came faster, and I Kieran's warmth crept up behind me. He ached to come to me, but left me to Roman.

"Roman," I said, head hung. "I can—see the other ends we could meet, Roman. What would have happened, if we didn't feed on our *unmei nashi*. For both them and us."

He came back to himself, then, instead of sinking into what he'd become. What I'd made him.

"You're *Shinigami* now," he said.

"Yes, that's not important. What's important is that I know what would become of you." My throat constricted. "The worst fate I can imagine, Roman. *This.* You'll never feed, never take the lives of your *unmei nashi*. You'll become a ghost of this place, and those humans will suffer hideously for what you won't do. Hundreds of them. I can see them." His blue eyes became clearer, pupils dilating. "And you. You'll never die, and you'll be this thing, that you are. Forever."

His face didn't change. "What I do makes everyone

suffer, anyway. I'm powerless to do anything but ruin lives, then end them."

"What if I told you that Nicholas will never be healthy without your help?" Please let that be enough to convince him.

"He will be restored with time."

"If he drinks your blood, he'll be whole again, immediately." Not enough. "Roman, Nicholas needs *you*. You're his brother. I can't make him happy enough, he misses you too much. You're his home as much as I am, and without you, we're falling apart."

It hadn't dawned on me until I said it. I never wanted to admit that Nicholas and I were drifting from each other, slowly, like the earth moving, imperceptible until the seasons die. But Kieran behind me was as much proof as I needed. And the clinging to me, the utter owning of me that Nicholas wanted these days—it spoke volumes that he was missing something. I knew who it was.

"He'll repair. You both will. But I never will, and I don't deserve to."

"Stop the pity party, Roman. I get it. You're in agony because of what you did, but you did it for us."

"I snuffed out a light so bright, I never want to see blue skies again."

Me, crying again. I hated it more than words could say. "Nobody understands more than I how much it hurts that Kat's dead. But think of how you feel, and that's how Nicholas feels without you. You were his light for so long, and now you've left him. He thinks it's his fault, I think it's mine, you think it's yours. We're monsters together,

Roman, but we're worse apart. Please, come with me. I'm begging you."

He clumsily rose to his feet. It was so sad to see the struggle in someone who'd been so angelic. He wasn't meant to be destroyed.

"Say it's true. Say I can help Nicholas. He'll never look at me the same again."

"Too bloody bad, man!" Kieran piped up out of nowhere. "You can fix wrongs here. You owe it to yourself. You weren't meant to live like this."

"I've done all kinds of things I wasn't meant to do," Roman said through a sneer.

"No, you did one thing you weren't supposed to do, and you only did it for me and Nicholas," I said. "You've made your point. Enough is enough."

He turned on me, snarling at me like a feral cat backed into a corner. "Stop trying to convince me I can do some good now."

I was getting nowhere.

"Fine," I hissed, my red cloud rising around me in my anger. "Sink into yourself, hide up here and think you can't change anything. I can tell you one thing—you've just proven that Nicholas French is a better man than you."

Roman sunk to the floor again. "You tell me nothing I didn't know already."

CHAPTER 37

Leaving Roman made me feel like the biggest failure and the worst person that ever lived.

"You didn't give up," Kieran said. "You did a great thing."

Snow melted in heavy drops all around us; I could hear it as much as see it. The rebirth of spring, coinciding with my rebirth into death. The crows circled high overhead, not wanting to come near me.

"What will you tell the golden boy?" Kieran asked me as we approached the mountain in leaps in bounds, envisioning ourselves closer and closer to the temple. If only I could envision other things, things that could actually help.

"Don't call him that. I'm not telling him about Roman."

"Lying to him?"

"No," I spat. "But I won't tell him I saw Roman that way, or that Roman refused to save his life. I won't tell him I failed. I'll tell him when I've succeeded."

"But Nicholas is leaving for New Hampshire."

My blood ran cold at the thought of him leaving me alone with this new power, and colder with the idea that he'd be without my blood to keep him strong in another country. Roman was supposed to heal him before he went to Ossipee, that was the perfect plan. My failure to bring him back didn't change that Lynch was out of control, or that I needed to breathe without Nicholas.

I needed to be alone to remember how much I wanted Nicholas French.

"Nicholas won't leave me if he senses that I need him. If he knows that I'm seeing things like this… He has to go."

Kieran was quiet as we moved, slower now, the temple and the surrounding dwellings in sight. Neither of us was ready to go back yet.

"Will you be telling him about us, then?" We stopped, looking hard at each other. He looked so hurt already.

"I can't."

There was so much guarded vulnerability there, hidden under tattoos and stubble and cigarette smoke, and he'd let *me* in. I'd wronged both him and Nicholas.

"I know you can't, lass," he said with a sad smile and a quick kiss on the cheek. "I'm not the kind you bring home to your family, and he is."

Ice formed around us on the melting grass. "I have no one to bring anybody to, Kieran. I make no apologies for caring about you, but I can't do right by anyone right now, and I certainly shouldn't be pulling you into my mess."

"I want to be here." He took both my hands in his, fire burning under his fingertips, ready to touch me and leave their mark. "Maybe once Nicholas is off babysitting the

Abomination, you'll be able to see what you want more easily." His lips on mine were unexpected fireworks, his fingers knotted in mine like he was afraid to fall.

I know I was.

He pulled away, smoke trailing from his lips between us.

"Now, time to report into the powers that be, before they come looking for us."

Like a solid shadow in the disappearing snow, Nicholas looked into the sky like it was going to answer his questions. I could see him without even trying in my vision now. The connection we had that was supposed to fizzle out was stronger than ever.

He looked sharply northwest, where I was, like he could feel me, too. I wondered if he could still hear my heartbeat miles away as he had when I was alive. I wondered if my heartbeat meant anything anymore.

Without warning, I couldn't find him in my mind, only the space where he used to be. It hurt, that sudden emptiness. Then it *really* hurt, a soreness that grew into a throbbing, that became a stabbing, then a scratching of healing skin around wounds. I doubled over with the intensity of it. I knew this pain like I knew death.

"What's wrong?" Kieran asked.

"Nicholas," was all I could say, shaking my head, not knowing what else I could say.

"I'm here."

Kieran took his hand off my back, and I straightened

up to see Nicholas next to me even as I smelled the peppermint brownie scent.

But the pain still wracked me, and I could see it was in him, too.

"Oh, God, Nicholas," I gasped, and threw myself into his arms. He was a deliciously warm blanket wrapped around me, all I needed to make me whole. "It felt like I lost you for like, a minute, and I wanted to die," I said into his ear, his dark waves brushing my nose. I could never die if he was gone, I would suffer it infinitely now.

He pushed me away before I was ready, and my shoulders slumped as he held them tight in his hands.

"How do you think I've felt since you took off on me?" he said with tense frigidity. My shoulders grew cold as the ice waves rolled from his fingertips. The ice in his eyes was worse.

I was stammering, looking at my feet, when Kieran came to my rescue.

"She needed to feed, and was tired of waiting."

"Well, thank Christ she has a womanizing Irishman to take advantage of her needs," Nicholas said, true to form.

"Maybe if you could get your head out of the Master's arse, she wouldn't have come to me at all."

"Maybe if—"

"Shut up!" I yelled at them. I pushed down my nerves and looked Nicholas square in the eye. "I'm sorry I left you like that, but you would never have let me go. I couldn't ask you to defy the Master and come with me."

"But you could ask *him*," Nicholas said, glaring at Kieran.

I looked at Kieran, too, hands in jeans pockets, chin on chest, eyes looking up at us, wide with innocent defiance.

"Yes, I could. He doesn't ask questions," I said.

"Is that where I've been wrong, then? Should I not question you, challenge you, treat you like a grown-up?" The ground was a solid brick of ice at Nicholas's feet.

"You shouldn't *doubt* her, man! She's more powerful than you or I will ever be, and was before she became a vampire."

My mouth gaped at Kieran, the sincerity of his words.

"Thank you, Kieran," I said quietly. He winked at me.

Wrong thing to do.

A sheen of shimmering frost filtered down Nicholas's body, chilling the air around him in slivers of ice. He growled low, teeth gnashing, fangs glistening. He was a wild animal, hunched over, broad shoulders rising and falling as he panted.

He was staring at my heart.

"Nicholas, calm down," I said slowly. He'd become more of a Mr. Hyde than at the most esteemed vampire among us.

"I spend my existence trying to convince you that you and I, this is forever. I've done everything I could to show you that you can't lose me, Eliza. I'm the one thing in your life that will be here always. Nothing can take me from you." His chill warmed up, and he looked so exhausted, so pained, so old. I'd done this to him. "You're the one running from me, Eliza. You're looking for a way out."

With one last sad glance, he left me with Kieran and the crows in the

woods.

CHAPTER 38

I t should have been easier to leave Kieran's side then. I should have run from him, telling him he was a bad influence, that being close to him was putting another brick in the wall between Nicholas and I.

But I needed him. He never judged me. Sometimes guidance was more like pushing.

Don't push me.

"I'm sorry, Eliza," Kieran said as we stood in front of my door, the sound of snow melting all around. The in between stage between wintry death and the life of spring.

"Nothing to be sorry for, Kieran." I sighed, afraid to go on, but I had to say it out loud. "Things are hard between Nicholas and I right now. You helped me in a lot of ways. This wedge between us was there before you were."

"But—" he struggled with the choice to speak. "But he most certainly is in love with you."

"And I'm in love with him." Slow, measured words.

"Love is the thing that makes you fear too much, make

you so afraid that you run from it, when it's the only thing that speaks the truth." He looked off into the distance.

"Who are we talking about, Kieran?"

He dragged his long-lashed eyes back to me with a grin. "Ahhh, quiet, woman. It frightens me when you speak the truth, too."

"What the hell do I know about truth?" Tears strangled me, but I wouldn't let them out. I wasn't sure why they were there at all, and that made it all the worse.

"I should probably be alone now," I said, motioning to the door behind me. "I don't think I'll have much time alone before the Master comes." Dread seeped in.

The fire in Kieran's eyes burned black this time. He was full of hunger, but for what it was difficult to say.

"I won't kiss you again," he said before he turned to leave me. "I want you to be alone with how much you want it."

And then he was gone, too.

I'd barely sat in front of the fire before Blue was beside me.

"I can't believe you just *left* like that," she said with no small amount of admiration in her voice.

"I have no patience for being told what to do when I know what to do."

"Why did you ask Kieran to go with you?"

I looked at her, but she wouldn't look back. She would have seen what we'd done if she had. And I was ashamed to admit that I hadn't thought of her at all when I kissed him.

"You know Kieran better than I do, Blue. He won't tell me to fall in line like a good little vampire. I needed that."

"I wouldn't have told you to fall in line," she said softly. It hadn't occurred to me that she wanted to be the one to run off to London.

"Oh, Blue, I'm so sorry. I *suck*." Just when I didn't think my body could contain any more guilt. Vampirism: Day One. "Of course I would've wanted you with me, but I was so restless, it happened so fast… And I know—"

"I know, I know I wouldn't have left the mountain anyway. I'm not sure I even could anymore." In a blur, she stood. "I'm tired of being afraid, El," she said, pacing the floor in her miniature royal blue slippers. "I'm crippled here."

"Blue, what if you just told Kieran he didn't have to bring you your *unmei nashi* next time? What would happen to you if you just *went*, by yourself? Or I could come with you, if you want me."

The half-smile on her face was disconcerting. "So that's how it feels, then?"

"What?"

"To be babysat like a child?"

"That's not what I—" *You're the one who has her meals brought to her in a mountaintop hotel suite, Princess*, I thought viciously. *You pretend it's a palace but it's a prison.* I sighed at my own thoughts, squinting my eyes as if I could dispel them and what a terrible person I was that easily. "Yeah, that's what it feels like, I guess."

She put her hand on my arm, an apologetic smile on

her lips. I couldn't look her in the eye. "Don't worry. I have my creator bring me back food like a baby bird, right? Nobody can snap me out of this fear, especially not myself."

I swallowed hard. "Does any of your fear have to do with Kieran, himself?"

"Meaning?"

"Well, I just wonder—I wonder if your fear of leaving the mountain is really your fear of leaving Kieran. Maybe this is your way of holding on to him?"

Suspicion crossed her face, making her just a little colder. "Are you looking for me *not* to hold onto him?"

"I'm either being interrogated or psychoanalyzed, but I can't decide which," I said, anger surfacing, the red mist not far behind. Always, so much anger.

"Join the club, Eliza."

I had no right to be angry at Blue, no right to resent her or blame her, but if there was one thing that pisses me off it's when the solution is *right there* and excuses are so much closer. Kat and I would argue about why I didn't talk to people, why she was always looking for Prince Charming, why we bought cake instead of fruit when counting the minutes until pay day. Then we gave up and did the things we were doing anyway.

Blue and I couldn't do that. Because if we gave up, it could be forever.

She brushed her gleaming ebony hair back, closing her eyes. When she was ready, she opened them again and said, "Kieran is a crutch. Until I saw you and Nicholas together, I didn't know. You're so much yourselves, and don't stop each other from anything. Kieran and I hold each other back. But I don't know how to be without him."

Connections forged by fate, and ripped apart by humanity.

I brushed her hair back on the other side, and said, "We'll live forever. We don't have to learn to be without each other."

CHAPTER 39

I went to the Master for two reasons: I wanted to throw in his face that I'd disobeyed, and I knew Nicholas was with him. Nicholas's desperation was like rusty nails down my back. He was ashamed of it, because he didn't think the feeling was mutual, but he was afraid to be without me now.

And he still needed my blood, no matter how hurt he was.

I entered the temple with the intent of a storming army, silk kimono swishing around my legs. The Master sat at the altar, the king on his humble throne, with Nicholas by his side. I was a little surprised to see Paolo with them. He looked so much stronger than Nicholas there, young and wiry, and clear-headed.

The Master's opaline eyes glinted, waiting for me to speak and put my foot in my mouth, but we both knew I wouldn't back down. I was, after all, Nicholas's *unmei fumetsu*, if not the woman he loved.

"I fed. It's done. Now if you want to have the ceremony, I won't stop you. But I don't want it."

Staff in his lap, the Master stared at me, as if trying to take me apart with his eyes. A few months ago, it might have worked. "I am not disappointed that you disobeyed me," he said in that controlled voice of his.

Nicholas cleared his throat and leaned over to the Master, eyes on me. "You're not?" he asked the old man.

The Master smiled in a warm, fatherly way. "I am not."

Nicholas pursed his lips to keep from smiling, but Paolo was unreadable. I tried not to pay attention to either of them, though Nicholas's mere presence made my undead heart race.

"Eliza is a singular woman, *Shinigami* like none before. She defies tradition. She makes fate eat from her hand." With a *crack* he stood in front of me, staff resting on the top of my foot, waiting to smash my toes if I did or said anything that didn't fit his plans for my rebellion. I didn't flinch, and he didn't expect I would.

The swell of blood in my newly immortal body told me things—and it told me now that my actions were part of the Master's world; he'd let me play my hand, but he was the dealer. I knew something else, too.

The Master was intimidated by me. It was all I could do to keep from laughing.

He'd seen the blasphemous look on my face, and my hands and feet went numb. Then my legs, my arms, my neck, as he searched inside me for something that I didn't want to let go of. My latent power was a slippery animal in my mind, trying to slink away as the Master closed his fists around it over and over.

"You know what your power is," he murmured, not hiding his surprise.

I held up my chin. "I know the beginning of it," I said.

"Eliza, what's going on?" Nicholas said. Fresh pain stabbed him, making his head twist unnaturally. A matching pain seared into my stomach.

Eyes still on the Master, I said, "I'm learning about myself, that's all, Nicholas."

Nicholas materialized between me and the Master. "Please don't shut me out," he whispered.

Nicholas took over the moment, like that first time we'd met, when he inserted himself in the middle of me, Kat and Lynch, when everything I knew was eclipsed by what he brought with him.

I was a new vampire, different from the woman he'd come to know, but he was with me. Our connection wasn't perfect, but he was still here. He ignored the Master behind him, as entranced by me as I was by him.

"You've been so far away, I can't stand being *me*, without you." Unblinking, steel in his words. "Eliza, don't let me go."

"Never."

One swift motion had me nestled in his arms, looking over his shoulder at the Master, who gave me a warm smile. I closed my eyes to eliminate anything but Nicholas.

"Please forgive me for everything I've done, Eliza," Nicholas murmured into my hair. "And don't say there's nothing to forgive, that's not what I need to hear."

I swallowed back the urge to tell him it wasn't his fault,

none of it, like I'd done so many times before. But this had to be different. It had to be true.

I eased out of his grasp so I could see his face register what I would say. "You blame yourself for Kat's death, and I blamed you, too. I blamed myself, and Roman, and Lynch, and Jenn. I forgive you for bringing all the dark forces that came with you. A thread connects you to Kat's death, but you weren't the beginning or end of that thread —you were caught in it. And there's nothing to forgive you for when it comes to me. I never wanted the life I had. This, I want."

"Thank you," was all he said.

"Now, I believe you should tell us about the things you've done and seen," the Master said, turning his back on us to walk unhurriedly to the altar—a show of apathy that I wasn't buying. Paolo waited for the old man, watching in stillness. His eyes met mine, and I looked away, ashamed without reason. Like God was right there judging me, ready to send me to Hell. I gasped to realize that Paolo was *doing* this, making me feel this way. He was doing it for the Master.

"I don't know enough myself yet, to give away all my secrets," I said.

"Tell us what you can, Eliza. This isn't an FBI debriefing." Paolo sounded clinical.

I'd been entirely betrayed.

Nicholas took my hand and we faced the Paolo and the Master. Pretending would be as good as me cowering and sobbing *I don't know anything* while they threatened me with a hot poker, like a deleted Tarantino film scene.

"My visions now are more...specific, and not limited to Nicholas."

"That's not new to us," the Master said.

"I don't have to tell you everything, do I? You're a dictator, not a teacher, if that's the case."

Nicholas squeezed my hand in warning, but I was done watching my words and actions.

"What do you have to hide?" Paolo said.

I coiled on Paolo, ready to strike. "What do you?"

He blinked rapidly, from guilt or fear. Either one reminded me that I needed to be less trusting.

"If Eliza doesn't want to talk about what she's seen—" Nicholas started.

"—then she shouldn't have come here," the Master finished.

I looked down to see that my feet had disappeared in a blink under the flaming red mist. It wound up my legs, around my waist like a secure arm, avoiding Nicholas's hand as it snaked up my chest and billowed around my head like a cobra's hood. My words came from within, channeling a depth of power from someone else. Maybe I was; Izanagi was never far.

"I'll go where I like. I came here because I was expected, and I won't play games. I face what challenges me, Master. I'm not afraid."

"You have no reason to be afraid," he said, unconvincingly. I saw right through him; he planned on using me for something and nobody but him knew what.

I rose from the ground, dropping Nicholas's hand, the mist hissing faintly underneath me with a life of its own.

Paolo watched in awe while the Master's jaw clenched and his eyes followed me into the air.

"You would reduce to trickery to intimidate me?" he spat, saber-tooth fangs protruding. "Now, tell me what you see! Tell me what happened when you fed!"

"Or what?" I said coolly.

"Eliza," Paolo interjected. I snapped my head in his direction. "There doesn't need to be secrets here. We're here to support each other."

"Paolo, the temple isn't a goddamn support group, or Arthur wouldn't have died here."

"We're a sanctuary," Nicholas said, "which means we don't force each other to do anything." I lowered myself beside him, the red mist dissipating only when I held his hand. "Eliza will choose anything and everything she wants."

Looking at Nicholas, I knew that meant a lot of things for us both.

CHAPTER 40

"You're ready to go?"

"No."

Nicholas was as warm as an Olive Garden bread basket, and just like one, I never wanted it to be gone. God, I missed real food. I anticipated crashing Blue's room to indulge in her endless stream of human, non-secluded world treats when I broke down over Nicholas's departure.

I wouldn't let him leave me without drinking my blood as I was now: immortal.

"Taste me before you leave me."

In a needy moan, he said what had to have been weighing on him. "You'll have visions about me, and us. Our futures..."

"I refuse to be afraid of something in my own head," I said.

I opened a vein for him, or maybe for me. If I could have crawled inside his skin, I would have. Wanting him to go and wanting him to stay created jagged edges in my heart, a sensation of both giving up and truly *starting* for the first time. It warmed me, and left me skinned alive.

When we were finished with each other, a pink sheen of watered-down blood covered us both from sweaty curls to naked feet.

"Are you crying?" I asked him, touching the half-moon circle under his eye. It wasn't dark anymore. I'd done that for him.

"I don't know," he said with an embarrassed laugh. "I do know I'll miss this like—like—"

"Like I miss pizza?"

He glowed with that laugh. A full sound, one of a man missing nothing. But the sudden lightning bolt of Roman in my brain, screeching through me like a missile, reminded me quickly of what he was missing.

"Eliza?" Nicholas said softly, his hands over mine as they held both sides of my head, trying to keep it together.

I was immortal, and this pain was a sliver of what I would know.

Shards of silver and black streaked across my vision as I opened my eyes and forced Roman out of my mind. God, Roman was in more despair now than before. I'd added to his entourage of ghosts, people he'd lost and given away.

"The visions are harder on you as a vampire when I drink, aren't they? Why am I sensing something bad's about to happen?"

"I have the same feeling," I said with a mirthless laugh. "And it's not just because you'll be withering faster with human blood that's not mine, on the other side of the world."

"My cryptic has worn off on you. Spit it out, beautiful."

"*I'm* going to be—different—when you do come back."

"So I will be able to come back eventually," he said with a deep sigh. "You let that one slip out. I won't be gone for good. I won't always be a crippled thing over there."

Crippled thing. Reminded me of what Blue had said.

"You'll be okay." *Better than okay,* I thought, and a flash of Roman slammed through me again.

"But you won't be," he said. Not a question—a statement. He'd caught on. I'd given too much away.

Another deep breath. "It will be hard for me without you, yes. But I need them to be. With you here, Nicholas—I can't see past you to know my own next move. Something is coming for me, something I have to be ready for. And whatever it is, I need it. Please understand that I can handle suffering, it's why I'm *Shinigami.* I need it to get to next."

He ran his palm over his face, like an angry father would do right before he said he wasn't mad. "It's enough for me to know that I'll be back for you," he said, his voice molten and dark. "No matter what state you're in or what you think you've changed into, it can only be more of you."

"God, Nicholas." My voice cracked and I fell into his arms once again. Every time I closed my eyes, I wanted to see him, in that translucent bubble we knew, where death didn't touch us. But I was assaulted by weakness, rained upon with horrible images, and tired. So tired.

Nicholas, my life and the very one draining the life out of me.

"I need Izanagi," I whispered, ashamed.

∾

"He's leaving you today."

Izanagi's words were robotic, exactly what I needed. Less emotion, more blood. Less loss, more growth.

"He'll be back," I said.

"Are you in pain?" the god asked me.

Pain like holding a glass that shatters in your hand. Pain I caused myself, but it was still somehow done *to me*.

"No. I'm not."

"This will help you when he goes," he breathed, his voice as ancient as the mountain breeze behind it. My mouth watered at his fresh death scent of wine and roses, and I sunk into him. His blood tasted like all the things I'd lost and all the things I wanted. It took away Roman, and left me with just enough Nicholas to keep me sane.

When I was filled, but wanted just another sip more, I took it, and my penalty was more than I could handle.

I pulled away, panting, the world moving in light speed. Simultaneous slide shows of past, present, future, worlds that didn't make sense together or apart, assaulted me from splices in the air that weren't there before.

I didn't know I was screaming until Izanagi whispered above the noise for me to stop, his voice the only thing that could penetrate the din.

"It is over," he said once. And so it was.

"I'm so sorry, I'm so sorry I took too much, I didn't mean to do it."

"Quiet. You did nothing wrong. The blood of gods doesn't lend itself to restraint." His words were an elixir for my panic. I took his hand and squeezed it, unable to speak for the overwhelming quiet in my mind.

"I didn't know how much the visions took of my mind until it was quiet. You quieted me."

He was having one of those milliseconds where he seemed almost human. "While you screamed, I saw through your eyes. Parts of my lifetimes, and worlds I do not know. The things that you will be and do, the lives of the fateless that you will touch, and many that you will not. Not but a god can see these things and expect sanity to survive."

He would save me in the treacherous weeks to come. I didn't know what they held, but I knew that without him, I'd be reduced to an animal.

"Thank you, Izanagi," I said, bowing low. "You honor me. The peace you give me now is more than I could ask for."

He said, "You did not ask for it, and it will not be yours for long."

CHAPTER 41

Nicholas and I walked like humans in the cold, early spring rain, going through the gardens, woods, well-worn walkways, bridges over half-thawed ponds. It had the tone of a date, but this was anything but a date.

"The Master wants you to have dinner with him in his room after I leave," Nicholas told me. I made a gulping noise and a face to match that was probably on the lines of pelican-ish. I didn't want to go to the principal's office, and yet, that's where I was going.

"What else did he tell you?" I asked suspiciously.

"He thinks my leaving will be too much for you."

"Why does he care?" The rain became a pelting, driving thing. I raised my head to let it soak my face.

Nicholas stopped to look at me with a disbelieving grin. "You're so smart, and so dumb. More dumb than smart maybe."

"Shut your mouth. Tell me what you're talking about."

The rain ended, or so it seemed; turned out I just wasn't

being rained on anymore. I looked up to see our snowglobe surrounding us, the rain cascading down its sides in blurry waterfalls. Translucent gray streams, never touching us. Maybe it was the proximity of his scent, the dark quiet that closed us in, but I wanted nothing more than to go home, wherever that was, and not be the future of anything.

Nicholas dropped his tattered duffel bag. It looked and smelled like Rocky Balboa's castoff, making me like it more. I smiled as he stepped closer. The world handing me a plate of brownies.

"Two reasons why the Master gives a crap about what happens to you when I leave," he said, holding up his index finger. "You're going to change everything. You've already started. Whether he likes it or not, it's his thing." Then another finger. "He loves me, and wants to keep you safe for me. It's that simple."

I smirked. "He doesn't like me. He's only doing this for you."

"And because of what you mean to the *Shinigami*. You're the first thing resembling change we've seen in countless years."

"But you didn't say he likes me."

He shrugged, cocky and dismissive. "How the hell could he? You've been a pain in his ass since you got here."

I toed my Chuck Taylors in the slush. "I'm not *that* bad."

Nicholas needled me in the ribs, laughing. "Are you serious? Even look at what you insisted on wearing today."

"I look perfectly fine. Like myself." No stuffy kimono,

no torturous wooden shoe-things. Me: cargo pants, black Converse, and a hoodie. None of the hidden pomp and formality of the Japanese temple.

I was a vampire, and I was Eliza Morgan, and I was done trying to be anything else.

"I'm not trying to fit in. If I'm—if *we* are going to move forward as a race, we should be comfortable in our own skin. This is my skin."

Nicholas leaned over and sniffed me with a sly smile. "You smell of Irish rebel."

"Kieran's one of us for a reason. And I think what you're smelling is Japanese god."

Nicholas lost the smile, and looked deep into my eyes. Izanagi's blood in me made me able to look past the entrancing mocha concoction, spinning like Nutcracker Suite dancers, into the man behind.

"Nicholas, don't be afraid of what's behind my eyes now. Izanagi lets me see clearly. No voices in my head, no other destinies fighting each other in there. He's elevated me."

He put his hands on the side of my head, pulling my forehead to rest against his. His mind whirred, working, his admiration and jealousy plain as day. "How can I not be a little afraid of you? Your existence threatens the only father I know."

I yanked my head back from his fast, electrified, the utter truth of what he said resonating in me with the weight of an entire race of creatures.

"Oh my god. You're right."

He did the rapid blinking, wide-eyed thing he does

that says he's surprised, while not too surprised to be sarcastic. It was familiar enough to help me not panic.

"I'm right?"

I looked at him like I was confessing to murder. Non-negotiable apology. "This is all his making," I said, looking around, stating only a half-truth. Izanagi made the *Shinigami*, the temple, the reason for our existence, even the mountain. But the Master claimed it as his, and had made the temple something else. "If I change all this, what else does he know? He doesn't even know his name."

The rain poured down our shield, and when Nicholas's shoulders sagged, a few drops broke through, hitting the ground with a sound that pounded my eardrums. I couldn't be sorry to Nicholas for the threat I was, for who I was. I couldn't be sorry that fate would have me take away from him someone so close.

Kat.

God almighty, fate knew how to twist the knife then throw hot coals on it and laugh in your face and say, *see? Could be worse.*

"An eye for an eye, my love," Nicholas said, eyes darting to avoid mine, to expose the anxiety there. Rain penetrated the globe more, drops hitting us with ferocity.

I pulled him to me and squeezed as hard as I could, for what I would do, for taking from him what I shouldn't, but had to. The shield he'd made over us weakened more.

I held his head to my chest and gazed up into the rain bulleting through the shimmering wall. I breathed in deep through my nose, smelling the fear of loss in the air around Nicholas. Closing my eyes, I imagined it seeping into me, a real thing that I could drink, eat, breathe.

His abandonment issues were edging in, and nothing had even happened to the Master yet. Nicholas's fear of losing the Master was worse than death.

With a roar from deep within, I consumed Nicholas's fear, letting it soak into me like the rain that punctured the snowglobe. My eyes snapped open, focusing on the places where Nicholas's shield faltered. I watched my red mist, thicker than I'd seen it before, rise and seep across Nicholas's shield, covering it from the inside, reinforcing it. The rain ran down outside again, the streams now pink through the red mist and the globe's shimmer. Rain and blood.

Nicholas's back straightened from the hunched position it was in. He looked above to the slithering mist that filled the space of the dome.

"Once again, getting all my strength from you," he said, smiling meekly.

I kissed him on the forehead. "I have plenty more where that came from." I picked up his duffel bag and we walked on.

CHAPTER 42

The Master's bungalow was greatly removed from the rest of the vampires' homes, like any leader would do. Establishing himself as one of them, but just a little apart, ever so slightly better. He loved leading the *Shinigami.* He loved his people, and he loved Nicholas. And he loved power.

Izanagi's blood was a hissing snake of knowledge in my veins.

Soundlessly, the door slid open to reveal the Master just inside. "Master," Nicholas said with a bow that I mimicked. The Master bowed back, his hands in the bells of his sleeves, and turned to go inside. Nicholas followed, stopping to remove his shoes. I took off my Chucks, determined not to be embarrassed by my holey socks.

Though the Master's home was more solid than any of the other homes at the temple, it was still extremely humble by any standard. Built of large stones from the mountain streams, and of a wood darker and thicker than what I was used to. A kettle was boiling in the fireplace. It was obvious this was the fireplace that inspired the one Nicholas had built in New Hampshire. This was home to him, too. The firelight flickered on the walls, illuminating weathered scrolls that hung there. The Master's home was cozy, cave-like. With the warmth and the rain tapping on the roof, it felt a little indulgent, something I'd been missing for a long time. I wanted to curl up under my afghan with a cup of tea in my sweats, a book from Birch Tree in my lap.

That afghan was still folded in my suitcase now, and I hadn't read a book since I got to Japan. I wanted that comfort now. I wanted all the parts of myself to be one.

The Master went about his business, his back turned as he tended to the pot over the fire. Nicholas walked past into a hallway, looking over his shoulder at me, beckoning me along.

That look could make me follow him into Hell.

"Your new room, if you want to stay here," Nicholas said.

"What? Stay here? Why would I—"

But the comfort of the room took me in right away. Smaller than where I'd been staying, and darker, it lent itself to hiding under the covers on the low bed, never looking out to see what new surprise I had coming my way. Never having to see that Nicholas was gone.

I swallowed back tears that pricked the corners of my eyes. I would not make this harder on Nicholas. But there was no hope of it not being hard on me.

"I'll think about it," I murmured, looking down.

A living apparition, Nicholas moved so quickly to be

in front of me and hold my hand that I forgot I was just like him for a moment. He was golden, good, soft as he touched me, my sadness reflected in his churning eyes. I didn't have the strength to erase it anymore.

"I trust the Master with you implicitly. I need to know the one I trust above all else is taking care of you." He swallowed, and blinked. It made my heart race, the emotion of the one second. In a pleading growl, he said, "I need your heart, soul, your blood, all of you to be protected. The thought of you being alone—unimaginable. Unimaginable."

I crumbled against him. "God, Nicholas, I'm afraid of the pain when we're apart. Not mine, but yours."

"I can handle the pain. It means you're still there." Another agonized swallow. "I love you," he said through gritted teeth, like the pain had already claimed him.

"I love you, too. If you need me to stay with the Master, I'll do it. Anything to make this easier on you."

His hands on my cheeks, he smiled, purely happy. "You'll be happier here than you think," he said. "He'll be here, but you'll still be alone. I know you need that." He kissed my forehead and turned.

"Blue," he said.

I looked over his shoulder to see Blue standing in the hallway, wide-eyed and trembling. I pushed past Nicholas to go to her and hold her hand.

"What's wrong?" I said, searching her eyes. Surprisingly, she smiled back.

"I've made a choice," she said. The hairs on the back of my neck bristled.

That's when I noticed the bag she held in one hand.

"Where are you going, Blue?" If I'd been human I might have hyperventilated. I needed her here now. Her eyes were on Nicholas behind me.

"I've thought too much about this, and you can't talk me out of it, El," Blue blurted, dropping her bag and pacing in two-step bursts, eyes on the floor. "I can't stand being afraid anymore. I'm going to New Hampshire with Nicholas."

I spun on Nicholas, waiting for an explanation.

"Eliza, I don't know what this is."

"Not really the explanation I was looking for."

"He didn't know," Blue said.

"And what is it exactly I should know?" Nicholas said. "Because I get the impression I'm swimming in trouble for it."

"Nicholas, I want to go to New Hampshire with you. You make me feel like I can leave this mountain, and experience this world, and I want that so much."

Jealousy stabbed me in the chest when Nicholas's face softened toward the tiny girl in front of him. She shuffled from one foot to the other, so vulnerable, but so powerful. Seductive.

What a mess I was next to her.

Please say no, Nicholas. Please.

"Okay."

"What?" I whispered.

They both looked at me like they'd forgotten I was there.

Nicholas flashed to my side. "She wants to do this, finally, and I could use the company."

I sneered. "Oh, could you now?" *Well, so could I,* I

wanted to say. I wanted to say that I needed someone to have pizza with, someone who would let me cry with them when it was all too much, someone who would give a crap when I told them I missed *Saturday Night Live* and moose crossing signs and going to work at a dumb tourist shop, and having coffee and nothing to do. I wanted a friend, and she was leaving with the man I loved; the same man who took friendship from me. Who'd lost his own friend, and the trust of his lover…

My mind ran away so easily since being imbued with vampirism, but it always came back to the same feelings I'd known in life: *Abandonment. Guilt. Anger.*

"Eliza," Nicholas said, lip twitching. "Are you actually jealous?"

Kieran would still be with me. I smiled as convincingly as I could at Nicholas. "No. No, I guess not. I just—miss you guys already."

Blue was on me with a hug that might have killed me. "I'll call this hug the Gorilla Killa," I squeaked out.

"Thanks for helping me get here," she whispered in my ear. "I can come back anytime I—can get up the nerve, you know."

"I know," I said. "But while you're gone, I'm using all your stuff."

CHAPTER 43

The agony that ripped through me at the sight of Nicholas walking out the door with Blue at his side had me bargaining with God or Izanagi, anyone who would listen, to please let the torture keep going for as long as he was gone. The pain that we shared when apart was how I knew I was insurmountably his.

He'd lifted me off the ground, his hands dimpling my fleshy curves, murmuring into my ear how much he loved me, how much words could never say it, how painful it was to let me go. I wanted to remember every syllable, but could only remember how it felt.

I longed already for the little signs of his presence. Hearing him open a drawer when my eyes were still closed in bed. Watching him sort through a half dozen black thermal shirts just to choose one that looked exactly like the rest. The sound of his old china cups clinking as he poured tea. The beauty outside the door that offered me silence, stillness, closeness to Heaven if there was one, was all just cardboard scenery next to sitting at a table with him.

I'd sent him away on purpose. This was a solitude I'd asked for. He left me with a creature that I didn't trust, and I all but begged him to do it. Asking for what plagues me.

Take strength from what consumes you.

I fell onto the bed that was mine for the time being, and curled up in a ball. My stomach was wrenched with the beastly pain that had been lingering out of sight, just waiting for a moment like this, to remind me what being human felt like when I'd had nothing to look forward to.

A strange coolness wrapped around me as I lie there, comforting me and making me feel both like I was outside in the budding spring, and held close in a warm blanket. I popped my eyes open to see my red mist embracing me.

"You're staying."

I leaped off the bed, chilled by the Master's silent approach, when I could hear anything, everything. So much for making myself comfortable.

"Are you offering or is this really Nicholas imposing?"

The Master smiled, but only a little. "You're important to us all for different reasons."

I stood, though there was plenty of effort involved in it. He needed to see that I could do this, face my choices on my own. Even if I couldn't.

"Did you see anything when you came in?" I asked, chin held high.

"Your mist is quite unusual, isn't it?" he said with a tight smile.

"I suppose it is. It makes me strong."

His face softened. He seemed just like a little old Japanese man then, one hand on his staff, treating it more like a cane, slightly hunched over. I sensed nothing behind his unexpected kindness, just that he knew I hurt. "It is quite difficult to see the one you love walk away," he said.

I laughed inappropriately, and my hand flew to my mouth. But he laughed, too, a rattling, pure sound.

"I'm sorry," I said. "I never thought of you..."

I saw why Nicholas loved him. It confused me that I'd not trusted him, and it confused me that I was giving up my suspicion so easily. His power thrummed through me with every false breath he took. Was it just that I was so desperate for companionship? Then again, wasn't that how he lured every single *Shinigami* to this place, isolating us all then giving us something to live for?

"It's hard to think of a strange old man like me doing anything except being strange, am I correct?" He was still laughing, and my shoulders relaxed. My head bowed, and I let out a deep breath.

The Master was next to me, hand on my shoulder. I gasped with surprise, but didn't pull away.

I wanted to give him a chance, whether it was his thrall or that I wanted him to love me like he loved Nicholas, like family.

I whimpered. The Master squeezed my shoulder, and I leaned against him. He laid his hand on my hair. Like calming a wild dog, the whole situation could be volatile at any second, but I didn't care.

"I will miss him, too," he said. "I'm sorry you're in pain."

"Thanks," I whispered.

He gently pulled my head from his thin chest to look at my face. "You can overcome the pain to grow into yourself. You are frighteningly strong. You quite frighten *me*, in fact."

Grinning, I said, "I know."

No sooner had I woken up than I found myself clung to the ceiling like a big, freak spider, a spray of scarlet around me like a—well, like a vampire shield. Even in sleep, my exhaustion couldn't keep away the emotions that were even more powerful than my senses, my strength. My mist had taken care of me in rest, and the pain didn't grip me until I felt Nicholas's absence again. I only feared for a moment before I opened my vision to him, desperate to be close.

Nicholas huddled in a dark seat, afraid to look anyone in the eye. His heart beat irregularly, each throb a stabbing pain. He could still feel my heart beating across all that distance.

He hurt worse than I did. Not one bit of him had wanted to leave.

Blue sat at his side, one hand on his back, staring straight ahead and biting her lip worriedly. Her worry made my own worry multiply about how fast my blood would wear off, how quickly he'd return to his former state of decay. My stomach buckled, and I crashed from the ceiling to the floor.

The Master crouched to help me to my feet by the elbow, saying, "Shhh, shhh, you're all right." It gave me another jolt of wonder at why I'd been rebellious since the minute I'd come to Japan, his home.

Then I thought of Izanagi, a hazy memory in the Master's sanctuary. The Master's thrall was so subtle, so enduring that it dulled even my senses.

The Master pulled me along to the main room and sat me in front of the fire on a stack of pillows. I groaned when he wrapped a blanket around my shoulders, and when the cup of tea was placed in my hand I thought I might pass out from the comfort it brought me.

"You're being so good to me," I breathed. I was apologizing, really. Jesus, I guess I should say sorry, then? Every second I fought with myself whether I was under thrall or genuinely reconsidering, or if I just missed Nicholas so much that I'd do anything to make my life easier.

He sat cross-legged next to me. "Why wouldn't I be?"

So, he was going to drag it out of me then. "I've been snotty and rebellious. I've second-guessed you, and challenged you and treated you like a mountain to climb."

He chuckled and sipped his own tea. "You have acted like no one that has ever set foot on this mountain. I would expect nothing less from Nikorasu's vampire."

Staring into the fire, I said, "I belong to Nicholas, but I am my own vampire."

That chuckle rose from his chest again. It was boisterous. *Loving*. "That you are, my friend, that you are."

I looked at him, trying to see inside, but only able to detect traces of his emotions through the pulses of power. It showed me nothing of what he really was. Izanagi was restless in the woods outside.

"Do you trust me?" I asked him outright.

Long white hair rustled as he turned his head to study me through blind eyes. "Trust is an emotion that I have tried to forget."

"But you trust Nicholas."

"And for that reason, you are still alive," he said with the same warmth he'd been speaking with all along. He rose and left me to watch the fire burn.

CHAPTER 44

The Master came and went as though I didn't exist. But for the pain, I might not have been sure I existed either. The longer I went without Izanagi's blood, the more I was attacked by visions of fates I knew nothing about. Surges of dread, restlessness, helplessness; the same dense despair when I stood in front of my parents' caskets and knew I was totally alone. The scent of wine and roses synonymous with death itself, with Izanagi, now a crouching predator waiting to slide itself into my thoughts.

These pictures in my mind were bits and pieces that belonged to other people, maybe other vampires, and I needed to find their owners. Nancy Eliza Drew, putting the clues together.

I threw on my hoodie and cargo pants with vampire speed and slipped outside, the Master nowhere in sight. The sun flooded my every pore, momentarily chasing away the dull, sightless fog the visions left me in. A pang of sadness came with my sigh of relief.

I could only stand the sunlight because I'd killed Clara Borden.

Nicholas loved the sunlight. It made him glow even when he was at his most gaunt and lifeless. With a deep breath, my mind opened up. Within a second I saw him carrying a stack of paperbacks with wrinkled bindings in Birch Tree Books—he avoided the windows. No sunlight for him then. I could smell the familiar must. The dust motes danced around the windowsill, the too-strong coffee from the old pot on the register, the peppermint-brownie of *him*, all things that sang of home. Nicholas looked up, his eyes dimmer than I liked, but still full of strength.

So my blood was potent in him, still.

"You're a shoddy replacement for Roman, the eternal babysitter, Nicholas. You can't make me check in with you like a grounded teenager."

"A grounded teenager wouldn't check in because he wouldn't be going anywhere. Keep up, Lynch."

Lynch showed up behind Nicholas in the vision, angry, fists curled. Nicholas didn't even turn around.

"You'll be happy to know my fangs haven't come out to play once today," Lynch said. He *was* checking in with Nicholas, like it or not. This wasn't the headstrong psychopath I knew.

This was a lost man looking for direction.

"Nice job. You can live to see another day." Nicholas stacked books on a pile of more books, his hands around

them to keep them from falling. They fell anyway. Nicholas turned to Lynch, who glared back.

"You won't kill me," Lynch said. *"I'm your only company,"* he added with a sneer. *"It wasn't enough for Roman to be errand boy for the great Nicholas French."*

Nicholas's eyes narrowed dangerously. The playful wit vanished, and his hand closed on Lynch's throat, fingers tight on his windpipe. A bead of sweat trickled down my own back as I watched Nicholas's lip curl in an animalistic snarl, his breath making puffs of cold smoke, frost crawling up Lynch's throat from his fingertips.

"It takes more than a lapdog to keep you alive, you ass. You should have thanked that man every day for your miserable existence. I would never have let you keep it. If not for Roman, the Master would have turned the other cheek long ago for me to stop this life of yours. If that's what you call it." Nicholas pushed Lynch back by his throat, leaving him gagging and smiling, as his personality dictates.

"You need me to focus on, or you'd have nothing," Lynch spat. *"But don't take it out on me that Roman deserted you. He didn't murder the woman you loved first."*

I shuddered, shaking the vision away, stomach rolling. The combination of Nicholas so far from me and Lynch showing actual emotion was painful.

"You're here," I heard from behind me.

I spun to find the only person on the mountain I wanted to see; Kieran. His eyes were red-rimmed, his five o'clock shadow a full beard, shoulders slumped. Reminiscent of Nicholas, actually.

"Kieran." I wanted to wrap my arms around him and

kiss him with all the energy I had left. "You don't look—like yourself."

He stepped towards me, hands in his pockets, head focused on the grass below. "I thought you'd left, woman," he said with a hint of shyness that made me groan inside. He looked up at me when he was close, the dull fire in his eyes flickering darkly. It seemed as tired as he did. "I am very alone," he said. And he put his forehead on my shoulder.

I put my arms around him, squeezing him as close as I could. "I'm so sorry, I've been, I don't know, mourning I guess? I'm sorry to have left you alone. I should have known you'd be like this, with Blue gone, and Leann, and now me—"

He pulled his hands from his pockets and placed them on my upper arms, head still resting on my shoulder. "Everyone else is so boring," he said with a grim laugh. "That Paolo boy has been all over me, and my God, I can't stand it."

I laughed, squeezing him tighter, then reluctantly letting go. I picked up his head by his fuzzy cheeks, and smiled to see the glint of fire in his eyes brighten.

"You've been staying with the Master?" he said, eyebrows furrowed.

"Yeah, actually. It just sort of happened. Nicholas asked me to, and when he left—well, I kinda collapsed in there and, well—I've fallen and I can't get up."

His mouth fell open, eyes blinking, incredulous. "It's been weeks, Eliza. You haven't been out of there for *weeks*. We all thought you'd left, too." He ran a hand through his spiky, messy hair that was in need of washing.

Weeks? How was that possible? My mind couldn't wrap around it, I had just fallen asleep, and vampires don't need to sleep that long... I had to change the subject, had to learn more without bringing Kieran into it anymore.

"Kieran, how have you been without Blue?"

A grimace that turned into a sad smile. "Don't worry about me, Eliza, I always burn on."

I squinted into the grass trying to replace the vision that popped up. Jesus, but they were frequent and without warning.

"What do you see?" he whispered, his fingers brushing my arm.

"I don't know. They hit me from all sides, and I don't know who or what—I don't know." With those visions taking me over, time was surreal, undefinable. Could I really have been in the Master's house for that long? Weeks, with Nicholas thinking I was...was...just fine without him.

He cleared his throat. "Rumor has it that you took off with Nicholas and Blue to hide your visions from the Master."

"Where did this rumor come from?"

Kieran glanced sideways, like he was waiting for the cops to break us up. "It seems to me Paolo knows something he shouldn't."

I'd been surprised by Paolo's sudden closeness to the Master when I returned from Clara. The way he'd turned on me when the Master was watching, it hurt me, but it was Paolo. I trusted him. We all had secrets, but we were still ourselves.

"No, no way. He's too loyal, if not to me, to Nicholas."

With a snort, "And to God. Rumor-spreading isn't in his nature."

Kieran licked his lips, a darting thing that was full of warning somehow. "No man is above his nature, woman, and no vampire can be tamed. Remember that. There's always something inside pushing out, wanting to prove itself. Paolo wants to be more, just like any one of us."

I found myself shaking my head at the beauty of his words, the darkness and heat of him. He was a remarkable creature, and waking from my slumber to him was like opening my eyes in a museum.

"So, tell me, gorgeous. Why are you hiding your bits and pieces from the Master?"

Kieran wouldn't have spoken a word about what happened that night with Clara to anyone. I believed this more than I believed in anything. He wouldn't want me to give any more of myself to our *cause*. Telling the Master that I could see the other fates of the *unmei nashi,* of the *Shinigami,* would be like putting a leash on me.

I wondered how long this dog could hide under his roof.

"I'd be the center of attention here, a sideshow. My purpose has to be *mine* for now."

Kieran swallowed, shuffling his feet. "The Master will make a slave of you if he finds out, Eliza."

My fangs splintered into my lip and the grass in front of me grew red with as my mist spread across it.

"He can try."

Kieran and I went back to my room, my *real* room, in the plain light of day, to the surprise and hissing of some of the *Shinigami* we passed.

"Their tunes change without Nicholas around, don't they?" I said with a mean-spirited grin towards a hulking beast of a vampire.

"They don't know if you're predator or dictator, dear girl. They know you have power, and they're more afraid of it than envious."

"Monster!"

I spun on a small group of vampires shying from the light in a doorway. They huddled together, hissing at me like the witches in *The Clash of the Titans*. The one who spoke stood a little taller, but still looked like an animal dragged through the dirt in the dark.

A whirlwind of red wound around my legs, spiraling up my body in a tornado of decay, the scent of wine and roses. The world emptied of emotion as I raised my hands up to the sky, as if I could make it grow to the clouds, and I rose from the ground like I was ready to try.

"You don't know what monsters are," I hissed at the quivering vampires below. They flashed away in shadows, leaving me to return to Kieran's side.

"Putting on a little show, are we, lass?" he said with a smirk.

"I won't let my power be bigger than me, and I sure as hell won't be intimidated."

He growled under his breath, and it arose a stirring in me to match. I snarled like a primal thing, and Kieran responded with an electric scent, eyes flashing when they met mine. Nature at its wildest.

Shaking it off, I tried to regain my humanity. These momentary bursts of unbridled force were addictive, and I wouldn't let them control me.

Kieran ran his fingers down my arm, a path of sparks left in their wake as they touched my skin, a sizzling clue to our magnetism.

"Eliza, we need to reel you in." He was panting, eyes following the jumping sparks on my skin. "It's like you fell asleep and woke up with a little extra magic. More than a little magic."

My power took over, and a blinding vision of Roman, shivering in the same spot I left him weeks, or months before, pulled into my brain like a train from Hell. I screamed with the intensity of it, the odor of dirt and neglect, the creaking of the floorboards from the wind outside, and him, a golem without the sense to hide from the horror. He flickered out of sight, reappearing at the door of a patient's room. His fangs came out, and he went inside with a deadly purpose, yet not one that called to him. Not his *unmei nashi.*

"Oh. When the hell did that get here?" I said, swatting my mist away. I flashed an insecure smile at Kieran, who didn't return it, just stared at me with grave concern.

"You have less control of yourself than I thought," he said.

"I was born yesterday, pretty much, and then was....what? In a coma or something for a few weeks? I'll get it. I'll get it." Of course I would.

He ran his hands through his hair a bunch of times, the pinup tattoo on his arm dancing with every movement. "We're missing something. These visions are getting stronger, and so are you, but it's like you're on two different frequencies."

I gritted my teeth and said, "They're incessant now that I'm *Shinigami.*"

"And when you drank from Clara, you saw not only her other fate, but Roman's as well." His eyebrows furrowed, and he groaned as if it hurt to think. "What if we experiment a bit?"

"I don't like the sound of that at all."

"Hear me out, now, you know I won't let anything hurt you. What if you drink a *vampire's* blood? Not Izanagi, he's..." He licked his lips, eyes filled with excitement. Such a child with a box of matches.

"I drank Nicholas's blood."

"Could you see anything?"

"I wouldn't let myself."

"So you *can* control this some." He breathed in deep through his nose. "You said when you drank from Izanagi that everything was clear. The longer you go without blood, the more muddled your mind becomes."

"It's more than that. These visions are missing pieces, waiting for me to find the right person to connect them with. But they aren't my *unmei nashi.*"

"Jesus, where is Blue when I need her wares? I could really use a beer."

I laughed, for what felt like the first time in months. "We could go to the, uh, *tea room.*"

His lips spread in a wicked grin, his arms crossed over his chest. He put the tip of his thumb in his mouth and I nearly passed out. Kat would have fallen over for sure.

"Eliza, you just woke up from a three week nap. You

need a night out carousing with me? Or do you need to figure out what it is that ails you?"

"Maybe what ails me is that I need a break."

He crossed the room in one motion, the scent of burning embers following him. "Let's break some rules."

The tea room seemed more like a bar this time. Vampires were laughing, lounged out on the floor and being more social than I knew them to be. The music was less traditional, more sultry, like it hid secrets of its own.

Kieran slapped his hands together, rubbing them greedily. "Now this is more like it!" His whole body relaxed, a strut replacing his protective hover over me. I watched him walk ahead, body equal parts lithe and rippling musculature, confidence a cloud of smoke around him. There wasn't a woman in the room who didn't have eyes for him. I kept myself from hissing.

"He doesn't belong to you," I whispered to myself. He glanced over his shoulder at me with a look the devil couldn't copy, and I bared my teeth in response. An animal's reaction, but the only emotion I was capable of showing.

We sat in the same place we'd been before, and a girl came right over with a pitcher of something that smelled like cranberry and heat. A low growl emitted from me. "What is that?" I said in a voice I didn't know to Kieran. He poured us both a cup, and my mouth watered, fangs tingling.

"Blood and beer, love. Can't be beat." He handed me the cup at eye level, eyes glinting.

My hand was too fast for even my eyes to follow. I grabbed it and chugged it down, throat filling with bloody, hoppy perfection. It dripped from the corners of my mouth; I wiped it with the back of my hand, then licked it off. I didn't stifle my grunt when I said, "More."

Kieran threw his head back with a gorgeous, sinful laugh, and did indeed pour another. I waited for him to tip his first back, slower than I had, and then we both gulped the second fast.

The room got lazy for me, the scene slower while my mind got sharper. An amazing contrast, the blood making me hyper-aware while the beer calmed me. I never wanted it to end.

"You've picked your poison, I see," Kieran said, leaning over the table. God, he smelled good. Fire and brimstone. Like everything that held me back, burned and left behind. It was simple now, to see what he was to me.

He incinerated everything I was told to be. He was my birth by fire.

I met him halfway across the table, the rich scent of blood beer wafting up between us. I grabbed him by the back of the neck and I kissed him like he deserved to be kissed. Like he was my savior and fury, passion and freedom. Like he was the smoke of burning villages and fired cannons.

He apologized for nothing and slipped his tongue inside. Every rule that shouldn't apply to me, broken.

"Well, aren't we friendly with the all the wrong people?"

We both looked up to see Leann standing there, like a spoiled brat kid catching her older sister with a boy.

"Leann," Kieran said throatily. He leaned back. "Haven't seen hide nor hair of you. Where have you been?"

She crossed her arms and tapped her foot like a real bitch. "It matters to you, *shugotenshi?*" she spat. "You've been occupied with someone else's woman." Her eyes on me were meant to be harsh, but they felt too empty, and I felt too full.

"Yes, it does matter to me," Kieran said. "I created you. I want to know that you're well."

She looked well, all right. The colors about her that seemed drab as the hidden human she'd been were vibrant now, defiant. Bright blonde hair, deep dark eyes, lips with an erotically pink pucker. So full of resentment and ferocity, she resembled a fallen angel.

My eyes were stuck on her jugular. I shocked myself with need to taste her blood.

A sneer revealed her sparkly new vampire fangs. "You did your job, Kieran. I don't need you to hold my hand in the afterlife, I'm doing just fine on my own."

"Then why are you so bitter to me, woman? Did you want something else?" he said huskily. Without looking, I knew he was running his eyes all over her.

"Don't flatter yourself." Her lips turned down with a childlike sadness. She shook her head a little, ready to regret saying what she would say next. "I don't want anything from you, and holy Hades, is it ever liberating to not have that *connection*, without supernatural handcuffs holding me to you, but it would have been nice if you hadn't cast me off so fast. If you showed you even *liked* me, even once. That I wasn't a chore for you."

That vein in her neck pulsed. I sipped my drink to keep myself from looking at it, and watched Kieran over the top of my cup.

He sat up, losing some of the rebel he'd been. "Neither of us wanted to be best friends. Neither of us wanted that blasted invasion-of-the-body-snatchers brain itch. You were as happy to be rid of it as I was. There's a reason you were chosen for me—we'll see it in time. Until then, we have our lives back. Easy come, easy go."

She looked away, making the tendons on her neck stand out even more. I shivered. When she looked back, she was smiling a tight smile, but the abrasiveness was gone.

"I guess I can live with that." She turned her body to me. "Why do I have the feeling you want to drink my blood?"

Kieran looked at me with surprise, but I only had eyes for Leann. When the words came out, I knew they were true, and that fate showed itself at the strangest times and in the oddest ways.

"There's something in your blood that I need."

CHAPTER 45

"You want to drink *her* blood?" Kieran's voice squeaked, and I laughed, but my gaze remained on Leann, whose eyes were darting, equal parts disbelief and scared rabbit.

"Where can we go?" I said to neither of them in particular, ready to imagine myself there and be there faster than any living thing could do. This was my world now.

I saw Kieran chug the rest of his blood beer out of the corner of my eye. "We go to Blue's," he said over the clank of the cup on the table, the liquid still thick in his throat. "Nobody will look for us there."

I dragged my eyes off Leann, as if being released from a hypnotist. "You're coming with us?"

He opened his arms, Jesus-style, giving me a look that was like Nicholas incarnate. "Like I'd miss this?"

Grabbing them both by the arms, I envisioned the three of us at Blue's, and we got there fast. Leann was screaming as if I'd brought her on a roller coaster, and

Kieran doubled over, hands on his knees, muttering that he was tired of Eliza surprises. I couldn't concentrate, Leann's blood singing a morbid chorus.

When he recovered, Kieran walked into Blue's room like he lived there. I had a gut-punch of jealousy that I willed away quick, replacing it with guilt.

Blue's place looked like she never left, and I missed her. There were still peanut butter cup wrappers on her otherwise sumptuous bed. The bathroom door was open and a fluffy purple towel lay on a heap on the floor.

Leann walked past me and sat on the bed.

"Dear lord," Kieran said beside me. I rolled my eyes.

"You're sure you can let me do this?" I said to Leann. "Because I think I'd do it anyway."

I *liked* the fear in her eyes. "I don't think I could stop you," she said with a reluctant sniff of laughter.

The hint of challenge was enough to make the red mist start to bubble around my feet, creep like eager fingers up my calves with a sickly warmth that begged me to do bad things. My sharp grin felt sinful, and I indulged it for a second before I willed it away to do what fate needed me to do.

"No, Leann, you probably can't stop me. So, enjoy giving in while you can."

With a movement that even I recognized to be a little too much like something from *The Ring*, I was leaning on one knee over her, pushing her back, her eyes blank in their trepidation. Kieran groaned behind us, but I couldn't pay him any mind. Leann's blood was a magnet for me, and I dove into her throat like a murderous machete.

Her scream was too far away, underwater. The instant

I tasted her life source, I was nothing but an animal, with no more thought but how to get more.

Until the image swooped on me, and it was all I could do to keep myself from echoing Leann's lingering scream.

I forced myself to continue drinking through the horror I saw. Leann's undead blood was decadent, an exquisite dessert when you'd had too much. Every mouthful was heavenly, but the path to the gate was lined with razor blades. I winced as I swallowed until I couldn't bear it another second.

With a thrust, I jumped off of her, my red shield in angry swirls. I hovered near the ceiling, as far from Leann as I could get, but never would I get away from what I'd seen. Never.

"Get out," I hissed at her, the words erupting through the shield like a bullet.

She sat up like a drunken sex toy of a girl, hair in her face, sticky with her own blood. "Wha—what?"

"Now."

She gaped at Kieran, who said nothing, before disappearing into the night, leaving the door open behind her.

I lowered myself to the floor, my eyes on Kieran, who was pale and shaky. Again, I should have been ashamed that I'd instilled fear in someone so strong, but it felt so *right*. This was how I was supposed to be seen.

It gave me temporary reprieve from what *I* had seen.

"What in blazes just happened, Eliza? You're making me doubt my own sanity."

But now that I was settling down, and the singular image stood in my brain like the Grim Reaper waiting for that final moment, I couldn't look Kieran in the eyes.

"I think should talk to the Master," I whispered.

Softly, he said, "I think you should talk to me first."

I stared at our feet, inches apart, and I let my eyes travel up his body to his face, a mixture of sadness, puppy dog vulnerability, and fierce protectiveness.

I became a little more inhuman in that moment. A little more beaten.

"What did you see in there?" he asked me, head cocked to one side.

My chest could cave in with the weight of my words.

"You. I saw you."

CHAPTER 46

Kieran's silence was built on fear, mine on confusion. Leann's blood left a trail of conflicting images as it rushed through me. Too many deaths. Deaths that would cripple me with loss, fear, and helplessness. Again.

"I wish you'd tell me more about my starring role in your vision before you tell the Master, who neither of us trust or even like." Kieran whispered this in my ear as we stood outside the Master's home, waiting for nothing. He knew we were there, I could feel it.

The Master appeared out of thin air in front of the closed door. "Why say the same thing twice?" he said. "Come inside."

I looked to the woods before going inside. I wanted Izanagi to be there, and he wasn't. Even the original death god ran from the war raging inside me.

"You must start at the beginning," the Master said, pouring tea. "Tell me everything."

I had no choice but to look for guidance, and the Master was it. Izanagi was who I wanted to lead me, but the Master was the one I had to have.

Short version. No time for pomp. "When I drank from my *unmei nashi*, I could see the other fate that awaited her. Another vampire."

The Master stiffened, milky eyes growing colder. He nodded, urging me onward.

"And I saw that vampire's other fate, too. What would happen to him if that fate was realized." Still, silence. "I can see the alternative for both *unmei nashi* and the *Shinigami*."

The Master stared, the cold chill of him radiating around him. He took a sip of tea.

"Why the urgency to tell me this now?" he said a second later.

I gulped, the taste of Leann still in my throat. "Because I just drank from Leann."

"You drank from the young one? A *Shinigami?*" The Master's anger caused the rays of white cold around his body to shiver.

"I did. That's not the problem. The problem is that…" Jesus, was I really going to let this go further than my own mind? I wanted to chain it up in my head and take control of it.

"Tell us, please," Kieran said. I was reminded with perfect clarity why I needed help.

The image jabbed my mind, bursting through the constant stream of swimming visions that I'd learned to block out. But not this one. Not this one.

"I saw Kieran," my voice cracked, "burning. In a pillar

of fire, his body consumed in it so all I could see was his outline, bright, brighter than the flames." I could see nothing in the room, only *this*. "He's in there, perfectly still, waiting to—to be *gone*. He doesn't even scream, but his pain is—unthinkable."

Kieran put a hand on my back, soothing *me*.

I couldn't look at him. "There's more," I said to the Master across the table. The world stopped. "Leann is there, just watching. She just watches him burn."

"Her blood showed you that," Kieran said in a small voice.

"Nicholas is there, too, watching," I said, ashamed.

"Nikorasu?" The Master's back straightened even more, the shock in his voice palpable. "He has such power with the cold, but he doesn't stop it?"

I nodded, looking down into my teacup.

"They want me dead," Kieran said.

My head snapped up. "No, I don't think that's— entirely—true." The maliciousness in the vision, a snap- shot of jealousy and venomous rage shook me, but it was so strong it was impossible to tell who it came from. I shuddered to think of that kind of hatred coming from my Nicholas, but the memory of him murdering that vampire at Leann's ceremony was vivid. "Anyway, you're safe as long as Nicholas is in New Hampshire."

"Ah, woman, you underestimate me."

"Never." I kept to myself how unnerved I was that Kieran didn't put up a fight in my vision.

He wanted it.

The Master stiffened, opaque eyes cruel. "Nikorasu is the most supreme of death gods, the best of us all. He would never allow himself to be reduced by such cruelty." The cold around him reached for me like icicle fingers. "And I am disappointed that you would believe it possible."

Guilt. More guilt. "I can't believe it either," I said. "But you asked me to tell you everything, and I did. It doesn't have to become truth, but you'd be foolish to think we aren't all capable of that level of viciousness. You're a greater being than that, to be so naïve."

The Master flew to his feet with an icy blast, rage shaking his body.

"What now?" Kieran said out of the corner of his mouth to me.

I rose to my feet, too, but kept my red mist at bay. This was not a time to intimidate.

"Master, you can't admit I'm right because you'd be wrong. Every one of us can change, and the world will change with us, one way or the other. If you aren't a part of that, then the world will eat you alive."

The air between us electrified with our tension, but the Master's chill subsided, leaving a small, ancient man standing alone.

Kieran's warm hand closed around my calf, shooting heat up my leg.

"What is it?" I asked, looking down at his puppy eyes.

"*Unmei nashi.*"

"You? Now?"

Kieran widened his eyes at me. "Yeah, right now, woman. I have to go."

"Can't it wait?" I hissed. But I saw the hollows under his eyes, and knew it couldn't.

The Master sat again. "He must go to his calling, and you must stay here where I can protect you."

"Me? Protect me from what?"

A surge of prideful anger welled in me as I answered my own question.

Leann.

CHAPTER 47

Kieran bolted off with such speed that it burned a black spot into the floor where he'd sat. The Master leaned over the table, and looked at the still-smoking stain.

"Hmph," he said.

I bit my lip to keep from smiling.

After several long moments of me wondering what to do next and figuring out just as fast that I didn't know, I realized that the Master was probably waiting for me to ask him.

"What do we do next?"

His thin shoulders jutted out as he tended the fire, long white hair dangerously close to the flames. "Do you need my help, Eliza?" he asked. Thank God I couldn't see the smirk on his face.

"I do. It's why I came." I had to take my own advice and be willing to change. I went to the Master for help and now I was irritated to have to ask for it. Childish. "I won't let Kieran burn."

The air froze behind him in his movement to me. He stroked his long beard. "Things become clear in battle. We train."

"We train? Now? Will there be a montage? The timing seems incredibly poor."

He ignored me. "You need to shed this shell and see what must be seen. It comes clear when the warrior kicks in the door of civility. You must fight."

I looked down at the clothes I'd been wearing too long. Such things just didn't occupy my mind space as a vampire.

"I'll need to change."

The sparring arena was laid bare, no longer under heaps of snow. As troubled as I was, I was taken aback by springtime newness jumping at my vampire senses like the pirates in that Disney World ride. Enjoyable, but disarming.

The falling petals from the cherry trees had a shushing sound all their own, as loud as the birds singing and the cry of my crows. The silence of the flowers bursting to life was deafening. The brilliant red roofs and intricate scroll-work and symbols that adorned the temple walls wriggled with sentient energy. Wind chimes carried a scent of life that mingled with the scent of death I carried, creating a blissful home where I was both stimulated and comforted.

But there was no time for comfort as I stood toe to toe

with a hulking *Shinigami* man, who stared at me like I was an alien. The muscles on his muscles had muscles. His fresh soil skin boasted black symbols tattooed on his neck and bald head. Gold hoop earrings hung from both ears.

And his fear of me was evident in every twitch of his fingers and musculature.

Pink and white petals rained around us. The Master slashed his hand through them silently, signaling for the fight to begin.

I'd never received formal training. I knew none of Nicholas's *katas*, had no long and drawn out smashing of my arms on a wooden dummy or carrying of water buckets for miles. For me, that would all have to come later, if at all. I was different, and my need was urgent. And Nicholas had once told me that to be good at form one had to be good at fighting, but not necessarily the other way around. I didn't question the Master's choice to pit me in a fight without training; I learned best when faced with the impossible.

We bowed, and my opponent began circling me like a wildcat. I mimicked him, curious to see if he would attack first.

His movements were fast, but not as fast as mine, which shocked me, frankly. It's not as if I was physically fit, even with the sparse diet of fish and vegetables. But I blocked one front kick, and a second, before he caught me with a jumping back kick, leaving me sprawled on the ground at least fifty feet away. With an ache in my gut that was definitely going to stick around for a few days, I grunted pulling myself up, only to be pounded back down with a powerful fist.

You really do see stars when you're hit that hard.

I shook it off, but my vision was blurry. My dead heart pounded in my chest with anticipation of the next bout of blows, and my legs ached as if I'd thrown countless kicks, but I don't think I'd thrown even one. I swayed, the multi-colored world spinning sickly.

To my horror, the Master barked out the order to continue fighting.

The dark blur came at me, and I threw a wild punch, catching him on the jaw. He stumbled back, giving me a second to regain my sight, but only just. As he tripped over himself, I followed up with a roundhouse kick to his kidney that made my thigh muscles scream with exertion. I knew the names of these kicks, the basic ones, because of Nicholas, but had no idea how to *throw* them. None-theless, they worked. The monstrous vampire fell back more, and with every last ounce of power in me, I leaped into the air, the dizzying colors and sounds making my stomach turn, and spun myself into a contorted kick that only an inhuman thing could manage. It landed on his face, knocking him out cold.

When I fell to the ground on one knee, I was seconds from sobbing. Every bone in my body hurt from our brief match. I'd been broken. Lost. Suffering like I'd known when Nicholas and I had parted in New Hampshire, when I couldn't bring myself to eat, or sleep, care that I was cold. Despair that dwarfed my physical agony. Failure. This was one millionth of the pain I'd suffered in my life, made worse because Nicholas wasn't here.

All becomes clear in battle.

That this pain is only a fraction of the pain I had felt in my life and would know in my eternity.

That all my suffering was for a purpose.

That being alone was my strength.

That no amount of suffering was too great if it helped my Nicholas somehow.

That pain was the way I learned and saw what was next. I was destined to suffer for that which consumes me gives me strength.

"Dokkoudou." Izanagi's voice, only for me, from a place deep in the woods. The words reverberated through my bones: The path of aloneness.

I stopped panting, because being out of breath was in my head. My opponent was stirring on the ground in front of me. I knelt by him, and wiped dirt off of his smooth skin, relishing the sensation of every pore under my fingerprints. *So alive, even now...* His eyes flickered open, and he looked at me with an admiration and fear I was growing accustomed to.

"You're terrifying," he said, his voice a booming, thunderous thing. His wide grin made me grin in return.

It felt ridiculous to offer my hand to help up such a giant of a man, but I did it anyway. He laughed and accepted, rising to his feet and shocking me with a bear hug.

I stood beside the Master as we watched my new friend flash out of sight. When he was gone, my knees buckled, and the Master threw one bony arm around my waist.

"Have you seen what you need to see?" he asked softly.

I met his eyes that scared and magnetized me, and

knew only respect for him. "Right now, the only thing I need to see is a bed."

The pain of Nicholas's absence and my mind-melting visions drove me through more rigorous training over the next few days, much of it with the Master himself. I didn't need to sleep, and was hungry to do something, anything. I stretched when I wasn't sparring, meditated when I wasn't stretching, and watched sparring in between. It took my mind off of Kieran, who I hadn't seen since my confessions to the Master, off of Leann, who was nowhere to be found, and off of Nicholas. But on the fourth day, the battling visions in my head came to the forefront again, wearing me down as much as the physical aches.

"You are pained today. Differently." The Master appeared next to me at the door where I looked out at the fresh life sprouting on the mountain. I breathed every creature's breath in those woods.

Where was Izanagi?

I cracked my neck in an unbecoming way. "I'm just tired," I said.

"Tired and weary are different things." He put his hand on my shoulder. It touched that place inside where kindness makes pain worse. I held my breath to will the tears away.

"Do not fight off how deeply you love," the Master said. His words made my tears spill over. "No one can abandon you as much as you abandon yourself. Do not let Nikorasu become less to you because he is not here."

I turned to him, captivated by how he could read my soul through the chaos of my mind. "I miss Nicholas so much."

"As do I. I always do when he's not here." He sighed, looking out at the rustling leaves, and gave me a rare, endearing smile of uneven teeth. "Few understand what an ancient thing like myself can be passionate about."

"Honestly, I expected you to say something anciency, like, 'We all share the same Earth and never truly miss each other.' It's nice that you just miss him like I do."

Without a reply, he disappeared and returned with the afghan out of my suitcase. I hadn't taken it out the entire time I'd been in Japan; it felt out of place. But when someone offers me my actual security blanket, it changes things.

"We miss our loved ones most in times of growth," he said as he sat me down on a stack of pillows. "And grow, you have. You've thrown yourself into your training with heart. It is clear you're learning more than just how to fight."

"I have much to fight for," I said quietly. Never mind that the ones I fought for also fought each other.

"You must sleep," the Master said, brushing the hair that fell out of my ponytail away from my neck. I didn't know he could be so loving, and that I could draw such strength from it. But I suppose, had I listened to Nicholas, if I'd seen what he'd tried to show me, I would have known.

"I don't want to sleep," I said. I'd loved a nap in life, but it was such a waste of eternity, and I'd rested plenty. Falling asleep with the warring visions, without Nicholas, hurt like a punched bruise. The pain already gathered in a knot at my throat, and my hand went to it. My companion watched, knowingly.

He said not a word as I ambled to my room in the back of his home, and soundlessly slid the door closed.

CHAPTER 48

V ampire sleep is like drowning in the dark. It took me over, smothered me, until I wanted it.

The Master came in to my room to wake me, silently handing me a glass of water, which I drank with eyes on him. I appreciated the crisp cold of the mountain water as much as blood, so vastly different it was than the tap water in New Hampshire; and *that* water was from a mountain.

There was no way he was getting me to fight. Vampire stamina coupled with *Shinigami* training was doing little for me, it seemed. I'd been death-ray blasted with exhaustion and I needed to sleep forever.

"You have a visitor," the Master said with a little smile. *Kieran.*

I shouldn't have wanted him to come to me as much as I did. But Kieran didn't want me to be anything I wasn't, or wasn't yet, or was supposed to try to be. I needed that. I always would.

The Master left my room, and I pulled the blankets up, even though I was fully dressed. I slept fully dressed all the time now, a testament to how much I didn't give a crap about clothes, I guess, or was just so exhausted I didn't care. I watched the door, patting my disastrous hair down, and waited for Kieran.

But it was Paolo who walked in. I hadn't seen him since I returned from feeding on Clara Borden. When he'd all but turned on me to side with the Master.

He gave me a sheepish smile as he closed the door behind him. He'd unnerved me at the temple, digging for information that I didn't want to give, and I sensed an ulterior motive. I hated ulterior motives. Now, he was the boyish, pious, peaceful young man that I'd warmed to immediately upon my arrival. The one that Nicholas had taken under his wing. My trepidation disappeared instantly.

He whisked across the room with more of a whisper than a *snap*, the way Nicholas did. Paolo worked alongside this world, while Nicholas exploded into it. I loved the difference between them, and the friendship they had in spite of it.

Sitting on the end of my bed, he blushed, and dipped his head. We laughed at his shyness together.

"Eliza, I apologize for how I behaved at the temple," he said, his Italian accent more pronounced with his earnestness.

"I was pretty irrational, in your defense."

"And frightening."

"I was not," I said, throwing a pillow at him.

"Oh, yes you were," he said, catching it. His smile

turned down, his eyes still on mine. "You must understand, Eliza. You're the closest thing I've seen to a miracle in my existence. I want to be part of it. I want to know what happens next, what it means." His blush returned. "What *you* mean to us all." The gold cross around his neck glinted in a stream of sunlight. He didn't shy away from the beam, like I did.

"Paolo," I said quietly, suddenly shy myself. "I'm hardly a miracle. I'm just different from what you know. And I'm not afraid to be different."

He smiled with infectious hope. "Change is miraculous when you've gone this long without it. You're a symbol of freedom for the *Shinigami* that we were unaware we needed." Springtime came alive in him as he spoke, the cherry blossom scent in the air lifting from his pores, the sunshine from his eyes.

Things were changing because the *Shinigami* wanted them to. I was the change they wanted. So, I told Paolo what I could do, the things I could see.

"Why didn't you tell us after you fed that first time?" The softness of his lips, his smile and demeanor was a comfort I needed.

"It was too raw, too much at stake. This is something in my *soul*, this ability. It's hard to let anyone, you know…see it."

He reached his hand across the bed and held mine, the priest in Paolo clothing. "Part of your gift is in the releasing of it," he said with a gentle smile. "This is your time to let the world see what you're capable of. Your anonymous days are over."

"I'm going to need a beer."

~

I drank a lot of beer. Not blood beer, Budweiser. I hated Budweiser, and the headache that lived inside the bottle, but it was what the Master brought me.

"I can't believe you drink Budweiser," I said to the Master, the fifth one going down easier than the first four.

The Master took a sip of his own. "It seems in my everlasting old age that only terrible flavors tend to linger."

"Thanks, Master," I said quietly, trying not to hate the vulnerability this showed. "For letting me stay here, for taking care of me."

His eyes didn't seem so terrifying as he looked at me then. Almost like he had pupils under that creamy haze. "Thank you for seeing past your fear of me," he said.

"I wasn't afraid of you."

Paolo stiffened. So, I'd said the right thing.

"Are you certain that's true?" the Master said with a sideways smile, showing his old man vampire teeth.

"Do you want it to be? Is fear the way you run the show?" I smiled back, the challenge accepted.

"Fear is not a sign of weakness, Eliza. Not admitting it is."

"I don't need to admit what isn't true. You unsettle me, but I'm not afraid." My smirk was jerky, and I shouldn't have done it probably. "Are you afraid of not being feared?"

My heart ached as I pictured Nicholas making a comment about me being better looking, but not as well-spoken as Yoda.

The Master didn't falter. "I am feared by all. But it is change that I fear."

Even I know when to shut up.

I don't know how long the three of us were together, but I do know that I fell asleep with a soundless certainty that didn't trouble me.

Until I woke up.

The Master hovered in my room again, glass of water in hand, smiling pleasantly. So why did I tremble with the fear I said didn't exist for me? He sat on the end of my bed, where Paolo had sat the day before. I'd become no more than an invalid getting hospital visits. "Eliza, you've made me think about things I've not had to consider for a very long time," he said.

Dread snaked into my bloodstream, raced through my skin.

"What exactly might those things be?"

"That those who do not accept change accept death into their hearts. I cannot make that mistake. We will move forward together, Eliza."

"Ooookay."

"I believe you should drink from another *Shinigami*. Let us see what you can see."

The churning of my mist begin inside, ready to create a shield around me.

"I guess I could? But I haven't had any *draw* to anyone since Leann. They only seem to call to me if they have something to show me."

"Eliza, I'm going to ask you a question and I do hope you will answer it. When you fed on the human, did you see which vampire would take her life had it not been you?"

I looked away fast, scared he would learn where Roman was, but I couldn't say why.

"Your apprehension tells me this is your secret to keep. You'll know when it's important."

I had the painful urge to get out of bed and run as fast as I could, run like a human being so every pounding footstep reverberated through my legs, and find Kieran. But I stayed there, not because I was paralyzed with nerves. Not because it was my duty to listen to the Master. Not because I had good reason to trust this man now, if I hadn't before.

I stayed because I wanted to know what exactly the Master had up his sleeve, and how deep the rabbit hole went.

CHAPTER 49

"I'll leave you to ready yourself for your guest," the Master said.

"Um, yeah. Okay, thank you? I mean, thank you." God, this weird scenario was making me trip over my words and sound like a moron.

Where the hell was Nicholas when I needed him? Right. Babysitting a psychopath.

I washed up in cold water, and opened my mind's eye to Nicholas. It seemed so long since the last time I'd seen him. The cacophony of visions that I couldn't piece together grew louder when I saw him, as if I opened a door to a mob in my head. But I needed him.

His woodsy warmth seeped through me, his peace and strength, his perfect unrest with thoughts of me. He was cutting wood in his massive back yard, out of sight of the cabin. Alone.

I'd spent half my life alone. It wasn't lost on me that

once I had Nicholas, I pushed him away, and resented that I'd never be alone in my own head all at once.

I dug a pair of yoga pants and Nicholas's old green sweater out of my spilled suitcase, taking a second to breathe in his scent. I'd washed it out a dozen times, but as a vampire, I could smell him in the fabric faintly again. Peppermint brownies. My whole life breathed a sigh of relief. He wasn't far, no matter how far he was.

Wet hair hanging down my back, I went out to the fireplace where I knew the Master would be, with whoever he'd chosen as my *guest.* They both turned to me as I entered the room. The vampire by the Master's side was full of suspicion and contempt. I didn't know him, and from the way he looked at me, he didn't want to know me.

"I'm Eliza," I said solidly, loud.

"Victor," he said, staring into my eyes. He made me think of truckers in horror movies, if they were glamorized a little. Like a hot actor playing a trucker. Same untouchable attitude.

"Okay, Victor," I said. He didn't flinch when I appeared next to him in wisps of red smoke. "Why you? What do you need from me?"

His Adams's apple rose and fell, and he blinked a few times. My mouth watered at his minimal show of emotion, his vulnerability.

When had I become a predator towards my own kind?

"I need to get away," Victor said, voice like crashing rocks. "Be my drug to get away."

I think he was meant to be *my* drug, but I understood

his plea. He needed escape that he couldn't find anywhere else.

I nodded, choked by the sadness in this strong man. His shoulders relaxed, only to tense again when I sunk my teeth into his neck without warning, unwilling to prolong or intensify our friendship. I knew more about him already than I wanted to, frankly. Death god or not, I had only so much capacity for pain.

His blood was oil-thick and *fast* somehow, the speed of a bullet in every molecule. It overwhelmed me with its sheer need in my mouth, like it always needed to be somewhere else, was always looking for the next thing, the next place, the next step away from where it was. Nothing in my life could compare to it.

Grunting with the labor of keeping up with its swiftness, I coughed against his skin. A torrent of blood cascaded down my throat, and as fast as his blood was, the visions he gave me came even faster.

A girl, of course. It was always a girl, wasn't it? *Foster.* Her name was Foster. Blonde braids, running-in-flower-fields fresh, and madly in love with Victor. Her heart nearly exploded as Victor mouthed an apology, and plunged a shard of wood into his chest, eyes locked on hers, not a tear shed in his own. Triumphant, he fell to the ground, his immortal life spilling out of him onto the tile floor. All joy evaporated from the girl's face as she fell to her knees, sobbing, screaming. The screams became groans, the groans became whimpers, and all were replaced by a vengeful howling that spelled revenge, and the souring of a ripened heart.

I didn't have to see her lap up the blood he'd spilled,

declaring she would do anything to avenge him, to know that she was able to unleash immense darkness. This was what fate could look like.

Victor slumped in my arms, all his tension gone like I'd given him a massage instead of sucking his blood.

All of his angst had become mine.

I fell back, flat on the floor, living the moment of Victor's death and the blackening of the girl's heart over and over dozens of times a second. The wild images of the anonymous fates that plagued my visions for so long faded, leaving only this perfect image of agony seared my soul.

"What the hell is that?" Victor said, clearly startled.

"Her shield," the Master answered.

"It's fucking weird."

I couldn't see anything, but felt my mist rising, the coolness of morning rain. The sheer crimson enveloped me in a familiar isolation.

Death, my only comfort when left blinded.

"You are not blind. You see with new eyes," the Master whispered in my ear.

"How—"

"Ssshh," he breathed. "You're safe here."

I went cold with the falseness of it.

My internal clock was powered by blood. The only thing that mattered past the abuse my mind took from the visions of Victor was that my body was stronger. My heart had a hummingbird whirr, begging for my body to move anywhere, everywhere. If I could have, I would have imagined over and over all the wonderful things my new immortal body could do, but inside my head fate and death held the reins, and I was lost.

Every. Second. Hurt.

"She's so beautiful."

I was paralyzed and blind, but sensed eyes on me. To be so strong inside an immobile shell terrified me.

Fingers on my cheek. "A beauty of fairy tales. Like Snow White in her glass coffin." It was Paolo.

"She has been this way for two days." The Master. He put down a pitcher of water on the table next to me, I could smell it. My senses were alight, even in this state. But all I could *see* was Victor bleeding out in front of the woman who loved him.

Paolo's breath on my face smelled of waterfalls. "What must she be thinking in there? Look at her eyelids flutter. She can hear us."

"I have tried to hear her, but I cannot. Her mind is a maze with no way out."

The Master left the room, his scent of earth and ancient stones going with him. But Paolo stayed.

"You are not lost, merely finding your way, Eliza," he whispered to me. "*You are* the light at the end of the tunnel."

The days came and went, though I only knew because my heart quieted when the daytime creatures went to sleep and the nocturnal ones burst into life. My skin vibrated with every molecule of the world for miles, but Victor consumed my mind, more real than the vampires in my presence. It was only ever the same two; Paolo and the Master.

To push Victor and Foster out of my head was like performing a self-induced lobotomy. The only other thing I recognized was Paolo holding me down, his tears splashing on my cheeks. It was the only thing that made me aware I was still part of something outside of Hell. In tortured desperation, I waded through the quicksand of my brain to pull out a vision of Nicholas.

When I was finally able to scrape back the scar tissue that was my connection to Nicholas, his pain came to me first. It was ever-present, always a dull ache; he needed me and I was too far. He sat on the sofa, feet up on the trunk that served as a coffee table, coffee mug on the sofa arm as usual. Gray sweatpants and a black tanktop with the elegance of a tuxedo, watching *Three's Company*. I missed *Three's Company*. I missed all reruns. I missed leaning against Nicholas's bare arm.

"Ha. Furley," he said with one shake of his head, and sipped his coffee. Old coffee mug, from some other time. The man drinking it from some other time, inserted perfectly into this time.

Just as perfect, the delicate beauty that was Blue swooshed through the kitchen door in a flannel shirt and jeans, carrying her own steaming coffee mug. A movement beyond her caught my attention. That's when I saw fingers clutching the arms of the shabby chair by the fire, holding on like it might get away. Lynch stared into the flames. A never-before-seen five o'clock shadow was almost as dark as his eyes. His hair was disheveled—another first—and he wore *jeans*. Sloppily.

Blood stained his ripped t-shirt, and he was crying.

I wished Nicholas would go to him, sit with at the fire as he would with Roman, but he just watched television. Blue ignored the Abomination as well, sinking herself next to Nicholas, laughing at Jack Tripper.

Their perfection stabbed me, heedless of the blemish across the room, but my pity for Lynch subsided fast. Jealousy bulleted through me, of Blue and Nicholas's comfort, of their togetherness, of their ignorance to the pain so close to them. Jealousy so strong, it drove my mind through the sea of visions to the surface.

"She's waking up!"

The Master joined Paolo at my side.

My eyes stung from lack of use, but I could see again. Paolo pulled me up into his arms. "I prayed every day you would come back to us, and I've been answered."

Leaning back to see his tear-streaked face, I let his purity shove my agitation aside. "Paolo, I heard you when I was—in there," I said. "You helped me not drift away."

He smoothed my hair, the knots rising against his hand. "You cannot drift away. Our miracle."

The Master appeared next to me in a burst of cold energy. "What do you need? How can I help?" Concern had the corners of his mouth turned down, and he was actually fidgeting.

"I think I'm okay," I said, smiling. My face hurt to smile. "Right now, there's nothing in my head." I laughed awkwardly and couldn't look them in the eyes.

The Master tried to keep me down, but I was

desperate to get up and move. "What did you see, Eliza?" he asked, his hand ice cold on my shoulder.

All he had to do was ask, and there it was again, brain-jacking me into a screaming convulsion. Victor, his blood in a pool, and Foster, becoming some other thing, a thing made of revenge and fury. And lurking behind it all, Nicholas, Blue, Lynch.

"No!" Paolo yelled, grabbing me by the shoulders. But the damage had been done. The wild mess of faceless images of fates returned, making a mush out of my thoughts as I tried to weed through them and find something familiar, something I could use. A pigpile of fleeting horrors, overrunning each other, then brought to an agonizing pinnacle by one of Roman, howling with his own madness.

"What do we do for her, Master?" I could still hear Paolo's panic, but nothing was stronger than Victor's blood pulsing through me in electric shocks.

I hoped they could hear when I moaned for Nicholas.

CHAPTER 50

The Master's answer for my madness was to bring me another vampire. And another. And another. Their blood would relieve me momentarily from the deluge of visions, replacing it with only one. Sometimes I found the strength to whisper the details of their fates into their ears, the worst secret there was. The secret that could change their eternity or leave them as powerless as I was.

When I was too weak to speak, the Master found a new way to divulge my thoughts. The gift was inside me, swimming in my blood and heart. And he found his way in.

He drank from me countless times, needling into my veins with his four snake-like fangs, leaving me captive to the horrors in my mind. Singular images of my latest feeds would be replaced once again by random ones in time, and then with those of Roman, and then back to feeding on another of the *Shinigami*. One torment replacing another over and over.

I could hear them sometimes, speaking about me like I wasn't there, the Master and the latest vampire who wanted me to open me like a fortune cookie. I'd always known, I *knew* it, that the Master would use me, and I'd let him do it.

My transformation to vampire made me a sideshow, the bars of my traveling cage my own mind.

Sometimes I heard Paolo, in the low tides of my visions. They ebbed and flowed, letting me hear just what I was missing in the real world, as if the torture wasn't enough. Paolo held my hand, brushed my hair, and for the love of God, he bathed me like an invalid. I could only make animalistic noises to let him know that I recognized he thought he was helping me, but this humiliation... I'd let no amount of kindness cripple my rage, no matter how desperately I needed it. Paolo was the only one who could stop this *torment*, but he didn't. Man of God or not, he didn't.

I wished for Nicholas, that he would sense my anguish across the world. But I learned that this was where our connection met its limit. Kieran's face would blaze in my mind's eye, but not for long. Nothing lasted long in that spiritual and mental chaos. I hoped that Izanagi would come to my rescue again, when I could hope. If I'd been remotely human, rather than that knot of turmoil, I would have missed them. There was no sense of time for me. Days and weeks may not matter when you have eternity, but stealing from the rich is still stealing, isn't it?

"Paolo." The word sounded like a curse, it was so thick and raw on my tongue after my silence.

"My God, I thought I'd never hear you say my name again."

My eyelids fluttered, shards of light blazing into them with each pass. "Why—why can I speak today?" I managed to say.

Paolo's breath was on my cheek as he said, "You have refused to drink in several days," he said.

My eyes stayed open at that. And when they did, I was able to acknowledge the relative quiet in my head, my own presence in it.

"Paolo," I said again, and he smiled, angelic as always. "What do you mean, I refused to drink?"

He stilled, unblinking, breath held. His words pounded like a monster up the stairs in a child's nightmare.

"You have attacked and shielded yourself against all of the *Shinigami* the Master has brought for three days now. You simply would not drink."

My blood sizzled with fury. And my mind was as clear as a crystal stream.

"You mean to tell me," I said, my voice gruesomely threatening, "that I was *fed* vampire blood until my *unconscious* body rejected it through my goddamn coma. You're telling me—that even though I pushed *one* away, that you. Kept. Bringing. Them. To me."

"Not me," Paolo said in a trembling voice. "The Master." This was no saint in front of me, this was a man, who feared for his very existence because of me.

I showered in his terror.

My body rose into the air, my shield pungent with the

scent of wine and roses, and the same color. An ache for Izanagi made me angrier. Where was he? Why had he let this happen?

Or had my captors done something to stop him?

I howled with animalistic pain as Paolo cowered from me, backing out of the room.

"No running," I hissed, gathering mist to my chest into a miniature wall. I willed it across the room to stop him in his tracks, dropping the semi-solid wall in front of him. A vibrating, scarlet cube, like a chunk of gaseous blood. Horrifying, and mine. The wall became more liquid in front of Paolo. Droplets of red fell from it to the ground, and with each passing second, the wall transformed more into an erect barrier of pure blood.

It made me buzz with vitality to see.

Paolo's eyes met mine. "Eliza, you don't understand what's been happening here."

"Make me understand," I growled.

He spoke to me like he was pleading with God. "You have suffered for your people immeasurably," he said. "And in your blindness you have opened their eyes." His own eyes glistened with tears, rendering me speechless. He let his fear dissipate, and I understood this trust in me, as vengeful as I was.

I had become his God now.

I pictured myself standing with him, and I was, leaving a path dotted in blood behind me from a dripping shield. He didn't flinch. The Master's outline stood in the door behind Paolo, and I thickened the red wall with a fast focus of my eyes, to keep him where he was.

Paolo took my hands in his own; I stiffened at the

touch. "The vampires of this mountain can see their options through your blood. You've given us choices we have never had."

My thick, misty shield faltered around me, dulling to a shade of weak pink.

My gift was to give options to the rest of my kind. And to take my own away?

"The *Shinigami* can see what will happen if they don't kill their *unmei nashi?*" I asked.

Paolo nodded, eyes welling more.

"I've given them the ability to be judge and jury. Nobody should have that kind of power."

"But you do. This is what you were chosen for, because you alone can lead us down the right path!" He swallowed hard, eyes spilling over. "Show us the impact of our blind decisions. We see the path in front of us. Because of you."

"And those who are choosing not to feed? Are they sick?" Pictures of Nicholas made me close my eyes. Nicholas's shoulder blades jutting out from under loose thermal shirts. Nicholas's eyes ringed in black. Nicholas's hair, dull in the sun that he had to shy away from. A race of withering gods, all because of me.

Paolo let out a laugh that reeked of disbelief. "They are not! They are as well as they ever were! It's a miracle, Eliza."

"What?" How could that be? How had I done that? The answer dawned on me behind a sickening red glare.

The wall of red that held the Master out, the most powerful vampire of us all, fell to the ground and disappeared in evaporating droplets of blood. The Master came inside, his soulless eyes on mine.

"It's been you, all along," I said. "You made them believe they had no choice. And when they saw another way, you lost your power over them."

Paolo and I watched the old man expectantly.

"Is this true, Master?" Paolo asked.

"The *Shinigami* needed a leader. I am that leader. You need someone to guide you, your powers are too great to be left to your own devices. I am that guide. You needed a deity to rest your faith in and give you meaning. I am that deity."

The mist boiled around me as I spat, "Izanagi is that deity. He created the *Shinigami.* Where is he?!"

The Master didn't answer, but Paolo did. "You needed to be alone."

"*You* saw Izanagi?" I asked. Things became clearer and clearer, and I hated it. "When you trusted in me, more than him," I shot a look at the Master, "Izanagi showed himself to you." I seethed with anger, wondering who else had been kept from me. "And Kieran? Has he been trying to see me?" I almost asked about Nicholas, but if he wanted to find me, nothing would stop him. Nobody could.

"Kieran is an upstart who has no place with you," the Master said icily.

"And I suppose my place is here, in a coma, being experimented on to see how much I can take?"

Paolo answered. "The Lord will not give you more of a burden than you can handle."

The room pulsed with my anger, the walls buzzing. "*The Lord?* You'll put your faith in anyone that doesn't make you accept responsibility for your own choices, won't you?"

He gaped, his heart pounding. I could feel it in my own, how deflated he was by my words. I meant them.

"I accept one thing," he said, tears thick in his voice, shoulders sagging. "I would follow anywhere you led me."

My knees grew weak, but I held myself up. This could not be my undoing. "You would want me, diminished, weak, barely alive, Paolo?" I said, shaking my head.

"I would want you any way I could have you," he said levelly.

"My God," I said. What else could I say?

The Master snickered, an ugly thing.

"When Nicholas finds out what you've done, he'll find a way to kill you," I said, snarling.

"Still a fool," the Master said with a laugh. "Nikorasu loves us both. You are the one who would make him choose. I have kept you alive because he needs you. He'll see that through your hatred of me."

I thought the Master had begun to care about me. I still saw it now, despite his cruel words, his terrible actions.

"You have your own reasons for keeping me here," I said softly. "Please, just let me understand what the hell all this is," I pleaded, blood tears masking my eyes. I couldn't hold them in anymore. The things that had been taken from me, the things I'd caused. "I don't want to disappear in my own head anymore," I said, my voice barely audible through the cracks.

The Master waited a long time to answer, and Paolo was dying to speak, I could see his jaw working. How hard was this going to be to hear?

"Shall I tell her or will you?" Paolo said, staring at me, through me. "I cannot see her suffer her ignorance any longer." And no matter how depraved, a rush of love for him flooded me at that moment, for the suffering he'd endured in his own way.

The Master sighed, and flashed across the room to sit in a chair by the window. The sun lit his face up, making him almost translucent. An ancient man with too many secrets.

"Nikorasu is my son in my heart. Everything I do is for him."

I nodded. Because I knew love could make a person do ugly things.

"Jenniveve came to me this winter," he said. I sucked in my stomach. I'd never wanted to hear her name again.

"Go on," I said. Paolo took my hand, but I pulled it away.

"She was a terrible creature, and more terrible with age, but she loved Nikorasu as much as a soul like hers could love anyone. She was desperate, and still my child. I couldn't fathom her pain to see Nikorasu, as filled with light as he is, taken away from her. She's never known anything but the darkness of her own heart." He focused on me, and the room went cold. I pretended not to notice. "Her pain at seeing you in his home, what you meant to each other, spun her into a world that no one should have to endure. I could not say no to her, my creation."

Mother of Christ, if I didn't despise myself for understanding.

"What did she ask you to do?" I asked. But I knew.

"Kill you, of course."

Paolo sat in the middle of the floor, drained. My heart went out to him. Compassion for people who would torture me.

"I was aware of you from the second Nikorasu found you, you know," the Master went on. "When you didn't know what you were, I did. I knew you would change everything I'd created." He smiled, and I smiled back. I still can't believe I did it. "I am a god to these people, but I am just an old man, Eliza. I fear change."

His admission sent more tears cascading down my cheeks. Emotion I'd held back in life knew no restraint once my mind had been opened, once I saw too much.

"Jenniveve and I both only wanted things to stay the same. I know no other life than this one. I would fight for it until the end of time. So, Jenniveve stayed quiet as long as she could, and—"

Paolo's sob broke through the Master's sentence, stopping my own tears. I was wracked with suspicion. Conspiracy.

When Paolo spoke, he could only look at the floor. "I didn't ask why they wanted my help," he said, trance-like. "I'm not one to question my God, no matter what form He takes. When the Master asked me to find a way to end you, I saw my purpose here, finally. But fate's plan for you was bigger than me." He looked up at me, eyes dry, but his heart broken. "You were invincible in my soul. How could I resist such a miracle? I love you," he finished with a sad laugh.

I fell to the floor next to him, unable to fight with myself anymore. I held him and he held me back like I was the only thing that mattered in the world. For him, I guess I was.

Looking over his shoulder at the Master, I asked, "Why did you kill Jenniveve, then?"

The Master cocked his head. "Because even I know when I am wrong."

CHAPTER 51

I asked to be alone, and they both left in silence. Seconds later, a heat emitted from the other side of the door so strongly that I pulled the blanket over my eyes, like that would stop me from burning. The shoji door went up in flames, incinerating in seconds. The door frame smoldered, the metal lamp near it melting into a deformed thing. My heart nearly exploded with hope and more joy than I thought I would know again.

Kieran was coming for me.

He appeared in the smoking doorway, his eyes a rippling orange, his skin vibrating with a radioactive energy that resonated in my bones.

"Eliza." Words in a wisp of smoke, Irish whiskey-scented longing.

I exploded across the room in a magician's burst of red death clouds, my emotions strangling me. I threw myself into his arms, our skin sizzling, a hiss between us.

I would heal from that. I could not heal without his arms around me.

He buried his face in my hair, I wound my fingers into his. We held on like both of us would burn forever without this moment.

"I'm so sorry," he whispered in my ear. My stomach clenched at his unnecessary guilt.

I moved my head as much as I could from his grip. "What could you possibly be talking about?"

"I left you here to find my *unmei nashi*, for god forsaken *blood*, and I couldn't get back to you." He held me so tightly that I could feel burn marks on his skin under his t-shirt. I tried not to cry. What had he done to himself? "Jesus, Eliza, I'm sorry I wasn't strong enough to save you."

Running my hands over his back, the heat jumped under my fingertips, making sparks. "This had to happen to me. Fate led me this way," I said.

He took me by the arms. "Don't let them own you any more than you have to."

The Master appeared behind him, and I glared over Kieran's shoulder, clenching my teeth at the onslaught of visions that came with him. I spoke over them, doing all I could to hide the pain.

"I will have this time with Kieran. You've kept him from me long enough." I held Kieran closer. Holding Kieran at that moment was as good as taking my life back, whether or not it gutted me with guilt.

Kieran released me and spun on the Master, smoke rising from his shoulders, his t-shirt growing holes where it burned. "She is no puppet. She's not your second coming, and she won't be your salvation. She is a woman with more fire in her spirit than you deserve to be witness to, and I will not be kept from her again."

The depth of Kieran's feelings for me came to life in his words, and my soul ached to hear it. Partly because I knew it would never become anything, and partly because I felt the same way.

"You are the embodiment of destruction that cannot be allowed to touch her," the Master said.

My anger might burn me alive, too. "Why not, Master? So you can *protect* me?"

"You need no protection, Eliza," the Master said. "He needs to leave you because you belong to Nikorasu."

An image of Nicholas, meditating in the spring sunshine by the fish pond in New Hampshire blazed in my mind. But I could still see Kieran through its vibrancy.

"I don't care what your reasons, I won't be enslaved for you or any greater good. You'll be lucky to survive my leaving here." I squeezed Kieran's hand and we brushed past the Master.

"We can't just walk out, Eliza," Kieran whispered.

"Why not?"

"Well, lass," he said, scratching his head with his free hand, face scrunched up. "I amassed myself quite a crowd on my way over here. Seems the townspeople knows their princess has awoken."

Sure enough, outside the door a throng of vampires stared back at me. Some cheered, some hissed. Others cried tiny rivers of blood.

"What the hell—"

The Master stood beside us, looking out at the

Shinigami. "They need your guidance, Eliza. You're here to provide them with it."

"I'm not their leader," I spat. "You are, right? Self-proclaimed."

Kieran cleared his throat. "Leaders are chosen, Eliza. You've done something for them that the Master can't undo," he said, nodding to the crowd.

I looked at the *Shinigami,* really looked at them, all of the faces I'd become familiar with. Others that rarely came out of the shadows of their mountain dwellings. They all wanted the same thing from me, even the ones that resented me for it. They all wanted to know what happened next.

The recognition of their need caused a volcano of a rupture inside me, an explosion of fates. All at the same time.

I screamed, digging my fingernails into the sides of my head, and so help me God, if I could have ripped my brain right out, I would have. Kieran's arm held me up, searing me with its heat.

Fate would take this last person from me—myself. Not part of this world, but a conduit.

"Bloody hell, Eliza, can you hear me?"

"Kieran, get the vampires away from here," the Master said.

"You get them away from here. I won't leave her side."

The Master's presence left the room, but it would take more than that to dispel the *Shinigami* that wanted me.

Not me. My visions. They didn't care if *I* lived or died.

"Croooooows," I groaned.

Through my closed lids I saw the swift shadows

descend the instant I needed them. The vampires cried out in alarm, my senses clearing as they sought cover.

"Well, okay then," Kieran said. "We'll fix this, Eliza," Kieran breathed, his hand under my head as I lay on the hard floor. "I won't let you get lost again." He kissed my forehead, searing and tender.

I wished I could scream for Nicholas to come. Then through my selfishness, I remembered that when Nicholas came back, my vision could become reality; Kieran would burn. And here I couldn't unburden myself of this slide show of images that meant nothing, when I needed to help what did mean something.

As the visions dragged me under again, I wished I could burn in Kieran's place.

CHAPTER 52

As long as Kieran held my hand, I could sense the world around me, but as soon as that warmth was gone, so was I; inside the nightmare world fate had built for me, plagued with lives I couldn't control.

The nightmare outside of my head didn't seem to be much better. Kieran would only ever leave my side to fend off *Shinigami* trying to force me to drink from them. Dozens of them, thundering in my brain before I heard them. Each one had a calling to an *unmei nashi;* and each vampire wanted to know if they were killers that made things better, or just killers. Vampires, waiting for me to make them heroes or monsters. Their faces swam in front of me in a scarlet haze, with a backdrop of hellish images of death: rape, torture, dreams unfulfilled, terrors unleashed because one death god made a choice. I was glad I couldn't hear my own screams.

Every time Kieran returned to me and took my hand, the world flooded back, adding to the things squeezed into my mind until I prayed for my existence to end, any way it could.

Only one could calm my butchered soul. When he arrived, I couldn't be angry that he didn't come before, my need for him was too great.

"Izanagi."

His name was a sigh of relief on my lips, the only thing I was able to say.

"Jesus, you spoke," Kieran said. "I don't know where he is, Eliza, I can't find him."

"He's here." My voice sounded scorched, like I'd been burned at the stake. The people's heretic.

"What? Oh! Mother of Jesus!"

My old friend, death, in the flesh. Wine-soaked sorrow, wilting roses, the end of things, here. The one thing I knew better than anything else—loss. Tears dried on my cheeks as the scent enveloped me once again.

That which consumes me makes me stronger.

Izanagi whispered in my ear, words with the impact of an avalanche. "You are not what fate would make you."

And life inundated me with a deafening rush of his blood, washing away the poisonous images at once. He tasted of overripe fruit and the beginning of the world. A musty richness of something that has lived too much life, and is more beautiful for it.

Izanagi's blood took away the hateful roar that made me nothing, and brought back the god in me.

I flew to my feet, my heart thundering with blood, a sheen of silky red over my eyes. I wanted to see nothing but Kieran and Izanagi. Kieran, perfect in his imperfection as always. Dirty jeans, plain black t-shirt, twenty-four hour shadow, knuckle tattoos bared as he clenched his fists with worry. Izanagi didn't belong in the same room, and there was nowhere better for him to be. Pristine *hakama* pants, bare feet, bare, smooth chest. Glistening midnight hair in a topknot, sword hilt visible behind it. One sob broke free of me, and I grabbed Izanagi first, holding him to me like he wasn't a supreme being, but a man. A man who'd known me when no one else did. A man who would always understand when I was disintegrating, and would bring me the darkness that completed me.

"I failed you," Izanagi said into my ear.

I pushed him off to look into his black eyes. I didn't ask why he hadn't come before, I didn't need to know. "My life isn't yours to save. You came when you could." I kissed him on the forehead, like an equal.

Kieran stood hunched a few feet behind him, hands on his knees, looking at the ground, panting like he'd just finished running. My Kieran, always running.

A ghostlike flood of red swarmed around my feet, propelling me towards Kieran. No time passed before my hands were on his warm, stubbly face, our lips brushing. I squeezed my eyes shut against the thought of him invisible in a nest of flames.

He rested his forehead on mine, hands on my cheeks, and we were alone. Without regret, without future or past. "Thank you, Kieran."

"Never thank me for my selfish needs, woman. I needed to be here more than you needed me here." He cast his eyes to the floor, one hand knotted in my hair, like it was the only thing that kept him from fading away.

"I'll repay you, Kieran. What I saw won't happen. I won't ever let you burn."

I hated what I saw in his eyes. The thing that happens before defeat, that voluntary hopelessness.

The two of them looked so utterly *inferior*, like they'd accepted failure. Two of the most magnificent beings I had ever known.

"Both of you, look at me," I said slowly, red mist a raging tornado around me, holding me steady while the world trembled. "You've been unerringly loyal to me, and if you think I'll let you wither into some depression because you didn't get to me fast enough, you're goddamn wrong. There's more than one way to be by my side. Because of you both, I'm stronger than I've ever been. Fate will try to destroy us from the inside out, all three of us. It doesn't stand a chance against me. I won't let either of you down. Just like you've never let me down."

Something was consuming them both, and I prayed I wouldn't have to choose between the people in my vision to save them.

All becomes clear in battle.

"Now. I need to fight."

CHAPTER 53

I needed to fight because immortal or not, love could always be taken away from me. I needed to fight to understand who I was fighting for and against. The image of Kieran burning alive, the realization that Izanagi depended on me, the distance from Nicholas, all of it fought with my own changing heart.

I needed to fight because the person that might let it all go was me. All it would take was one…wrong…move. One second of hesitation. One poor choice.

My blood senses awoke the world for me. The sparring arena was filled with more springtime beauty than I wanted to see; none of it was on fire. I wanted that fire. I wanted to face it in real life, not in my head. I was ready for it to pick on someone its own size. Instead I was faced with a flurry of falling cherry blossoms and singing birds, while in my mind were burning trees and screeching crows.

Its timeless peace warred with the change that was coming, and it felt like a lie.

In the center was Paolo, meditating, trying to grasp a higher meaning I wasn't sure existed. My higher meaning stood next to me, stronger than the mountain itself, the god who created it all, while Kieran leaned against a pillar, pulling a crumpled cigarette from his back pocket. I grinned at how much he looked exactly like he had that first day I saw him, right in this same spot.

With a smile, I left them both to watch me. I flashed across the arena, and sat cross-legged with Paolo. We didn't look at each other.

"Kind of a shitty day. Want to spar?" I said.

He laughed, a despairing thing. "Love to."

We stood in a single motion, and faced each other. My breath caught. With Izanagi's blood in mine, Paolo's eyes were warmer and sweeter than usual. So full of faith. In me, in God. A trust I longed to have.

This was one vampire that was more dangerous than I'd realized.

We bowed, our friendly smiles never leaving each other. My speed dizzied me as I bolted across the ring and threw a series of punches and kicks in a blur. I was stronger than before, but Paolo's unhurried strikes nearly matched me. We laughed, reveling in each other's strengths, and it felt like diving into cool water to be with him. This was what balance felt like. I never wanted to stop until I finally crumpled to the ground dramatically, exhausted, sore and sweaty with a pink sheen on my skin. I tapped the ground.

"I'm done," I gasped through a smile, my hair spreading around me in the dirt. "You've made your point."

Paolo laughed heartily. "What was it?"

"Eliza weak. Paolo strong."

He sat next to me again, full circle. "You're far from weak, my dear," he said, rubbing his chest and wincing. "I've been too afraid to spar with you since you arrived. Nicholas was right—even as a human, you could have laid me out." His face was as friendly as the first time we'd met, like we were at a wedding or something, not like we'd just exchanged blows. Not like he wanted me for himself. Not like we were just showing each other that everything was okay between us despite that he'd helped trap me, that he was challenging his own faith; not like everything was going to change even more than it already had. He was still an ointment to my emotional wounds. The odd part was, even with all that had happened, I still seemed to soothe him, too.

He stood and pulled me to my feet with an outstretched hand. We stood face to face, two priests of different churches.

"I don't want to change anything except the ability to change," I said, a meaning that came from the blood inside. "It's all any of us really want." I glanced behind me at Izanagi, and saw to my surprise, the Master not far behind him. I kept my eyes on them as I said, "We're death gods, Paolo. We shouldn't only be able to change, we should initiate it. We should not be denied choice."

My own choices were ganging up on me, but I refused to be powerless against them.

Kieran swaggered over to us, flicking the cigarette butt

and incinerating it in the air with one look. *He could do that?*

Kieran didn't stop until he'd pulled me to his body and kissed me with a fervor that I didn't think I could survive. His hands on my hips, bending me back, not questioning if I was his to have, the taste of rebellion on his lips, complete control of his lack of control.

I lost myself in his lips, my heavenly blood coursing into every sinew, to take in every molecule of his love. Letting him know I was filled with it, too.

It lasted for as long as I could stand it. Eternity isn't for all of us. I pulled away, aware of Paolo's eyes on us, but Kieran pulled me back again, his fingers digging into my skin.

"This," he said into my lips, "is what love feels like. Letting go, and taking back. A burning inside that won't stop." He pressed his lips to me harder until they stung. "Burn with me, Eliza, until I'm all you breathe."

I nipped his bottom lip, tasting a speck of blood that made my dead heart pound. I groaned, and pulled away, afraid. A predator with a heart as full as mine was the worst kind of animal.

A white glimmer appeared in the air around Kieran, distracting me. I squinted and watched it hover by his shoulders, cling to the tips of his mussed up hair, then to the dirt at our feet. I got a chill and saw it on the sleeves of my shirt.

Frost. Sticking to me, melting right off of Kieran.

Hair whipped into my mouth, across my eyes, as I tried to find the only thing missing. My mind's eye opened to search for him. Gasping and sobbing, I focused, desperate to find where he was in the real world.

I spun to see the top of the great stone stairs, and found Nicholas. A white flurry raced around him in his own personal hurricane. His dark curls, black wool coat and swirling eyes were just visible to my own preternatural ones behind the storm from inside him.

In a white streak, Nicholas was inches from me. Traitorous wretch that I was, I threw my arms around his neck, inhaling the smells of home. He was so cold to the touch, and stiff.

He didn't return my embrace.

"I couldn't stay away any more," he said dryly.

I pulled back, ice snapping from my arms. His caramel and chocolate eyes that I'd dreamed of, that I couldn't bear to see in visions, were sedentary and sludge-dark. His neatly trimmed beard didn't hide the clench of his jaw, lips pursed, chin up, shoulders back.

"Nicholas," was all I could say.

He swallowed, but didn't blink. Didn't falter. "I hated every second. Every second of my life without you. I listened to your heartbeat from halfway across the world." He punched his chest, breathing in through his nose. "It never left me, no matter how far I was."

He didn't have to say any more.

"Nicholas, I'm sorry."

"There is such a thing as self-fulfilling prophecy. You never believed I could want you forever, and you worked your hardest to make it true, didn't you?" he spat, turning on me to look at Kieran.

"No, God, no, please."

The image of Kieran burning crashed in my mind, making me stumble. But goddammit, I would not take my eyes off Nicholas.

The Master appeared next to me, and put his hand on my shoulder, holding me up with his infinite strength in this small gesture. It snapped me back.

"Nikorasu," he said. "You don't know what she's been through."

"She made me leave!" he shouted, pointing at me.

"It was necessary. She couldn't breathe enough to see what she needed to see. She needed to see it alone."

"She wasn't alone much," Nicholas said.

"Watch it, man," Kieran said, raising his hand up. "That woman's heart beats only for you."

I squeezed my eyes shut, itching to close myself off, my heart stiffening against Nicholas's accusations. "That's not true," I said.

When I opened them, all eyes were on me. It was then that I saw Blue and Leann at the edge of the ring. I wanted to cry out and throw my arms around Blue, but her face showed me it wouldn't be welcome. She shook her head at me in disappointment. And the idiot I am, I was blind with jealousy that she'd been with my Nicholas, when I hadn't been. Leann stared at me blankly, as unknowable as ever.

"Nicholas, my heart bleeds with how desperately I love you. But Kieran," I glanced at him, the innocent rebel that he was, "sees me another way. He helps me break free. No desperation. I love him for it."

The heat from Kieran was the only thing to stop the world from freezing when Nicholas heard those words.

"And Nicholas," I said, crawling inside myself with every revelation. "I know where Roman is."

"No," he said, shaking his head. Blue rushed to his side and took his hand when it looked like he would lose control. My sharp look at her was enough to make my shield extend from my open palms and the bottoms of my feet, fluid like blood, light as air. I didn't try to reel it in.

"You'd keep that from me?" Nicholas whispered.

I wasn't going to say I had to. It was my choice. "I did. He didn't want you to know, Nicholas, and if I told you, you wouldn't have gone to New Hampshire."

"Why are you doing this?" Blue said, squeezing Nicholas's hand tighter. The mist became a solid thing.

"Because now that Nicholas is here, I can see what happens next." The swarm of visions that plagued me were gone, and now with him here in front of me, I saw what they'd covered up. "You have to go to Roman, Nicholas. You have to go, and I can't come with you."

The Master seemed to grow bigger in my peripheral vision. "You will not leave Nikorasu for *this*," he said, nodding his head at Kieran.

"Tell me how you really feel," Kieran said.

"Blue is going with him," I said.

It was Nicholas's turn to look apologetic. "Eliza, things aren't like that with us, and you know it."

"I do know it," I said with a sad smile for him. "But Roman needs you, and I know he needs her, too," I said, smiling tightly at her. "I'll be waiting for you, Nicholas. But our paths have to part again. Not just because fate says so, but because I need to work through my own heart." The mist swirled around me, wrapping me in its comfort. Blood welled in my eyes, tears I couldn't hold back.

"No!" the Master roared. We all stared at him, unsure which of us he was angry at. Big surprise, it was me. "You will not send away the only one who knows what I'm worth here! You will not take over this place, *my* place! You will not stay here to replace me and destroy what I have built. You will not stay here to abandon Nikorasu for the Irishman! You will leave, and you will leave with the man who loves you."

"He's right," Kieran said. "You belong with Nicholas, and as long as I indulge your finer tastes, you won't love him the way you should."

"This isn't about you, Kieran," I said gently. "I've seen the alternative, and this is what has to be done. Nicholas leaves. Blue goes with him."

"It doesn't matter what you've seen, dear heart," Kieran said, next to me with his hand on my cheek. "I see your heart, and I cannot live without it. You may leave me, but I will never leave you."

Nicholas was to my right. Leann had found her way to my left. Kieran between them both. When he stepped back, it would be exactly the way I'd seen it. Fate's fingers were clawing down my back. My vision was coming to life.

"No," I whimpered, blood tears thick on my cheeks.

"Ssssh, lass," Kieran whispered, kissing me swiftly on the lips. Cold blasted me from Nicholas's side. "If I had a purpose in this life, it was served the moment I found you. There's nowhere for me to go from here, Eliza. I can't let you go, and I won't watch you stay."

"You listen to me, Kieran. You told me that which consumes you gives you strength." I swallowed, but the pain was still there. "If your love for me consumes you, *let me give you strength.*"

"Keep giving and you'll have nothing left. Don't do that again," he said with a grim smile. He took his hands from my face, and backed up, eyes still on me, but all I could see were the flames waiting to engulf him.

Cinders crackled under his feet, and I sobbed again. They licked up his legs, his arms, tore through his body. He made not a sound.

"Nicholas!" I pleaded. "Please, stop him!" But Nicholas's fury had him staring back at me blankly. In a billow of red mist I rose from the ground and flew to him, grabbing him by the shoulders. "Don't let my choices keep you from doing what's right. Please," I begged.

"How much betrayal should I take before you don't ask me for favors?" Nicholas said to me. Of all the coldness I'd seen from him, never had I been so frozen. I turned my back on him.

"Leann," I said as calmly as I could while Kieran's body burned to ash. "Show me why you're here. There's a reason."

"What reason do I have to save someone who wants nothing to do with me?" she said, sneering.

"He's your *shugotenshi!* Please, don't watch this happen. Make something better happen."

"I owe you nothing."

"Please!" I screamed, but nobody was listening. I looked at Paolo, who looked back at me with wildly anxious eyes, shaking his head. Nobody could or would help, and Kieran didn't want it anyway. The orange streaks reached for the clouds, the air crackling around Kieran's body, invisible in the inferno.

A deep hum filled the air out of nowhere, and Izanagi materialized in front of the flames with an electric blue shield around him that pulsed with bolts of ice cold lightning, freezing the ground instantly and the feet of all those who stood on it. The trees above turned glassy with ice.

The flames around Kieran dimmed ever so slightly. This was what hope looked like.

"You!" The Master howled through the air at Izanagi, knocking him to the side with his staff, letting it fall to the melting ground, while the flames grew. The two *Shinigami* erupted, becoming what gods of death were meant to be; enormous, too terrifying to look at. They took to the sky, their bodies assuming translucent shapes, cloaked in the apparitions of dragons that consumed the sky, too otherworldly to look at or understand. Shimmering, thundering, ghostly fire poured from their mouths, their monstrous claws shredding one another. Destruction greater than time.

And Kieran burned.

The red mist wailed like a possessed tornado, lifting me higher into the air than I'd ever been. I twisted my arms in a circle over my head in an ancient dance that I couldn't know, spinning red mist like the twirling scarves of a bellydancer. Izanagi battled with the Master, and I summoned his blood inside me, feeling it bubble, rupture, until it spouted from my fingers, twisting blood streams into the raging red wind. Rivulets of blood splattered the sky and hung suspended, until there was no more mist, only a whirlpool of pungent blood. Airborne over Kieran, the blood rained upon his flames.

His fire hissed and bit at the sky, dwindling.

Kieran's face, scorched black, looked up at me from beneath, more afraid of me than the flames that destroyed him.

"Don't leave me," I whispered through my storm.

The notion of losing him, of losing anyone else, plowed into my heart, and my fountain of blood overwhelmed the sky, cloaking the spring newness in my abandonment. My very own gift of isolation, working my will. The Master and Izanagi stopped tearing each other apart with ghostly claws.

When my power exceeded both of theirs.

The wretched *aloneness* ate through me as the embodiment of it fought his own battle with the Master, his presence the most comforting threat that I loved to despise. I screamed, and mist the color of warfire, the odor of wine and roses, poured from my mouth, taking with it all of my horror at being left without Kieran, without Nicholas. Being *me*, alone. The red cloud tore itself apart, like my heart, the explosion of it transforming into hundreds of blood-sculpted crows, blind and screeching. Their liquid wings created a deafening wind, pouring my life's desolation into the air with every beat. I spread my arms wide, torrents of blood thrashing around me, and with another scream I felt my skin stretch, blood being ripped from it like hooks into my flesh, curdling into another flock of bloody crows, taking my emptiness with them.

Fueled by the desolation that lived in me, their wings

pounded the air, and nothing could be mightier. They would all feel how I felt.

Kieran's flames of self-destruction extinguished below.

The Master recovered from his shock when he saw, and sped towards Kieran, his dragon form dissipating into the hellishly determined vampire, leaving Izanagi behind in my recoiling shield.

Leann flashed to the ring of embers, screeching like an eagle, and met the Master with his own *bo* staff, driving it into his heart, straight through his body. Impaled, and sputtering, he asked for only one thing before his body stopped moving.

"Nikorasu."

And then he vanished, like the ghost of the world he'd made.

CHAPTER 54

When you hunger for the death of things, and it gets delivered, you think it will be a weight from your conscience. A wintry kiss on scorched skin that brings newness by utterly destroying the ruin that came before it.

I didn't know it would show me how much I'd decayed.

We weren't heroes. We were birds of prey, and the world was our carrion.

Nicholas wouldn't or couldn't speak to me. He'd try, in an empty monotone, but never finished a sentence. I couldn't know what trumped what—his disappointment and anger at me, or his grief for the Master. It was an awful reflection of myself not so long ago, and the hollow that Kat left inside me.

Maybe Nicholas was just like the rest of us; afraid of what would come next.

Two days had passed. With the Master gone, I

expected the birds to be quiet, the trees to stop moving, but apart from the silence of the *Shinigami*, spring bloomed as usual. Vampires left the mountain to pursue *unmei nashi*; I refused to exchange blood with them, to give them a choice.

What had choice ever done for me?

As a matter of fact, I was making another bad choice right at that moment. I slid open the Master's door, noticing immediately how *missing* he felt. But the place wasn't empty.

I cringed as I sat next to Nicholas in front of the fire. I could only see Kieran's face in the flames.

"You pulled me apart in so many ways, I don't know if I can put myself back together," Nicholas said.

I straightened my back and looked at him, even if he couldn't look back. I'd deserved no better than to watch him unravel.

"You deserve more than apologies, but the only other thing I have to give you is my blood. You need it for your trip," I said.

"I can't go anywhere, and I don't want to taste you."

My heart stopped. "Nicholas, I get that you don't want to let him go," I said, motioning to the room that was all Nicholas had left of the Master. "But I've seen what you need to do, and there are reasons for the choices I make."

"You had a reason for Fire Boy, did you?"

"I have a reason for most things," I whispered.

He turned to me with a set in his jaw and a darkness in his eyes I didn't like. "So, tell me, prodigy. What plans have you made to get me out of your way this time?"

"It's not like that. Exactly. Look, I needed you to leave

because I felt as much as you did that we were waiting for something to happen. I didn't know that the something was going to be me imprisoned by the Master, or that Kieran would be the one to come for me. But if I've learned nothing, I've learned that fate guides us, but it's up to us to decide what to do with it."

"And what you decided to do was push me away. You *took* from me. You knew where Roman was. You took the Master from me. And you took you."

"All true. But I won't apologize anymore, it's what I had to do. Not because it was written in the stars or whatever...but Nicholas, before you I went my whole life without feeling, and then, then..."

"When I had to do something, I didn't. I didn't because of what it would do to you."

"You're going to make this about Kat?"

"Isn't it always? She's all you see when you look at me. Now you'll only see that I would have let Kieran burn."

My mouth went dry. "That's in your heart, not mine. You have to go, Nicholas. It all falls in place like the world's suckiest puzzle," I blurted. "We need to heal from what we've done to each other, and we can't do it holding hands. You can feed from me first." *Please say you will.*

He put his head down. "It can be a terrible thing, when your taste lingers," he said slowly, like each word hurt. "Like waiting for the world to end one second at a time." He looked up at me, eyes filled with sorrow. "You've made me wonder if change is the worst thing that can happen to us. Just looking at you makes me think of what we've both lost. We've made monsters of each other."

My throat constricted, and the pain I'd long since

forgotten, that connection between us, threatened to take me.

"You told me you'd love me after I became—*this.*"

He looked at me, and I knew he was seeing the blood and the crows, the storm, and that he didn't recognize me. "It's the person you were already that hurt me this way."

I hated being ashamed. "I'm sorry about Kieran." My voice cracked. "My reasons don't always make sense, even to me, and I won't blame my choices on fate. Fate gave me options, but my choices were mine." There was no more for me to say about the things I'd done and hadn't said. It was time for change. "You have to go to Roman now."

"Roman," he said, running his hands through his hair. As much as he didn't want to leave the Master's place behind, he desperately wanted his brother. The notion that I could be successful in making him go was a debilitating success. So, I continued.

"Roman's blood will restore you once and for all, and fix his mind in the meantime. And when he's done fixing you, and needs a new reason to hide and brood, Blue will be there to drag him out."

"Blue?"

I nodded, smiling weakly. His heart pounded, reminding me of all the times he gazed at the spot where my heart beat for him. I took his hands, and held them over my heart, hoping he would feel how much it belonged to him no matter what came between us.

"I'm yours forever, and nothing will change that," I said, tears choking me. "But I have somewhere to be, sweetheart," I said.

The man who held my heart pulled his hand from me, and turned away.

～

"It's been two bloody days. Nice of you to show up. He's been asking for you."

"I know, I'm sorry."

Blue left me at her open door, and I followed her in. Her frustration with me was clear, and I was eager to talk to her, but all thoughts stopped once I saw the black ash that was Kieran lying in her satin bedding.

I ran to him, putting my hand on his forehead like it would do something, and pulling it away as it seared my skin.

"Right, don't touch him," Blue said. I rolled my eyes at her, cradling my wounded hand.

"Woman, look what you've done to me," Kieran said in a hoarse breath.

"Yeah, I've heard that already today," I muttered. "I'm sorry I didn't come sooner, I didn't know what to say."

His charred skin split as he turned his head to me. "You came to say goodbye."

"What?" Blue said, coming to my side. "Where are you going? You can't leave the *Shinigami* now! The Master is *gone*, they'll all be looking for you and Nicholas to show them what to do!"

"Exactly," I said. "They'll never make choices on their own as long as I'm here, and Blue, you're leaving, too. With Nicholas."

Kieran and Blue blinked at me, wide-eyed, mouths agape.

"I won't leave Kieran like this," Blue said, shaking her head, black hair flying. "And neither should you."

"Blue, if Eliza says you have to go, you have to go," Kieran said. "You can't say she has to lead us in one breath, and deny what she tells you in the next."

"Who will lead *them*?" Blue said, looking out the door.

"Someone who can rise from his own ashes," I said quietly, looking at Kieran.

Kieran stared at me, white eyes in black ash. "Woman, Izanagi's blood has made you mad. The *Shinigami* don't trust me, never have. I'm no leader. Look at Paolo for that."

Blue's voice was so small, it barely existed. "Paolo—"

My heart froze with dread. "What about him?"

It scared me more when Blue softened, her anger subsiding. "Paolo is a man of faith. The things that have happened…they've taken it from him."

"Where is he?"

She licked her lips, held her breath. Jesus, what could this mean?

"He went to the part of the mountain we never see; the Master never wanted us there. And when Paolo came back, he was *dark*. He drank from bad things there, and now he can't come outside, he can't look me in the eye. The only one he'll talk to is Leann."

"Sounds like he went looking for a little slice of Hell," Kieran said, his voice smoke-dry.

Falling dominoes, every one of us. And I pushed the first,

second and third one. "Paolo will work his way through his faith. He and the *Shinigami* have been sheep long enough. They need to make their own way, guided by someone who isn't afraid to find his own path. That's you, Kieran."

He craned his neck to kiss my wrist. "You're just afraid to do it yourself."

"I'm not afraid of anything anymore."

Kieran sat up, his skin crackling as he moved. "You're afraid of being alone now more than ever, it's all over you. You're afraid I'll leave you, but I'm the one who should be afraid." He held my hands, steam rising from between them. A thin layer of red mist wrapped itself around our hands, and he breathed a sigh of relief. "Don't tell me to fall down the rabbit hole and leave me to do it alone. I want you by my side. That rabbit hole has teeth."

I smiled at him, kissing his hands. "Kieran Coughlin can climb out of that rabbit hole bloodied up to hell," I said, laughing. "But I have to go. Something's calling me," I whispered. "Something is begging me to burn who I once was."

He put his head back against the wall. "Is this because Nicholas doesn't want you now?"

I gasped, and Blue appeared at my side.

"Don't listen to him," she said, glaring at Kieran, patting my hair. "That's not true."

Red tears blurred my vision. "No," I said, my voice far away, but my words close to me. "It's true. You both saw what I became. I'm something different now. He doesn't want this. He doesn't want me."

Kieran sat up fast, pulling my face to his in a kiss that made me sizzle with a hundred emotions, all of which hurt. His hands on the side of my head, he looked into my eyes. I don't know whose hid more in their flames, mine or his.

"He'd be blind if he didn't see what a magnificent thing you are. It's time for a change, for you, too. Don't let anyone decide who you're going to be." He rested his forehead on mine, burning my skin, leaving his mark. "Get away from here, from me, from all the things that would hold you back. Only death and fire live here, Eliza. Time to burn it all down."

CHAPTER 55

The woods were dark, but not dark enough to hide the murder of crows, perched on every branch. The only thing darker was the god who stood among them.

"Your mind is in a turmoil that I cannot save you from," Izanagi said as I approached him.

There was something incredibly different about him. My blood cooled as I reached for his mind, still so connected to mine.

"But yours isn't," I said.

He smiled, wide and bright. The crow closest to me cawed. "Tell me I had something to do with this. Did I do something besides cause a goddamn catastrophe here?"

"Do you know why you were brought here, Eliza?"

"To make my own path. To take back my choice," I said before I knew I'd said it.

He smiled knowingly. "And because my wife, Izanami, wanted it to be so. She wanted you to give me the same." He looked at the crows surrounding us. "These are her creatures," he said with a smile, reaching out to one of the black birds. It nuzzled its head into his fingers. "And now they tell me to leave here."

"What? I don't understand."

A stream of images from Izanagi's mind trickled neatly into my own as he told me his story. "I created this mountain, and it created me. There is a place on this mountain that leads to Yomi, the gate of Hell. I left my Izanami there in a moment of mortal weakness and fear, and in her vengeance, she vowed to destroy one thousand men each day. I vowed to create the *Shinigami*, a breed that would not die. My first vampire creation was what I wanted to be, to have given her. Strength, stability, for nothing to change."

"The Master," I whispered.

He nodded once. "But we were blind to how destructive never changing can be. When you believe something for so long, it becomes real. The *Shinigami* believed many things that the Master believed."

Pictures of Nicholas, losing his strength. "That they would wither away if they didn't feed on the right humans," I whispered. And with pain I could barely fathom, that dwarfed all the other agony I'd been through, I realized the truth. "That they would be in agony if they didn't turn their *unmei fumetsu* into vampires. That there was no choice in any of it." The pain of separation from Nicholas; it wasn't real.

"The choice you are about to make, Eliza, is one that you can refuse. All of your choices are."

I didn't have to think about it. The churning temptation deep in my gut, the screeching need in my blood rose to the surface, clawing into my consciousness to feed it.

"Fate has shown me the way. It knows what it wants to do with me, but it can't tell me who I am." The ache in my heart told me there was more to know. The same sensation when Leann's blood called to me, imploring me to drink and see what I could see.

To give me the gift that would make me a hero or an abomination. Blood sang to me now, of truths and pains, and a life unled.

Lynch's blood.

"I choose to go to New Hampshire," I said. Izanagi nodded solemnly.

Smiling felt so strange.

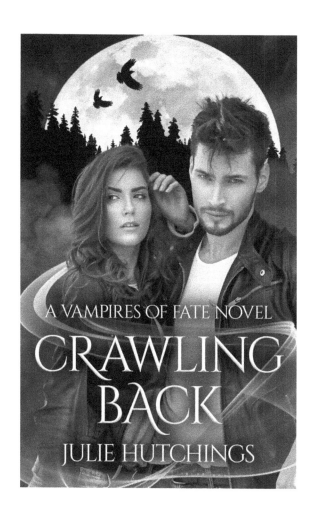

BOOK THREE, CRAWLING BACK, WILL BE OUT
IN 2020!

ACKNOWLEDGMENTS

Writing isn't easy, we all know that. Continuing to write is harder. Publishing is an industry riddled with draining choices, loss of trust, putting faith in others and ourselves at great risk to our stability in every way. We remain vigilant. For that, I want to acknowledge my brothers at Books of the Dead Press. Mark Matthews, John F.D. Taff, Justin Robinson, Bracken MacLeod, James Michael, Weston Kincade, and T.S. Alan. Keep writing. Make your passion matter.

Never Miss A Release!

Thank you so much for reading **Running Away**. I hope you enjoyed it!

I have so much more coming your way. Never miss a release by joining my free newsletter where I'll be sure to keep you updated on upcoming books!

To sign up, simply visit
https://juliehutchings.net/

Thank you for reading RUNNING AWAY! If you enjoyed the book, I would greatly appreciate it if you could consider adding a review on your online bookstore of choice.

Reviews make a huge difference to the success or failure of a book, especially for newer writers like myself. The more reviews a book has, the more people are likely to take a shot on picking it up. The review need only be a line or two, and it really would make the world of difference for me if you could spare the three minutes it takes to leave one.

With all my thanks,

Julie Hutchings

JULIE HUTCHINGS

Charity Blake survived a nightmare. Now she is the monster others dream about.

By day, punk-rock runaway Charity Blake struggles through a stream of dead-end jobs and the haunting memories of her past. But at night she is the Harpy, sprouting wings with black feathers, and claws made for tearing the flesh of her prey.

Having survived a lifetime of abuse and torment from a sadistic man who broke her spirit, Charity's physical manifestation of her grief and anger allows her to hunt down those like her abuser. Only this time, Charity isn't a helpless little girl praying for things to end. Now she is the monster, and hell hath no fury like a harpy scorned.

Power always comes at a price though, and Charity's inner predator craves to take over. Torn between a life with no feeling other than the sweet satisfaction at ripping evil apart or suffering through her days to stay with the two people she cares for most, Charity must choose between her human existence or the wild and feral freedom of a flying avenger.

A perfect read for fans of Joe Hill, Anne Rice, and Chuck Palahniuk, THE HARPY is the first book in the chilling and deeply disturbing world of the Harpyverse where victims become vigilantes and power is a thing to be played with.

Get your copy of THE HARPY today and delve into the deliciously dark paranormal horror everyone is talking about.